WATCH YOUR BACK

CROSSROADS SUSPENSE

Take My Hand—Book One
Hold Your Breath—Book Two
Watch Your Back—Book Three

WATCH YOUR BACK

CROSSROADS SUSPENSE: BOOK THREE

BY

KRISTEN HOGREFE PARNELL

Dedication

To my Noah,
May you know that with God,
All things are possible.

Acknowledgments

When my publisher asked me to write a third book in my Crossroads Suspense trilogy, I hesitated. I wanted to write Avery's story, but my son had just turned a year old and was starting to walk. My days would be filled with chasing him, savoring each exciting new milestone, and turning in for the night with the exhaustion that only moms of young children can understand.

I asked my husband, anticipating that he would probably agree that now wasn't the right season for book three. Instead, he said, "You need to say yes."

James has always supported my writing, but I figured he would give me an "out" since my plate was already full. Instead, he knew my heart better than I did and that I should—and somehow could—write this book.

He was right. I figured out how many words I needed to write each week to reach my deadline. The word count would look embarrassingly small to most authors, but for me, it was all I could do to stick with it.

But I finished, and I'm so thrilled this story is now in your hands, only possible because of my encouraging husband, the grace of God, and the support of so many.

Thank you, Miralee Ferrell and the team at Mountain Brook Ink, for asking me to write this book and helping make it the best it can be. Thank you, Kristen Johnson, for fielding my questions, and Tim Pietz, for being such a helpful publicist.

Thank you, Stephanie Alton, for representing me and coaching me in the publishing journey. I am so grateful and blessed to be part of the Blythe Daniel Agency.

Thank you to my family for believing in my writing and being my constant cheerleaders.

Thank you, Ashley Jones and Amberlyn Dwinnell, for asking how I was doing and letting me be honest with you—about the highs and lows of both motherhood and the writing life.

Thank you to all my friends and readers who celebrate my stories, invest in them, and leave reviews. It is such a joy to hear from you in person and online.

Thank you, Jesus, for the gift of words and stories. I pray that I steward this "talent" well so that I may one day hear You say, "Well done, good and faithful servant" (Matthew 25:21).

Chapter One

Tampa, Florida

Not even the Buddy Brew barista could have noticed the subtle tremble in his fingers as Ethan Bridger accepted his quad espresso shot. His therapist would call that progress and God's grace in his life.

He called it will power—and the skill to razer-focus on the job.

If only those traits hadn't abandoned him in Guantanamo.

Nodding his thanks and ignoring the long lashes the barista batted his way, Ethan turned and slipped out of his favorite coffee shop. His G-Shock watch beeped a warning. Less than fifteen minutes remained to pick up his colleague to work security for the private concert. Somehow, he had to make the drive to Ybor City and back to Tampa in record time.

He would have been early if Jake had given him more notice, but Ethan didn't question his boss—or his other colleague for calling out on short notice. All the Coast Guard veterans at Semper Security had each other's back and didn't ask for an explanation when their past demons delivered an uppercut.

They simply stepped in and got the job done.

A cool October drizzle coated his brown leather jacket as he clicked the key fob to his oversized, navy Dodge Ram. After a swift check to his mirrors and back-up cam, he swerved out of the parallel parking spot and revved toward Luke's place at ten miles per hour over the speed limit.

The light misting continued as traffic crawled down one of Ybor's less-desirable streets. It was a shortcut he seldom used, but time wasn't his friend. Shadows covered the dingy streets and alleys. His pulse quickened the way it often did in his nightmares.

Not that he wasn't prepared. His concealed carry handgun was seated in his inside-the-belt holster. But the last thing he wanted was the need to use it—

Movement to his right caught his eye. A woman shifted side-to-side on a concrete bench in front of a boarded-up restaurant. She tugged at the sleeves of a tight beige sweater, which exposed her midriff but hung half off her slender shoulders.

A siren wailed in the distance as traffic inched toward the temperamental stoplight ahead. Once through it, he would be at his colleague's place in no time.

His gaze kept darting to the woman who shuffled back and forth on the bench. Her lips were blood red, her hair was curled like a doll's, and her features looked too young for her to be dressing like that. But her mini skirt, fishnet stockings, and stilettos sent a signal so explicit that any buck within a mile would notice.

His truck crept past her bench, but Ethan watched her in his rearview mirror. Why did she keep pulling at her long sleeves? What were they hiding?

The knot in his stomach doubled as a white box van with black windows jerked onto the sidewalk behind him and stopped in front of her. A hooded man jumped out the side door and yanked her to her feet. The woman's body stiffened, but she didn't protest as the man wrenched her toward the van.

Ethan's stomach twisted as his fingers tightened on his steering wheel. He was no stranger to the reality of Tampa's trafficking problem. The sunshine state's dark side included ranking third in the country for the illicit trade.

The only thing necessary for the triumph of evil is for good men to do nothing.

Ethan swerved his truck off the road onto the sidewalk and shoved open his door. Springing off the pavement, he raced toward the bench behind him.

The woman was disappearing inside the van's sliding door.

"Stop!" He threw his left shoulder into the gap and shoved it back. The hooded man cursed but still gripped the woman's arm. She screamed. Her eyes held a look of confusion—or was that anger?

"Let her go!" Ethan growled.

"It's a sting!" The driver shouted from the front of the van.

The hooded man shoved the woman into Ethan. She screamed again as the force propelled them onto the sidewalk. Ethan grunted as she slammed into his ribs, and the concrete connected with his spine.

The white van cut its way back into traffic, creating a domino effect of horns and screeching brakes. The woman rolled away from him, and Ethan shoved himself off the pavement to his feet and tried to ignore the pain in his chest. Probably cracked a rib.

Shaking his head, he focused on the woman who stood facing traffic with her back to him. Was she trembling? Understandable, given her close call.

He placed a light hand on her shoulder. "Are you okay, miss?"

She spun to face him—and her blue eyes flashed in rage. "It's *detective*, and no, I'm not fine. You just ruined my chance to nab those perps."

Chapter Two

Avery Reynolds yanked her hair into a tight knot on her head, unlocked her office, kicked her stilettos into the entryway of Reynolds Investigations—then slammed the door behind her.

Her private firm might not last the year if she couldn't get a handle on the case that made her open it in the first place.

Of all the bad luck—

Her cell vibrated in her bag, and she dug it out with one hand while disarming her security system with the other.

"What happened?" Liam Bracken's concerned but calm voice did little to slow her pulse. He was her first hire, and of the few professionals she employed, understood the complicated mess that the Casale/Russo/Eddie case, what they now dubbed CRE, had become. Though not even he knew how personal it was.

"Some security officer tried to rescue me from the John. The guy shoved me out of the van, thinking the officer was part of a sting operation." She snorted as she flipped on the light to her office. "Little did he know *I* was the sting operation."

"Wait, where was this security officer? I thought you were waiting outside an abandoned restaurant?"

"I was." She pinned the cell phone between her ear and shoulder while peeling off her fishnet stockings. "He came out of nowhere."

"Then how do you know he was security?" Liam asked.

She sighed into the phone and sunk into her leather desk chair. "Because his shirt read *Semper Security*."

"Sounds like a well-meaning vet tried to save your life. Maybe we shouldn't be too hard on him."

Avery scooted her chair to a mini fridge in the corner and selected a Dr. Pepper. "I didn't need rescuing."

"He didn't know that. Any other woman would thank him."

She popped the lid open. "Yeah, well, he didn't have to call the Hillsborough County Sheriff and explain that I bombed my part of the undercover sex trafficking op. Liam, this tip was my chance to prove to Hannaford that I haven't lost my touch since resigning from his force."

"Sheriff Hannaford knows better than anyone that not every op goes as planned, and you didn't burn your bridges when you started your own firm. He won't think twice about using you again when he needs to contract out work," Liam said. "If his tip was right that Big Eddie is expanding his trafficking ring and using the cover of sporting events to draw more business, we'll have other opportunities. We're only a month into NFL season."

The cold beverage fizzed down her throat, coating the bad taste tonight had left in her mouth. She didn't pay Liam to be an optimist, but maybe he was right. Hannaford had been disappointed but promised to let her know how the other undercover agents fared.

"Bucs are ahead too."

Avery rolled her eyes and took another gulp of her drink as Liam rambled about the football game highlights. She didn't care whether the Tampa Bay Bucs won or not. She just wanted to win at her game, and tonight set her back 0-3.

Strike one—Big Eddie had disappeared in January even though she'd managed to catch and imprison his Hollywood girl, Russo. Strike two—Avery had uncovered his drug trafficking disguise, a fishing LLC that connected her to one of his top transporters, Rolles. She had been about to catch up with the Bahamian drug runner—when the resort owner Mario shot him before taking a fatal bullet himself.

The thought of Mario and her final promise to him made her shift in her seat. She would sort that out once she saw justice served. She owed him. She owed Casale. Her list of IOUs was stealing any chance of a good night's sleep.

Strike three—botching tonight's sting. Avery pulled open a desk drawer where she kept civilian clothes. No chance was she going anywhere else in this ratty disguise that reeked of failure.

"… Beech Mountain this weekend."

Avery's fingers hovered over a lightweight hoodie that would be worlds more comfortable than this mini sweater. "Come again? Sorry, I'm multitasking here." It was better than the truth—she hadn't been listening to Liam at all.

He chuckled on the other end. "Have you forgotten that Reef and Kaley's wedding is this weekend?"

She pushed the speaker button on her cell to free her hands for changing outfits. "That's this weekend? Yeah, guess I'll have to send a gift card or something."

Her colleague stopped laughing. "Avery, you RSVP'd that you were going, and I already said you could ride with Jayna and me. This is a small wedding of just close family and friends."

"Then I probably shouldn't have been on the list in the first place," she snapped.

There was a pause on the other end. "We went through a lot together in the Bahamas. Reef and Kaley count you a valued friend. Don't take your relationships for granted because one sting didn't go your way."

"Good night, Liam." Avery disconnected the call and pulled on her jeans. She trusted Liam's professional advice, but he tended to veer too close to preaching when it came to her personal life. Maybe faith and friends worked great for him.

So many people had come and gone in her life, and once-upon-a-time, her eleven-year-old-self had discovered a hard truth there was no point denying. She was a loner and always would be.

Chapter Three

A couple of bruised ribs and not even a thank you.

Ethan grabbed two ice packs from his freezer before rolling onto his king-sized bed. His lab Blackie trotted to his side and nuzzled a cold, wet nose into the palm of his hand.

"I'll be okay, girl. Just need a break." He slid the ice packs under his shirt and winced. Bruised ribs weren't as bad as broken ribs, which he'd had before, but they were no picnic. With a grimace, he reached for his phone on the nightstand.

He had popped a couple ibuprofen and pushed through the pain for his security shift, but now, he felt the force of that spitfire woman from his tailbone to his sternum.

Her intelligent, blue eyes might be beautiful if they hadn't been so furious. C'mon, how was he supposed to know she was an undercover cop?

It didn't matter. He would never see her again.

Besides, a woman who would understand his past and be patient enough to live with the ramifications—yeah, she didn't exist. The women who flashed attention his way saw only his physique and the good looks he'd inherited from his mom. They weren't willing to look beneath the surface, and if they dared, they would run.

Scrolling through his calendar, Ethan relaxed at how clear his schedule was. He had decided to take PTO the next two days to rest, and after that—

Wait. No. Not this weekend.

With a groan, he swiped to his inbox, searching for the invitation.

Save the date. October 17.

That was why his week was so clear. His time-off for the wedding next weekend had been approved weeks ago, so he'd forgotten about it. Now, the idea of driving eleven hours sounded miserable.

No, he wouldn't let his friends down. Kaley's counseling had given him a lifeline and more coping skills than anyone else he'd met with. Her fiancé Reef had become a true friend, someone who didn't judge but showed up when he needed him.

This weekend was their big day. He'd make it work, even if his own bruised dreams and ribs made it hard to breathe.

He had a few days to rest, get his suit dry cleaned, and attempt to snag enough sleep so Kaley wouldn't see any bags under his eyes. His therapist noticed everything, and the fact she was getting married wouldn't change that.

Sliding his phone onto its charger, he reached for a water bottle and pill case instead. Tonight called for melatonin. He might have to fight the nightmares he couldn't remember later, but he wouldn't have to fight falling asleep.

Maybe one day, he wouldn't wake up in a cold sweat, crying like a little boy who had the worst nightmare of his life.

Kaley said perhaps he wasn't dreaming at all but that his body was stuck responding to the traumatic event in its own way. She had told him he wasn't alone, that other PTSD veterans had similar experiences—waking up with night sweats and tears and not knowing why.

He had asked if there was any hope his nights wouldn't look like this the rest of his life. She'd quoted him some statistics he couldn't remember, and he'd brushed those aside. What he really wanted was hope.

What she said next continued to rub the back of his mind.

"You want my personal take? On a professional level, I'm not permitted to share my beliefs, but if you ask me, I can tell you."

He had wanted to know.

Kaley had scrolled on her phone for a moment. "The Bible says in Romans 8:38-39, 'For I am persuaded that neither death nor life, nor angels nor principalities nor powers, nor things present nor things to come, nor height nor depth, nor any other created thing, shall be able to separate us from the love of God which is in Christ Jesus our Lord.' Nothing, not even your unrelenting symptoms can separate you from God and His love."

He had tapped his fingers together. "I grew up in church. I've heard all that before. But can God heal me—and if He can, will He?"

Kaley had set her phone aside and taken a deep breath. "Ethan, God can heal anyone, and sometimes He chooses to do so. Other times, He doesn't in this life. Either way, He works through our pain and struggles to accomplish a purpose greater than anything we can imagine, a purpose that is ultimately for our good and His glory."

He snorted. "No disrespect, but that sounds selfish."

"It's not selfish when you realize He created the world perfect, and we're the ones who messed it up. You've been to church. You know the redemption story. I can't tell you what God's plan for your life is and how your trauma plays into it, but I can promise you He has a plan. My clients who find the most hope— and healing, in one way or another—are the ones who believe that."

Their session had ended, and even though he didn't believe her, he did respect her and how much she cared about him and her other clients.

Blackie now snored on the floor beside his bed, and Ethan's own eyelids began to feel heavy. The melatonin was kicking in, stilling his restless mind.

One last thought nagged him. If God truly cared, He wouldn't let such awful things happen in the first place. He wouldn't let him spend the rest of his life regretting how helpless he had been to save his best friend.

Chapter Four

The drive to the Devant Dance Company near Hyde Park offered a sharp contrast to the dingy section of Ybor where her sting had gone south last night, but the manicured scenery did little to soothe Avery's frustration.

She had expected a call from Bella, but the timing couldn't have been worse.

After parking in the large lot, Avery started the familiar walk to the rehearsal studio. The company's modern two-story brick building with its vintage black and white sign, private garden, mini theater, and adjacent reception hall made clear these ballerinas had the best—and their parents had the deep pockets to pay for it.

Passing the garden, she couldn't help but overhear a woman talking to a young girl in a pink tutu. The girl's eyes were red and puffy, and the woman, perhaps her mother, wiped her tears with a tissue.

"Shush, now, don't listen to what the other girls say. You can be anything you want to be."

Avery winced and hurried to open the studio door. Her foster mom had once told her the same thing.

You can be anything you want to be.

Eleven-year-old Avery had believed Mrs. Casale. Thirty-one-year-old Avery was doubting if she should've.

After checking in at the front desk and confirming she was Bella Ricci's guest, Avery cracked open the studio door and slid inside. On the large open floor, an instructor conducted a class of maybe two dozen miniature ballerinas, while parents and guardians watched from the comfort of cushioned chairs and couches offset by mahogany coffee tables.

Her gaze landed on Bella's dark, wavy hair that fell below her shoulders. She scrolled on her phone, no doubt working remotely with real estate clients during Gianna's lesson. If only Bella's brother Anthony could have pursued a respectable living and not been sucked into the crowd that had ruined his reputation, broken Mrs. Casale's heart—and ultimately taken his life.

After Mr. Casale unexpectedly lost his job, the foster system moved Avery from the Casale's home. She lost touch with the family until reconnecting with Bella in college and forging a deepening friendship since then. Avery hadn't personally witnessed Anthony's descent into Tampa's dark underbelly, but when she was assigned as detective on his murder case, since gone cold, Bella begged her not to let the man responsible for her brother's death remain unpunished.

As if sensing her, Bella glanced up and smiled. Her former foster sister's genuine smile doubled the knot in her stomach.

Bella motioned for Avery to join her on the velvety blue couch and circled an arm around Avery's waist. "Thank you for coming. I wish we could grab coffee somewhere, but this is the last free time I have on the calendar today."

Avery resisted the urge to pull away. Bella was one-hundred-and-ten percent Italian, like her mother, and physical touch was a way of life to her. She had never understood Avery's resistance to touch, and Avery had stopped trying to explain. Better to let her hug and get it over with.

"It's no trouble. I love watching Gianna." Avery shifted to search for her goddaughter on the floor. The ten-year-old girl was a spitting image of her mother Bella, but her dark curls wrapped into a tight bun. Her full lips pressed tightly together in concentration as she pirouetted and pointed her toes.

Bella didn't voice the reason she had invited Avery here but let the silence do the talking.

Avery sighed and turned back to the woman who was the closest thing she had to a sister. "I'm sorry, but I don't have the good news I'd hoped to report. The lead I was working met with— let's just say I hit a wall." There was no point telling her the wall belonged to a six-foot-something security guard with a heart of gold but the worst timing ever.

Taking a deep breath, Bella set her phone on the coffee table and took Avery's hands. The gesture would have been repulsive if anyone other than Bella had done it.

"Avery, you know that my mother—God rest her soul—had absolute faith in you, and so do I. Setback or not, you will find the mastermind behind Anthony's death and bring him to justice."

After a gentle squeeze of Bella's hands, Avery pulled back. "I want to be worthy of your trust, but this case is so much more complex than anything I've worked on before. The man I'm hunting is—invisible most of the time, relentless in expanding his reach, brutal beyond words—" Avery stopped herself. Bella didn't need to know the odds against her.

"I won't stop, Bella. Not unless I have to shut down my agency and go back to the sheriff's department for work, but even then—"

Bella shook her head and reached for her phone. "No, I believe in you. I'm wiring you extra this month."

"Stop." Avery bit her lip. Bella's advance for taking her brother's case had helped her open Reynolds Investigation in the first place, but she couldn't accept more, not now.

"Even a private investigator needs a bonus every now and then." Bella's dark brown eyes twinkled. "We're leaving tomorrow for Cancun. You should take a vacation too. The distance will do wonders for your perspective on the case, and getting some rest couldn't hurt you."

"Bella, I don't need a vacation."

"Yes, you do. You need a breakthrough in the case, and the best way to start is by getting some rest yourself. Trust me. I know what burnout looks like." She chuckled and tossed her phone in her Kate Spade purse. "I'm the worst offender."

Avery pressed a hand to her cheek. She should've applied more under-eye concealer. "When will you be back?"

"Next Tuesday." Bella reached for a flyer on the coffee table and passed it to Avery. "Gianna's recital is that Friday. You will come, won't you? It will be here in the performance theater."

Avery glanced at the flyer with the recital date and details. "I wouldn't miss it." She stuffed it in her bag and cast another look at the ballerinas. "I'm sorry I can't stay longer, but I have another meeting in less than an hour. Please give Gianna a kiss for me, and tell her I can't wait to see her performance."

"I will." Bella's purse vibrated, and she groaned. "This vacation can't start soon enough."

Avery rose from the couch and waved goodbye as Bella reached into her purse to dig out her phone. Missing out on a farewell hug was fine by her.

Gianna's recital was just under two weeks away. She would have a new lead by then. She had to. Disappointing Bella—and the memory of her beautiful mother—was not an option.

Her thoughts elsewhere, she nearly collided with an older man with a cane who was also leaving the studio.

Avery stepped aside and reached to open the door for him. "I'm sorry. I wasn't paying attention."

The gray-bearded man dismissed her apology. "It is nothing. Those *stellas*—they are everything."

Avery smiled at the Italian endearment for *stars* she had heard Bella call Gianna before. It was a fitting way to describe the ballerinas. "Yes, they are."

He adjusted thick-framed glasses and nodded his thanks for getting the door. "Even stellas must learn that practice doesn't make perfect. Only perfect practice does. Too many mistakes— and poof! Failure. Unacceptable."

She held her smile in place as he shuffled past her, but inwardly she rolled her eyes. These children were too young to carry the burden that came with disappointment and failure. Why did some grandparents hold children to such unreachable standards?

The old man probably meant well, but his words made her wince. These days, she was no stranger to failure.

Avery cast one last glance over her shoulder at Gianna. The girl was almost the age she had been when she entered the foster care system, which shattered her sense of belonging and self-worth.

Gianna was blessed with parents that loved her, but Bella was increasingly distracted and driven to avenge her brother. Avery had to finish this case once and for all. She couldn't let anything cast a shadow on Gianna's bright future.

First, she would take Bella's advice and get some healthy distance and perspective. She could work remotely for a few days reviewing the files Hannaford had shared with her about the sting. When she got back, she'd tackle every potential angle with fresh determination.

Avery unlocked her car, started the engine, and pressed the voice command button on her steering wheel. Grimacing that he had been right and she might have to apologize, she sighed and then said, "Call Liam Bracken."

Chapter Five

The South Carolina drizzle held a chill much different from the Florida weather they had left nine hours ago. Avery pulled her jacket hood over her head and gripped her newly purchased iced coffee bottle. Then, she jogged from the well-lit gas station store entrance to the overhang where Liam was filling up the tank of Jayna's small SUV. Jayna had insisted they use her car since it was roomy enough for three.

Why these two lovebirds wanted a third wheel on a road trip was beyond her, but it saved Avery the trouble of driving eleven-hours by herself.

She stepped next to Liam as he topped off the tank. "I'll take the last shift. You've done the lion's share of the driving."

He shook his head. "You've got to be more tired than I am. You were already at the office when I got there at seven this morning."

They had agreed to work a half day before starting the road trip, because yes, she was a workaholic and felt better about missing only part of Friday. Little did he know she'd started her day at five.

Avery held up the iced coffee. "I've got caffeine, and I don't need a lot of sleep. Go join your girlfriend in the back. She's been out since ten o'clock."

"It's past eleven, Avery. Are you sure you want to drive the mountain roads in the dark?"

She stretched out her hand, palm open. "I promise to drive better than James Bond. Keys, please."

"All right. But I'm going to keep you company from the

passenger side." He nodded toward the side window. "Jayna has pretty much taken over the back seat anyway."

Avery snorted. "Your girlfriend sure can sleep. Amazing, considering all she's been through."

A soft smile lit Liam's face as he handed her the keys. "She's come a long way in three months, thanks to God's grace and Kaley's counseling."

"Uh-huh." Avery opened the driver's door.

"I need to use the restroom. I'll be back in a minute." Liam jogged away as she closed the door, started the engine, and searched for the seat warmer. Being tall for a girl, she didn't need to adjust the seat.

She checked her rear-view mirror, and her gaze settled on Jayna. Her wavy dark hair half concealed her face, pressed against a pillow on the seat. The woman had gotten lucky to escape her controlling fiancé and the drug-running web surrounding his resort. But Liam hadn't given up on her, and now, the woman clearly held his heart.

No wonder she could sleep so peacefully, knowing that a good man cared about her. Avery had never let men get close to her—relationships were too much of a risk. They hadn't worked for her parents, and where had that left her?

In and out of foster care homes until she'd finally aged out and learned to stand on her own two feet.

Liam pulled open the passenger door, his own glass coffee bottle in hand, as she chugged half of hers and popped in an earbud.

Avery shifted to drive and navigated toward the station's exit. "Don't drink that. Get some sleep. If I feel woozy, I'll wake you."

"Nonsense, it will be almost one in the morning before we get to the Airbnb."

"Exactly why you should get some sleep," she said. "I've got Pearl Jam on my playlist. I'll be fine."

Liam opened his mouth to argue, but Avery pointed to her ear. "Not listening to you. Go to sleep."

For a few minutes, he fussed about making sure she had the directions plugged into the GPS and then said he'd be "resting his eyes" if she needed him.

Ten minutes later, he was out cold.

She glanced at him and grinned to herself. He was a good man, but no one could top her stamina where caffeine was involved.

Besides, she planned to sleep through the morning festivities anyway. No one would miss her. How she had merited an invitation to a small, private destination wedding was beyond her. Most of the family and guests were staying in a big Airbnb, but Kaley had insisted she join them. She'd be sharing a room with Jayna, who wouldn't be in it most of the time, which suited Avery's solitary self just fine.

She'd go to the wedding. Take in the mountain scenery and fresh air. Eat a slice of cake. Toss some confetti or whatever they tossed at brides and grooms these days.

But her mind would be mulling over the case to find any angle she might have missed. In the mountains of North Carolina, she would have nothing to distract her.

Avery squinted her eyes together and blinked again. The dashboard clock read one in the morning, but the blue digits blurred. Maybe she had overestimated her alertness. The music thudding in her ears no longer was enough to keep her blood flowing. Man, she was tired.

She shook herself. Her GPS said they were close. Gripping the wheel, she focused on the pavement, shrouded in fog. Her headlights illuminated deer on the side of the road, and the last thing she wanted was to hit one.

Liam hadn't been kidding when he described the winding

mountain roads. She couldn't imagine driving these switchbacks in icy conditions.

Finally, the GPS guided her to turn off the main road, and she sighed in relief. ETA was less than two minutes.

Several cars parked on the side of the road, and she pressed her brakes. This might be the place. Lots of cars made sense for a wedding party.

She found the driveway and maneuvered past a few more cars to a parking spot. Her GPS said this was the place. Shutting off the ignition, she nudged Liam. "We're here—I think."

He mumbled something incomprehensible in reply and turned to the backseat where Jayna remained passed out. She would leave the job of waking her up to him.

Reaching below her seat, she popped the trunk and then opened her door. She would grab her small bag and see herself inside. Kaley had told her and Jayna that their room was the first one on the left on the main level. It couldn't be too hard to find.

Slinging her duffle over her shoulder, she waved at the motion light on the side, and it bathed their surroundings in light. Her feet crunched on rocky gravel, and the crisp mountain air sent goosebumps down her arm. A shadowy pavilion around back promised a relaxed hang-out spot, probably with a firepit. No doubt this place would look stunning in the morning.

Right now, the one thing she wanted was the pillow on her bed.

She helped herself up the porch steps and twisted the door open. A massive great room greeted her. Thanks to a small light in the kitchen off to the side, she made out a large fireplace, plenty of couch seating, an antler chandelier—and all she cared about right now, two bedroom doors separated by what she presumed was a bathroom.

Left door, right?

Her phone was about dead, and she didn't have the energy to double check. Her memory said *left*, so she grabbed the knob and twisted.

She stepped into the pitch-black room and pressed her hand along the wall for the switch. There.

Light flooded the room.

A man bolted from the bed, and she staggered against the door. "Wrong—room—"

In a flash, he drew a handgun from beneath his pillow and aimed at her. His eyes were wide but not awake.

Her own firearm was locked in its case in her bag. "Stop!" She held up a hand. "There's been a mistake—"

Her voice died in her throat. The man pointing a gun at her was none other than the security guard who had botched her sting.

Chapter Six

Sleep evaded him most of the night. Ignoring the pain behind his tired eyes, Ethan slapped for his cell phone on the night stand—and his fingers grazed his firearm instead.

What a nightmare. A living one. He'd drawn his gun on a detective and not just any detective. What was that spitfire of an undercover agent doing here?

It was a miracle she hadn't arrested him. The glare in her eyes hinted that she had wanted to.

He groaned. It had been a mistake. He hoped she would accept his apology this morning and not press him for an explanation. If she did, he'd try to shrug it off as the instincts of a security officer.

Not the side effects of PTSD.

Turning off his alarm, he slid onto the cold hardwood floor. His toes protested at the chill, and he dug out a pair of socks. What he really needed was coffee and lots of it.

He also needed to find Reef or Kaley and confess he had almost shot one of their guests. Yeah, he definitely should drink some coffee before that conversation.

The large two-story cabin was quiet. Most normal people would still be asleep at five-fifty in the morning on a vacation. Too bad he had lost touch with normal.

He wanted to brew and drink his own pot, but a small Keurig offered a temporary solution that would be quieter. Selecting the boldest k-cup on the rack, he started the single-cup setting and glanced out the window toward the outdoor seating and firepit.

Not a soul in sight. He could decompress there before the others woke up. If the floor were any indicator, the air would be cold. As his cup brewed, he retrieved a jacket and then took himself and his black coffee to the outdoor retreat.

He paused at the circle of chairs around the fire pit. Each one had some point of weakness, leaving his back exposed to—

Ethan shook his head. He wasn't in danger here. If only he could shut off his training. Picking his way to the far end, he selected a chair that gave him a view of the kitchen and main house. At least if that agent showed up, he would see her.

"You can't sleep either?" Reef's voice made him jump.

Spinning in his seat, Ethan glanced to where his friend exited the suite separate from the main house. A few other guys were staying there with him, but Ethan was grateful for his own room where his night demons couldn't bother anyone but himself.

"You could say that." Ethan tried to relax in the wooden chair. "I'm guessing my reasons are quite different from yours."

Reef grinned and folded himself into a chair beside him. "Dude, I'm getting married tomorrow. I'll be amazed if I sleep at all tonight."

What would it be like to know that in one day, he'd get to spend forever with the woman he loved? Ethan sighed and sipped his coffee. That day might never come for him, because what woman would understand him?

"If you need company, text me. I'm a pro at insomnia." Ethan forced a lightness he didn't feel into his voice.

Reef's smile faded a little. "Sorry, man, sleep isn't any better for you these days?"

The image of the agent's shocked face sprang back in his mind. He needed to confess before she told her side of the story. "About that—"

"I see I'm not the only early riser around here." The bright, breathy voice suggested someone who had just finished a jog.

Ethan jerked his head toward the woman who had somehow managed to surprise him. The agent was hiking up the yard from the street. Her light reddish-brown hair was pulled into a high pony tail, her cheeks were flushed from exercise, and a smile lit up her face—until she spotted him. The smile vanished, and she froze in her tracks before reaching the patio.

He jumped to his feet. "I'm sorry about—"

She narrowed her eyes. "About pulling a gun on me?"

Now Reef sprang from his chair. "Whoa—what?"

Ethan ran a hand over his face. "It was a mistake. She barged into my room—"

The detective closed the space between them. "I did not *barge*. I was being as quiet as a mouse not to wake anyone."

He held up his hands. "You scared me to death and woke me from a sound sleep when you flipped on my light. It was my training coming out."

"Training? What kind of training?" She poked a finger toward his chest. "You should always be sure of your target before you aim a gun."

Ethan shook his head. "No, that's before you pull the trigger, which I didn't when I saw you."

Reef stepped between them. "We-ell, sounds like you two had a, uh—surprise—meeting last night. Glad you're both okay. Let me officially introduce you."

The woman stuffed her hands in her red jogging hoodie and snapped, "Oh, we've already met."

"Ribs are still sore, thanks to you," Ethan shot back.

Reef raised an eyebrow but cleared his throat. "So anyway, Ethan, this is Avery. Avery, meet Ethan. You're both mutual friends of Kaley's and mine, and we're so glad you both made the trip to be here for *our special day*."

His emphasis on *special day* brought the surroundings back into focus for Ethan. He wasn't here to make a scene or prove who was more in the wrong. This weekend was about Reef and Kaley, and he wouldn't be the one to spoil anything.

Ethan took a deep, steadying breath. "Thanks, Reef. Any friend of yours is a friend of mine."

The frown on Avery's face and arms crossed on her chest indicated she did not share that sentiment.

Right then, the side kitchen door opened, and Kaley appeared with a glowing smile on her face. She wore jeans and a white shirt with the word *bride* spelled in bold blue lettering. In her hand, she held a black paper bag.

"Morning, Ethan," Kaley said. "Avery! So glad you made it."

She moved toward Avery as if she might hug her, but the agent waved her back.

"I need a shower—just got back from a jog." Avery edged toward the now-open door. "Since I got in late last night, what's on the schedule today?"

"We'll leave for breakfast when everyone's up," Kaley said. "Then we'll explore the Woolly Worm Festival together, come back and relax here, and get ready for the rehearsal this evening."

Ethan bit his lip to keep from chuckling. Avery's face looked lost. "The Woolly what?" she asked.

"Oh, it's a tradition around these parts. People race woolly worms, there's food, lots of vendors, should be fun. Reef and his dad went to it when he was a kid, and I was beyond thrilled to find out it's the same weekend as our wedding."

Avery's eyebrows couldn't climb any higher, could they? Ethan choked down a laugh and glanced at Kaley. "Sounds—interesting."

Avery thumbed toward the kitchen. "Right, so I'm going to shower now. See you kids in a few." With a last glare at him, she disappeared inside.

Reef strode toward Kaley. "Morning, beautiful. I like your shirt. Where's mine?"

She reached for a hug, and Reef circled her in his arms. "Guess you'll have to open the bag." She kissed his nose.

That was Ethan's cue. Three would always be a crowd.

"I'm going to go—make a pot of coffee," he excused himself. Those two lovebirds needed some space, and now that people were up, he wouldn't feel bad about making noise in the kitchen.

Maybe he'd offer Avery some coffee when she reemerged from her shower, but something told him the agent would not be remotely interested in any peace offering from him.

Chapter Seven

Avery shoved her arms into a red flannel shirt and buttoned it over her black tank top. The flannel was two sizes too big and the perfect cover for concealing her Glock.

Not that she would have any need of it in sleepy Beech Mountain. But that kind of thinking was what caught agents unprepared, and unprepared, she would never be—especially when a gun-slinging security officer shared the same air space.

She ran a hand through her blow-dried hair and resisted the urge to tie it up and out of her way. The air carried a chill, unlike the sticky humidity that Florida offered on most days. Wearing her hair down might feel nice and not like an itchy mess.

Her stomach rumbled, and she hoped whatever place Kaley planned for breakfast was good—and not far. Her body craved calories after her run, and she'd forgotten her breakfast bars.

Jayna poked her head in the door as Avery pulled on her boots. Her roommate's dark wavy hair fell just below her shoulders, and she was wearing a green flannel that offered a stunning contrast to her olive skin. "Everyone's getting ready to leave for breakfast. You want to ride with Liam and me?"

"Yep, coming." Avery grabbed her small backpack-style purse and paused. Should she bring her laptop? She didn't care to visit the woolly-whatever festival that Kaley was ecstatic about. Maybe falling in love made people lose their senses.

She wouldn't know.

"Oh, lose the laptop," Jayna said. "This is breakfast, not a business meeting."

"Yes, but—"

"C'mon! This is a fun day. Be present."

Avery gritted her teeth but forced a smile. "Fine. Let's get some food. I'm starving."

A dozen or more people buzzed around the main room. Avery paused by a wall and observed as she did best. There was so much hugging and laughing. Some must be family, and others, close friends.

Was this what a fish out of water felt like? In her work, she felt at ease. Here—well, this group had a sense of home, of community she would never understand, could never understand.

Resentment tugged at her heart, but she shoved it aside. No, she didn't belong here. She didn't belong anywhere.

That was her reality. It didn't bother her when she existed in the quiet confines of her office, but here, she felt exposed.

Hugging the wall, she edged toward the kitchen. She needed something to relieve the tightness in her throat.

"Coffee?" A quiet, deep voice intruded into her thoughts.

It was Ethan. He held out a travel coffee mug while sipping from his own. He had a lot of nerve speaking to her after—

But when her gaze drifted to his face, her ire faded, for he surveyed the scene just like her.

As an observer, not a participant.

She frowned. How annoying that he should turn out to be decently good-looking in the daytime when he wasn't ruining her plans or aiming a gun at her. Dark stubble edged his jawline, and intense gray eyes surveyed the room, though the bags underneath them hinted at someone with an insomnia problem.

"Feels kind of like looking in on a Norman Rockwell reunion painting that you didn't get painted into," he said.

She stared at him. A security guard with an artistic sense? Weird. Even weirder was how he had expressed her sentiment exactly.

Clearing her throat, she accepted the mug. "Black, the way I like it."

"I thought so."

Avery glared to hide her surprise. "Lucky guess."

He shook his head. "Nope. People like us don't have the taste or time for sugar and cream. Coffee is fuel, not a frou-frou drink."

The brew burned down her throat. People like *them*? She didn't belong in the same sentence with the man who had destroyed her last lead.

For that matter, she didn't belong in the same conversation either. "Thanks for the coffee." She surveyed the room to find her exit. "But don't think this makes us friends."

"I wouldn't dream of it." The lilt to his voice suggested he was smiling at her or teasing her, neither of which were acceptable.

Avery stalked to the closest corner where Jayna chatted with an older couple. Jayna caught her gaze and waved her over. "Have you met everyone yet?"

She hadn't met anyone yet, which was fine by her, but she had to lose her raincloud mood since this was a happy occasion. "No."

"This is Kaley's mom and dad," Jayna said. "Her brother is around here—somewhere." The woman looked like an older version of her daughter with bronze-blonde hair that fell in waves to her shoulders, but Kaley had gotten her green eyes from her dad whose no-nonsense, black-framed glasses didn't quite seem to fit the jovial smile lines on his face.

"Nice to meet you, Mr. and Mrs. Colbert," Avery said.

"And which of Kaley's friends are you?" Mr. Colbert asked.

Avery paused. How exactly did she answer that?

Jayna saved her the trouble. "She's the agent who helped get Kaley back—and I owe her a heap of thanks too."

Before Avery could object, Mrs. Colbert wrapped her in a bear hug. "I have wanted to thank you in person for so long. What you did for our daughter—"

"It was my job, and I'm glad I could." Avery patted her shoulder and pulled away. "I just wish everyone had such a happy ending. I mean—look at this." She gestured to the room. "It's like the fairytale wedding that ends a story."

"God has blessed Reef and Kaley, but I don't think they're under any illusions that life is a fairytale," Mr. Colbert said. "Marriage won't always be easy, but they are committed to each other and to Christ, so I'm confident they will be better together. We couldn't be happier for them."

Avery nodded to be polite and took another sip of her coffee to spare herself from thinking up a trite answer. Concepts like commitment and Christianity were nice for some people but didn't ring true to her life experiences.

Liam appeared next to Jayna as the Colberts excused themselves to get jackets from their room. "Reef said we should head out soon and hope to beat the lunch rush at Banner Elk Café. With the Woolly Worm Festival in swing, restaurants are bound to be packed."

"I'm ready whenever," Avery said. Lunch would … give her more opportunity to spend time with this chummy group. Great.

At least she could do so while eating food. Her stomach reminded her she needed more than coffee after her morning run.

Liam waved at someone on the other side of the room and wrapped an arm around Jayna's shoulder. "Have you met Reef and Kaley's friend Ethan yet? He's got some bruised ribs, so I told him he could ride with us."

"Sure, that's fine," Jayna said. "I'll ride in the back with Avery. Poor guy. That has to hurt."

Avery snorted. Not as much as losing her most promising lead did. Now, she would have to spend most of her morning with the man. This day could only get better.

"Did you say something?" Jayna asked her.

"Nope." Avery chugged the last of her coffee. The less she said, the less she would have to choke up an apology for later.

"Hey, thanks for letting me ride with you guys." Ethan strode toward Liam but halted when he saw Avery.

Jayna's gaze darted between the two. "Oh, have you two met?"

"Yep." Avery jerked a thumb toward the door to avoid any more niceties. "Let's get this circus on the road."

Chapter Eight

The town of Banner Elk offered good food, even if it was also home to the quirkiest festival he had ever witnessed.

Ethan couldn't help but stare at someone dressed in a full-body, orange-and-brown worm costume posing across the street with some kids. Kaley wanted everyone to explore the festival after their early lunch, but he was in no hurry. He was quite content sitting in this lodge-like restaurant eating some of the best chicken and waffles he'd ever tasted.

At least one other person didn't want to visit the Woolly Worm Festival, and that was the enigma of a woman who'd been on a phone call for most of the meal. Avery paced a small rug in front of a fireplace in the corner of the room. She'd left her hair down, and its reddish tint emphasized her fair complexion and blue eyes.

Right now, she ran a hand through her hair, as if it were a trial not being pulled back. Something agitated her, and he hoped it wasn't the business he had botched.

He shook his head. The woman was quite the looker. But the handgun that his trained eye had noticed imprinting inside her flannel shirt reminded him she was lethal.

"So let me get this straight." Liam's words pulled Ethan back into the conversation, and he redirected his gaze toward the agent. During their car ride, Ethan had been able to piece together that Liam and Avery were colleagues, which probably made this group the most protected wedding party he'd ever attended.

Not that they needed it. He couldn't imagine anyone here having enemies.

"People actually race worms—woolly worms—during this festival as part of a competition?" Liam asked.

Reef nodded. "Sure do. If you look out the window, you can see the yellow stage. You can't tell from here, but there are several strings tied to the top, and people race their worms to see which one will get to the top first."

Liam laughed. "I've seen a lot of races in my day, but never a worm race."

"You'll get to change that today." Kaley cupped her hands around her coffee mug.

"But what's the point?" Ethan asked. "I mean, why race worms?"

"Just a sec." Reef waved over the waitress and asked for the check before leaning forward to answer him. "You're familiar with Groundhog Day, right?"

"Sure."

"Think of the woolly worm as Banner Elk's version of the groundhog. The worm that ultimately wins the most heats, wins the "race" and is used to predict winter. If the winning worm's brown segments are lighter, winter will be milder. If they're darker, winter will be colder and snowier."

Ethan rubbed a hand over two days' growth of beard. "How accurate is this method for predicting weather?"

Reef shrugged and wrapped an arm around Kaley's shoulder. "About as accurate as the groundhog seeing his shadow."

Kaley laughed and leaned her head against Reef's shoulder. "I still think it's a super fun concept for a festival, and I can't wait to explore it."

Reef kissed her head. "I'll pay the tab, and we can head over."

"What about Avery?" Jayna nodded toward the fireplace. "She's been on that call for so long I don't think she had a chance to eat."

"I'll get her a box," Kaley said, "and drop it off on the table by her. Hopefully, she can join us soon."

Ethan sipped his water and tried to hide a smirk. What little he knew of Avery suggested she wanted nothing to do with a festival about weather worms.

The next time she decided to go on a vacation, she would fly to a deserted island and stay there by herself.

It would certainly not involve navigating a worm festival to find a wedding party.

The kicker? She had to *pay* to get into the darn thing.

Oh, and her lunch was cold.

That part, at least, was her job's fault. She had forgotten about Russo's hearing date, but her office manager Tasha had not. The woman, a capable agent herself, should have called her yesterday, but that was Avery's fault too.

For taking a vacation in the first place.

The verdict didn't surprise her, but Russo must be none too happy with a life sentence. Would knowing her fate make her more willing to talk? Avery would schedule a video visit next week and find out.

For now, she had to find Liam somewhere in this maze of vendors and food trucks. He would want to know about Russo.

Someone bumped her side, and she arched away. Crowds always made her nervous, because she saw all the potential problems. Missing child. Theft. Assault.

This town had its charm and seemed like a place full of pleasant people, but she didn't have an "off" switch.

"The funnel cake's good."

She spun to see Ethan taking a bite out of his funnel cake. Powdered sugar coated the corners of his mouth and clung to his stubbly chin.

"Where's Liam?" She scanned the people around him, but he appeared alone.

He shrugged. "Everyone's off doing their own thing. Some people are getting junk food, others are shopping around. Kaley bought a woolly worm and somehow convinced her younger brother to keep it until after her honeymoon."

Avery frowned. Since when did this security guard get to be so chatty? "I'll find him."

"Oh wait, I see him." Ethan jutted his chin to indicate somewhere behind her. She turned to spot Liam and Jayna popping their heads in plywood cut-outs of life-size woolly worm caricatures.

Liam's pale Irish skin blushed from the sun or pleasure at Jayna's laughter or both. The two had recently made their relationship "official," and Avery was happy for her colleague, but right now, he clearly wasn't in the right headspace to talk about the Russo hearing.

"Is something wrong?" Ethan finished his funnel cake and tried to brush the powdered sugar off his chin.

She wasn't about to tell him. "Nothing I want to talk with you about."

"Ouch."

"Listen, we might be part of the same wedding party, but—"

"Hey, Avery!" Kaley's voice was an octave too high.

Avery spun to see the bride-to-be jogging toward her. Kaley's cheeks were flushed, and she kept glancing over her shoulder.

Her senses went on high alert, and she scanned the crowd. "Where is Reef?"

"That's just it." Kaley paused a few feet away and tried to catch her breath. "I don't know, but someone dressed like him grabbed my arm a few seconds ago. When I realized it wasn't him, I shouted and yanked free. The man mumbled an apology and disappeared."

She hugged her flannel sleeves. "Avery, it felt like what happened with Valentina Russo all over again."

Chapter Nine

Ethan leaned against the railing outside the intimate reception hall at Overlook Barn and checked the building's perimeter from the bird's eye view. He had planned to spend the late afternoon taking a nap to make up for last night's lack of sleep.

Instead, he was offering security services to his therapist during her rehearsal dinner. The laughter coming from the room behind him suggested the wedding party was having a wonderful time—and had forgotten Kaley's scare from earlier in the day.

A few more friends had arrived, including Kaley's and Reef's pastor-friend TJ who would be officiating, the maid of honor Olivia, and half a dozen other people whose names he would never remember. After this weekend, he'd never see them again anyway.

He gazed over the mountain scenery in front of him. Golden hour transformed the trees on the mountain into shades of gold, orange, and yellow. The evening seemed to promise that tomorrow would be the perfect wedding day.

Kaley deserved no less. Ethan still couldn't wrap his mind around the fact someone had abducted her on this very mountain last winter and that she had never said a word to him about it.

Sure, he was her patient, but he understood trauma. Perhaps it was a code of therapists not to share their personal experiences with clients. That made sense, but now, he felt like her words to him offered that much more credibility.

She'd been through a horrific experience and made it to the other side. The way she lived her life suggested she was stronger and more secure in spite of it.

Even so, there was no denying the fear he'd read on her face at the festival. Avery suggested the man had simply mistaken her for someone else, and maybe he had, but Kaley's reaction proved that even a survivor like her wasn't immune to triggers.

He turned back to face the room of family and friends. If his presence could provide them with peace of mind, he was glad to be here. The group had made him feel like one of them, including him in the catered barbeque dinner from a local place.

Food aside, he now knew every step Kaley would be walking tomorrow. He'd memorized the path she and her dad would take to the outdoor wedding overlook, examined the barn where the happy couple would have their "first look" photographed, and inspected the reception areas and adjacent facilities. He would arrive early before the ceremony tomorrow for a final walk through and to meet the rest of the venue staff.

Liam nodded his direction and slipped away from Jayna's side to stride toward him. Ethan hadn't met Liam prior to this trip, but they had talked several times in the car today, and he could see why Reef picked him for a best man. Liam was thoughtful, attentive, and easy to like—except on the one count that he was competing with Reef for luckiest guy in the room. Man, Liam's girlfriend was hot.

It was hard not to feel insecure about his hopeless relationship status around here.

"Thanks again for being here tonight." Liam unrolled his cuffed flannel sleeves. The evening chill was creeping in.

Ethan had to give it to Kaley—hers was the first casual rehearsal dinner he'd attended. Almost everyone was in jeans and flannel shirts. Even Kaley wore dark-washed jeans and a light blue flannel shirt over her white t-shirt which read *bride*.

"My pleasure," Ethan said but directed his attention to a staff member who had entered and was now speaking to Kaley.

"Avery is convinced what happened earlier is nothing," Liam continued.

The staff member seemed to acknowledge something Kaley said and then turned to leave. Kaley stood and waved Reef over. It must be about time to head back to the Airbnb.

"She may be right, but I believe in preparing for worst-case," Ethan said and closed the balcony door. The evening temperatures were dropping fast, and the wedding party was moving toward the front exit. "Usually, worst case doesn't happen when you're ready for it."

Liam bobbed his head in agreement as they followed the others out front to where their cars were parked. "Always ready, right?"

"Semper Paratus," Ethan said, but his chest clenched at the words of his Coast Guard motto. The evening sunset faded on the horizon, heralding the arrival of night and whatever torments it held for him.

The one time he hadn't been ready had cost him everything.

Thud.

Avery bolted from her bed and smacked her head on the bunk above her. She bit her tongue to hold back the words forming on it. Somewhere above her, Jayna was asleep.

Blasted bunk beds. She had hated them in the foster homes where she once lived, and she hated them to this day. Tall girls like her always banged their heads.

Rubbing a sore spot on her scalp, Avery twisted to her side and stuffed her head back into the lumpy feather pillow that completed the less-than-ideal sleeping arrangement. It had taken her forever to fall asleep.

Now, what was responsible for waking her up?

There was a noise, like something large had fallen. She should ignore it.

No, she couldn't. Kaley had been so on edge after the incident at the festival. Although Avery was sure it was a mistake, she could at least make sure there was nothing potentially off the night before Kaley's wedding.

Careful not to knock her skull on the wooden frame, Avery pushed her pillow aside and scooted to the edge. The hardwood floors were cool to her socked feet, and the air temperature was probably in the sixties.

A shiver ran down her spine, but she didn't dare fumble

around in her suitcase in the dark for something warmer than her short-sleeve shirt and lightweight sleep pants.

The door creaked for a moment as she slipped into the hall. Silence greeted her, but a dim light shone from under the partially ajar bathroom door. It had to be two o'clock in the morning. Who in their right mind—

The heat kicked on, and the change in pressure inched the door further open. Maybe someone had forgotten to turn out the light. She could at least do that before going back to bed.

She pressed her hand against the door and pushed it open the rest of the way.

And froze.

A man was picking himself up off the bathroom floor, crawling up the bathroom vanity as if dependent upon it for support. His tank top was drenched—in water or sweat?—and clung to his muscled torso.

Avery's throat went dry as he turned haunted eyes her direction.

Ethan.

What in the world?

With one hand supporting himself, he twisted the faucet on with the other and splashed handfuls of water onto his face and into his mouth.

She didn't wait for him to speak but spun on her socks and fled back to her room, not caring if the door creaked as she opened and then locked it.

Maybe he was sleepwalking. Is that why he had fallen?

Those eyes of his— She pressed her own shut and tried to forget their disturbed, glazed look.

Either the man had a medical condition or was tormented by some secret she had just glimpsed.

And now, she couldn't forget.

Chapter Ten

His hand trembled as he poured his coffee mug. Ethan gripped it tighter and willed his nerves to steady.

If only willpower were enough.

Today was Kaley and Reef's wedding, and a glance out the window at dawn's first light suggested it was going to be perfect. He had to keep himself together and not let another miserable night impact their day.

Someone's light-colored hair flashed in his peripheral. No doubt it was Avery. He closed his eyes, hoping she wasn't the one who had seen him in the bathroom last night. He couldn't handle her scorn, not now.

Why did he agree to come in the first place? He should have known he couldn't keep his PTSD under wraps.

She entered the kitchen but didn't glance his way. White earbuds poked out from under her hair. Maybe she was back from another run. Damp hair clung to her face, and she had shoved her long-sleeve shirt up to her elbows.

Without a word, she placed a water glass under the refrigerator dispenser and filled it to the brim. After gulping it down, she set it in the sink.

"You know you sleepwalk, right?" Her words pierced the silence. Her tone was matter-of-fact but hinted at concern.

"What?"

"Sleepwalk. As in, when you walk in your sleep." Avery selected a banana from the fruit bowl and peeled down the sides. "You should get that checked out."

He exhaled. She hadn't come close to the truth. "Yeah, probably should."

She swallowed a bite and surveyed the empty space. "Last piece of advice: Warn your friends so they don't get freaked out."

Ethan couldn't suppress a grin. "Did I freak you out?"

Avery glared at him. "I don't get freaked out—easily. But normal people do."

"So you're not normal?" He couldn't help himself.

"My mistake offering you advice," she muttered and sped out of the kitchen space.

He sighed. He shouldn't have riled her, but there was something about pushing her buttons that he couldn't resist.

Part of him ached though. He didn't want others believing lies about him. Why couldn't he be brave enough to fess up to the truth?

The back door creaked open, and Reef's face poked into the kitchen. "Hey, man, Kaley's not up yet, right?"

Ethan shook his head. "No, the coast is clear, though I did hear her say something about hair and makeup starting early."

"Then, I don't have much time." Reef stepped inside and snatched an orange and granola bar off the snack counter.

"Yeah, you'd better get out of here," Ethan said.

"I need a favor first." Reef rubbed his chin, already freshly shaven. How long had he been up?

"What can I do?"

"I was hoping you'd ask. Kaley's parents were going to pick up the cake, but the order has been delayed an hour. It's no problem with the wedding, but her parents will already be at the venue for family pictures before the wedding. Is there any chance—"

"Sure, I can pick it up. Text me the pickup information."

Reef hesitated at the kitchen door. "We also appreciate you helping with security. It really eased Kaley's mind last night."

Ethan shrugged. "Glad to help. I'll keep tabs on things once I get there with the cake."

"You're the best."

No sooner had Reef disappeared outside than Kaley appeared in the kitchen, wearing a button-down flannel, yoga pants, messy morning hair, and the bright smile of a woman on her wedding day. "Morning, Ethan. Please tell me that's coffee."

"Fresh pot. Want some?" Ethan opened the cabinet for another mug.

"Pleeeaase." She ran a hand over her face. "I could not fall asleep. At all. Until maybe three in the morning. And then my alarm went off at six."

He grunted and selected the biggest mug he could find. "Welcome to my world."

Kaley leaned her elbows on the table-sized island in the kitchen. "I'm sorry, Ethan. I shouldn't complain when you deal with sleep troubles all the time."

"It's okay." He slid the coffee mug toward her. "Wish I could say I was used to it, but I'm not."

She thanked him for the coffee and twisted toward the fridge. "How have you been on this trip?"

He poured himself a second cup. "It's your wedding day. Don't ask and make me say something that might spoil it."

"Wedding day or not, I care."

His hand stilled on the now half-empty pot. "I know you do."

"Then don't pretend with me. I'm a good listener."

Ethan stalled by sipping the hot, bitter brew. "I think I scared one of your guests last night. I had an episode and woke up in a full sweat, so I went to the bathroom. But I tripped and fell on the rug."

He waved his hand. "Anyway, I'm fine, but she now thinks I sleepwalk. Guess that's better than the truth."

Kaley stirred cream into her mug and then leaned on the opposite counter. "The truth is always better, Ethan, even if it is harder. The Bible says the truth sets us free. It might be painful, but admitting what is real can be a step toward acceptance and healing."

She hurried on. "I'm not saying you need to explain anything to whoever saw you. I'm saying that in general, you shouldn't make up a story to cover what you're going through. You can be honest about it."

"It's easy to be honest around kind people like you, but other people judge. I hate it." The shaking in his hand returned just thinking about what Avery—or anyone else—would say if they knew the truth.

Kaley nodded. "I respect that. You are a strong man, Ethan,

and you feel that your PTSD is a flaw, a weakness that detracts from that strength. What I'm praying for you is that you'll realize that what you perceive as weakness can become a strength for you and for others."

"How?" He growled. "There is nothing good about what happened to me."

"May I speak as your friend?"

"Of course."

"What I'm about to say isn't going to make any sense right now, but I hope it will in time. The Bible talks about a man named Paul who had what Scripture calls 'a thorn in the flesh' that tormented him. He begged God to take it away. You know what God did?"

"A good God would take it away," Ethan said.

Kaley shook her head. "No, our good God did even better. He told Paul that His grace would be enough and would sustain Paul in spite of it. God's strength would be perfected through Paul's weakness."

Ethan choked on his coffee. "You're right. That's nonsense."

"The truth sometimes seems to take the shape of foolishness," Kaley said. At that moment, laughter filled the room as Kaley's bridesmaids appeared.

"The hair stylist is here!" One of them called to Kaley.

"I'll be right there!" She replied, then lowered her voice and offered him a final smile. "I'll look forward to talking more with you when we get back from St. Thomas. I'm so thankful you're here to celebrate our day with us. Know that I'm praying for you and will keep praying for you—and for God's healing in your life."

Her words echoed in his mind, even after Kaley had left to join her friends in the makeup and hair traditions that only brides and their girlfriends could get excited about.

Why couldn't she talk in plain English? She was such a wise woman, but nothing she said made sense.

Nonsense or not, his heart burned with something that felt strangely like hope.

And he needed to know why.

Chapter Eleven

Where was Liam?

Avery tapped her cell phone as she stepped into a low pair of heels that would put her at right around six-feet tall. She couldn't remember the last time she'd slipped into the black heels and her emerald cocktail dress. Probably some other poor soul's wedding.

Liam still hadn't returned her call, and unless she had misread the invitation, the wedding started in two hours.

He was the one who had guilt-tripped her into coming. "So help me, if he leaves me behind and I miss the wedding, it's on him." She secured her thigh holster. After seating her concealed carry in the holster, she smoothed the full skirt of her dress down and snatched the one clutch she owned.

Jayna had disappeared over an hour ago, but Avery had been too absorbed in work emails to register that she should ask when Jayna and Liam were leaving—and when Avery needed to be ready.

Was it too much to assume her employee wouldn't forget her?

Tapping her door open with her shoe, she surveyed the empty hallway. The cabin was eerily quiet. When had that happened? Maybe she shouldn't have stuffed earbuds in her ears to tune out the bridal party gushing over Kaley.

Of course, Kaley was a beautiful bride. Every bride was beautiful. The real test came after the wedding, when the festivities faded.

When wedded bliss turned into a daily grind.

When kids entered the picture.

When stress rose and pay checks didn't.

Would one of them throw in the towel and leave behind a spouse and kids who didn't understand what they had done wrong?

The door across the hall from hers swung open, and Avery

snapped to attention.

Good grief. Of all the people who had to be left behind with her, of course it was him.

Ethan froze in his doorway when he spotted her, and for a moment, they stared at each other like deer caught in headlights.

The sleepwalking security guard cleaned up nicely and matched her height, despite her heels. He wore a black suit, white-collar shirt, and had a tie slung over his shoulder.

"You—um—look nice," he said.

Nice? Good grades in school were nice.

"Where is everyone?" She glanced once more to her phone. Still no notifications.

"I think they left. Reef said they were doing the bulk of photos before the ceremony while everyone looked the freshest." He pulled some keys attached to a carabiner from his pocket. "You need a ride? I've got to pick up the cake, but then I'm heading to Overlook Barn."

Avery swallowed the *no* forming on her tongue. As much as she may not care about weddings, she had driven eleven hours to attend one for a couple who had shared some pretty intense action with her over the last year. The least she could do was show up to their wedding as she had promised.

"I'm not sure," she said. "Liam isn't answering my calls. I was supposed to ride with him and Jayna." That was what she had assumed anyway.

"Oh, those two left when the bridal party did." Ethan broke the silent match of chicken, hallway style, and strode past her toward the kitchen. "I thought you were riding with one of the bridesmaids, or I would have mentioned it to him."

Avery bristled and straightened to six-feet-and-half-an-inch. "I had work to do. Besides, I don't take six hours to get ready for anything unless it's research on a case."

He shrugged and picked a bottle of water off the counter. "I'm leaving now. You're welcome to ride along if you're ready."

The last person she wanted to ride with was Ethan, but he was apparently the last ride out unless she wanted to pay for an Uber. Who knew if one could even get her to the wedding in time.

"Sure," she said. The *thanks* got stuck in her throat. She'd give him gas money.

The one car left in the driveway was a black sedan.

"This one yours?" Avery was careful not to let her heels catch in the uneven gravel.

"Not mine, just a rental." He pressed the key fob to unlock it. "I like my truck better, but it's not exactly fuel efficient for a road trip this long."

She helped herself into the passenger door. Oh yes, she remembered his truck. It helped complete the scene of that disastrous evening.

They backed out of the driveway in silence, which strangely felt more oppressive than conversation.

Avery cleared her throat. "Where's this cake?"

"Downtown, doesn't look far. It will be good to have a second person to make sure I don't drop it."

"Why would you drop it?" She tilted her head to glance at him. "You don't sleepwalk during the day, do you?"

The minute the words left her mouth, the car's interior seemed to drop ten degrees.

"I mean—" she stammered.

"I know what you mean." His tone was tight and low. "But I don't sleepwalk."

Avery bit her tongue. He was definitely a sleepwalker, but if he wanted to deny it, whatever.

She just needed to get to this wedding, get it over with, and get back to Tampa. She had enough problems of her own to solve without adding a sleepwalking security agent to the list.

Ethan gripped the steering wheel. Why did this woman make his palms sweat?

"I don't sleepwalk," he repeated as Kaley's words from earlier rang in his ears. *The truth is always better.*

The silence that met his statement told him Avery's eyebrows had shot to the top of her forehead.

He took a deep breath and continued. "I'm a Coast Guard veteran with PTSD. It makes my nights a living hell sometimes." *Most of the time.*

She blew out of a breath. "I'm sorry. That must be hard." Her tone was surprisingly sincere.

"It is."

"Have you thought about letting people know—so they aren't surprised?"

He stiffened at the advice. Everyone was always too quick to give it and less willing to understand. "Kaley's my therapist, and Reef knows too. I didn't expect to wake you or anyone else."

"Of course," Avery hurried to add. "I didn't mean to trigger you like that."

"Thanks, I know." His shoulders started to relax.

"Does talking with Kaley help?" Her voice held an unusual warmth. Even Avery had a heart.

He sighed. "Yeah, I guess. I don't really find answers, but it's nice that she cares."

"That's rare," Avery muttered. "Most shrinks stick to a script."

Ethan glanced at her. "You've gone to counseling too?"

Avery tensed, and the air in the car became electric. "What? You think I need it?"

"Wait, no, that's not—" Ethan couldn't back-peddle fast enough.

Avery threw up her hands. "Never mind. Let's not talk about this anymore."

He gripped the steering wheel and glanced at his GPS. They were almost there. What a relief.

Minutes later, he pulled into the parking lot, zipped into a space, and shifted to park.

"You coming or want to wait?" He popped open his door.

"I'll wait," was her terse answer.

Fine by him. He was a seasoned veteran at doing everything by himself.

Chapter Twelve

What a relief. They had delivered the cake and arrived to the wedding venue with half an hour to spare. She and Ethan parted ways, and she made herself at home in the screened outdoor reception area which was blissfully empty. The family, friends, and other guests milled about in the outdoor ceremony area, but she would rather not wait in the direct sun.

After all, she might be walking back to the Airbnb afterward, which would give her more than enough fresh air. No way was she riding with Ethan again.

Her curious nature wanted to know what could have happened to a man in his prime to merit a medical discharge. However, Avery hadn't brought up the topic again and didn't plan to. Experience had taught her that the more you knew about a person, the more entangled you could become.

Look at the Casales. It was true that being their foster daughter for a year had endeared her to Bella, who was now one of her closest friends, but it had also introduced her to Anthony, whose wayward actions had ended in his tragic murder—and left her with the most impossible case of her career.

The reception porch door swung open, and Liam burst into the space. Creases lined his pale brow, and he ran a hand across his red beard, which he had regrown after their stint in the Bahamas.

"There you are. You need to see this." He held open the door and waved her over.

She snatched her water bottle from a high-top table and strode toward him. "What's the matter?"

He led the way on the gravel road that wrapped around the barn giving Overlook Barn its name. "You know it's my job as the best man to decorate Reef's vehicle."

"Sorry you got stuck with that chore," she said.

He shook his head. "I don't mind, but Avery, something's wrong with his SUV."

"What do you mean, *wrong*?" She frowned his direction.

Liam pointed to a sand-colored Subaru. Scrawled on the back window were the words *Just Married*, and strung from the back were empty cans.

"It looks like you did a fine job vandalizing Reef's vehicle," she said.

"No, it's underneath the car," Liam pointed. "There's a puddle, and it hasn't rained since we've been here."

A man stood up from the other side of the SUV, and Avery stiffened. That would be her luck–Ethan was here.

He brushed off his dress pants, though dirt still clung to them. "Liam, you're right. It's brake fluid. Someone cut Reef's brake lines."

Avery cursed her heels as she spun to scan the perimeter. Other than a few wedding guests, no one appeared out of the ordinary. "How long has Reef's car been here?"

Liam shrugged. "It's probably been about two hours, give or take. We were doing photography for a while, so anyone could have come and gone."

"But why?" Ethan asked. "I mean, it's the guy's wedding. Cutting brake lines is a mean and dangerous prank, especially in the mountains."

"I don't think it's a prank," Liam said. "Maybe what happened to Kaley yesterday wasn't either. Avery, you told me Russo was freshly sentenced."

"This can't be connected—" but she stopped short. She didn't believe in coincidence. The timing was alarming.

"What if Big Eddie is collecting his debts, so to speak?" Liam crossed his arms. "What if he's sending a message that you don't mess with his people?"

Avery connected the mental dots. If that were the case, at least five people here were on his hit list. What better place to exact revenge than what should be the happiest day of Reef's and Kaley's lives?

"There you are!" A breathless Jayna ran barefoot toward them, her heels flapping in her hands as a mid-afternoon breeze twirled through her curled dark hair and navy-blue dress.

"What's wrong?" Liam rushed toward her.

"It's the cake," she gasped.

Ethan straightened from where he had been inspecting the SUV. "What about it?"

Jayna bent down to catch her breath. "I think it's been tampered with."

"It was fine when we delivered it." Ethan seemed to bristle at the suggestion.

"No, I mean afterward," Jayna said. "I saw it when you brought it in, and it looked perfect. But someone either dropped it—or almost dropped it, and did a shabby job patching it up, because the frosting details around the edges are much thicker. They also added sugar beading to help try to hide the patch-up job."

Avery shook her head. "The problems are adding up too fast to be coincidence. I don't think someone dropped that cake. Jayna, don't let anyone eat it. Save a sample I can get tested and then throw it away."

Jayna's dark eyes grew wide. "But what about the reception? The wedding starts in half an hour, and the ceremony isn't much longer than that."

"Cake will be served after the dinner," Liam piped in. "That gives us easily two hours."

"But how are we going to get a wedding cake—" Jayna cut short her own question and shook her head. "I mean, I can make one, but I'll be so sad to miss the ceremony."

Avery bit her lip. The ceremony would be the last of the happy couple's worries if their cake were poisoned.

Liam wrapped an arm around Jayna's shoulder. "I'll ask Matt to record it. I'd offer to help you, but I've got to hold the rings— and I promised Reef I'd stand by his side."

Jayna kissed his cheek. "Of course, babe. You're the best man. You're rather indispensable."

"You are too, even if you're not in the wedding party." Liam released her. "And when I tell Reef and Kaley how you saved the day with their cake, they will be so grateful."

"Don't tell them before the ceremony," Jayna said. "I don't want anything to spoil their moment."

"If they ask about you, I'll say something happened with the cake, and you're fixing it."

Jayna tweaked Liam's nose. "Babe, when Kaley walks down the aisle, Reef will have eyes only for her. Those two won't notice if I'm missing. They wouldn't notice if a gorilla were in the audience or not."

"Well, you're a long shot from being a gorilla," Liam laughed, "but I get your point."

Avery tapped her heel impatiently. "We don't have time for this. Right now, we're playing defense, and someone is on the grounds here, and we don't know what their next move is. Ethan, do your security thing around the perimeter. Liam, you're in charge of security for the bride and groom."

"I won't see Kaley again until the ceremony," Liam said. "She's probably hidden in the barn right now with her dad."

"Then I'll stay with them until then." Avery spun that direction, then paused. "Jayna, are you good with the cake?"

"I need ingredients." She tapped Liam's shoulder. "I need my keys back."

"Reef's going to need a substitute getaway vehicle," Liam said. "I'm afraid I need to decorate your car."

"Then how—"

"Take my rental," Ethan turned to Jayna and pulled a key from his pocket. "I'm parked right next to you."

"Be careful," Avery said. "If Big Eddie is behind this, you might be a target too."

"I'll be careful." Jayna accepted Ethan's keys and hurried away.

"Any questions or concerns, call me." Avery tapped her smart wristwatch.

Ethan coughed. "I don't have your number."

She hesitated with her finger poised on her watch. She would much rather keep her number out of his contact list, but this wasn't personal. This was business—the business of keeping people safe. "Don't call it unless you absolutely need to." Avery rattled it off and then beelined for the barn.

The day's bluebird skies and afternoon sun made its white paneling seem even more—white—than any barn she'd even seen. But this barn hadn't housed an animal in its recent history. The polished black marble floor and overhead porch lights belonged more to a resort scene than a barn.

It was probably what Kaley would call perfect for a wedding venue. Maybe it was.

Right now, every stall housed a possible person of interest, and every noise in the vast space made her tense.

In the far back, a white shape drew her focus.

Kaley.

In her wedding dress.

Romantic pessimist that she was, even Avery had to admit the woman was a vision. Her full princess-style skirt wasn't what she had pegged as Kaley's style, but it suited her perfectly. The lace detail on the bust and delicate veil falling past her shoulders completed the dress.

Kaley glanced her way and beamed. Beside her, Mr. Colbert was talking to someone with a DSLR camera in hand. She assumed it was a photographer, but she had since learned in her work never to assume anything.

"I'm so glad you're here," Kaley said. "This waiting part has me losing my mind. I'm ready to go, but the ceremony is some twenty minutes away."

"Are your bridesmaids hiding in the stalls?" Avery used the question as an excuse to peer into the closest ones. "Aren't they supposed to keep you company?"

"They're getting the bouquets and should be here any minute. Oh, Avery, I can't believe today is finally here. I'm getting married."

Chatter alerted Avery to the appearance of two bridesmaids

in floor-length, blush-pink dresses. One carried an extra bouquet, the largest of the three.

"Sorry it took so long," the curly-haired bridesmaid said. "Someone was in the kitchen when we got there and fussing over the bouquets. I guess a worker must have accidentally bumped one of the vases, and she was making sure the flowers were fine."

She. Avery made a mental note that their suspect might be female. She focused on the bridal bouquet the bridesmaid was about to hand to Kaley.

Had it been tampered with too?

Chapter Thirteen

Ethan paused his perimeter walk at the back corner of the barn where he could survey the outdoor chapel.

The so-called "chapel" consisted of a simple wooden platform with the mountains as a backdrop and a dozen rows of folding chairs facing it. "God's chapel" Reef had called it.

If Reef were right, God sure knew how to paint a background. White clouds dotted the clear blue sky behind mountains ablaze in shades of orange, yellow, and red.

It all begged the question—why was he acting as security in such a place? Sure, Kaley had filled him in on her abduction story from last winter, but who were the people who had taken her? What bone to pick did they have with her and Reef now?

Liam and Avery had mentioned a hearing and someone named Big Eddie, but they hadn't provided any context. None of it made sense to him.

He glanced at his phone. The person with the answers was now in his contact list, but did he dare call her to find out?

A faint crunching of shoes on pebbly gravel behind him drew his focus. Maybe he didn't need to wonder about that call.

At the other back edge of the barn, Avery concentrated on something in her hand. Her dark green dress showed off her tight waist and toned legs. No doubt there was a holster under the full skirt. The woman had the build of a volleyball player. Did she play? Did he dare ask?

Ethan squinted. What was she studying so intently? Avery had kicked off her heels and stood barefoot in the gravel. Although she had twisted up her hair, several strands framed her face. She was beautiful, even in all her intensity.

He blinked. Where had that thought come from?

"You can stop staring and start helping." Avery growled.

Though her back was to him, she must have caught sight of him in her peripheral.

"I was observing—trying to figure out what you're up to now."

She turned to face him, revealing a bouquet in her hand. "This is Kaley's bouquet. The bridesmaids said someone dropped it, and now I'm worried it's been tampered with too."

He closed the distance between them. "How did you get it from Kaley?"

"Shh! Keep your voice down," Avery hissed. "I told her there was a bee on it, and I'd scare it off. What on earth could someone do to a bouquet? Poison powder? Some kind of tracking or explosive device in the stem?"

"It is wrapped super tight," Ethan pointed at the base.

"But it seems perfect, professionally wrapped." Avery tilted the bouquet so he could see better. "I'm worried if I undo it, I won't be able to fix it."

"Then assume it's a normal bouquet, and give it back to the bride who wants to hold it." He scratched his chin.

"But what if something's wrong with it?" She shot back.

"Do you always assume the worst?"

She glared at him. "Yes, when Big Eddie is involved."

He crossed his arms. "What does that even mean? I'd like to know who or what I'm supposed to be on the lookout for."

"You might as well know. We're dealing with Tampa's slippery mafia. They're impossible to pin down, flawless at covering their tracks, and the one that Kaley helped put behind bars just got a life sentence." She paused to adjust one of the buds that had drooped. The gesture was surprisingly delicate. Maybe this woman did have a gentle side.

Ethan glanced toward the parking area and Reef's vehicle. "With all due respect, cutting someone's brakes doesn't seem like the mob's style. I would expect a car bomb or explosion— something flashier."

Avery shook her head. "Not this one. The reason no one even knew of their existence for so long is because they are subtle. They blend in with the scenery. They don't draw attention. They make deaths look like accidents. They make millions using organic covers."

"Then how do you know they really do exist, and it's not someone else?"

Her frame went rigid. "I've seen a man hanging from their rope. I've chased their drug lord through shark-infested waters. I've watched a resort owner breathe his last breath because he crossed them."

Ethan felt his eyebrows climbing. "Sounds gnarly. It also sounds personal."

Avery bit her lip and lowered her eyes. Everything about her nonverbal communication suggested it was.

She cleared her throat. "I've got to get this bouquet back to Kaley. Keep an eye out and call me if you see anything that looks off."

"There you are!" Kaley called to them. She had emerged from the barn's cover into the sunlight, which made her dress sparkle, matching everything else about her.

Ethan swallowed. Wow, Reef was one lucky guy.

"Bee's gone." Avery stepped toward her and returned her bouquet, though she released it with a hint of hesitation.

Kaley grasped it and smiled. "Thanks, it is a beautiful bouquet." She winked. "Maybe you'll be the gal to catch it, though I think Jayna might fight you for it."

Avery backed away and half-chuckled. "Ha, she can have it. I haven't tried to catch a bouquet in my life, and I don't plan to start now."

Her words shot through him and struck a chord. Did she have a reason like him to be closed off to love?

The bride glanced around them. "Speaking of Jayna, have you seen her? She told me she would pray with me before the ceremony started—and that's in ten minutes."

Ethan exchanged a look with Avery. "We didn't want to tell you before the ceremony, but Jayna is fixing up your cake. There was a little accident with it after we delivered it."

"You know she's an expert baker," Avery chimed in. "It's going to be more perfect than when we picked it up when she's through, but she might be late to the ceremony."

Kaley clutched her bouquet. "That is so good of her, but I'm sorry she isn't here." She motioned to her father and bridesmaids inside the barn. "Jayna can't make it now, but I'd still like to pray. Will you all pray with me?"

Pray was the last thing Ethan wanted to do—and from the grimace on Avery's face, it wasn't high on her list either—but no one could refuse a bride on her wedding day. They joined the bridal party inside the barn and circled up.

"Dad, would you pray?" Kaley dabbed at her eyes. "I'm so happy, but I'm also about to cry. I've wanted this day for so long."

Her father wrapped an arm around his daughter's shoulders, though he seemed careful not to crush her curled hair. "Of course, sweetie." He took a breath. "Dear Father, thank you for bringing Reef and Kaley together."

Ethan glanced around the circle. Everyone's eyes were closed except his and Avery's. She scanned past him, not meeting his gaze, but there was something lonely, empty to her stare.

"You know they have waited on you for this day, and I pray you would bless them as they start their lives as one," Mr. Colbert continued. "May today be a day they will treasure, but even if something doesn't go as planned, help them remember that today is the beginning. The wedding is wonderful, but the marriage is what matters more. Give them a marriage with You in the middle. Bind them fast together, and use them mightily for Your glory. We thank you for them."

Kaley's dad paused, getting choked up himself. His words made Ethan pause too. He'd always considered the wedding most important, but what Mr. Colbert said made sense. A lasting, strong marriage should be the focus. Not that it mattered in his case. He was never getting married, a reminder that burned.

"And now, Lord, for my little girl who's not so little anymore. You know she's excited and nervous. Fill her with your peace and joy, and may her first day as a bride be beautiful, just like she is."

Her dad wiped his eyes. "Amen." He laughed and hugged Kaley again. "And you thought you were the one who was going to cry."

Ethan dared another look at Avery who was flicking her finger at the corner of her eyes. She wasn't fast enough to conceal that she'd shed a tear too.

Buried somewhere beneath her cold exterior was a heart. Despite his better judgment to ignore her, Ethan wanted to know what Mr. Colbert had said that penetrated its hardened shell.

Chapter Fourteen

For better or worse, the wedding had begun. A solo violinist started playing a song Avery didn't recognize, but she knew it signaled that the bride and her father would soon appear and walk down the grassy aisle a little girl had sprinkled with rose pedals.

Along with the other guests, Avery rose and cast her gaze toward the barn where Kaley appeared next to her father with her arm tucked into his.

Avery flicked moisture around her eyes and told herself it was because of the glare and the fact she had forgotten her sunglasses.

Her heart, though, she couldn't deceive.

The last memory of her father was of his broad back to her as he stalked out her front door, out of her life—and never looked back to acknowledge his seven-year-old daughter pleading with him to stay.

The love and pride on Mr. Colbert's face as he led his daughter to meet her groom was something she had never seen and never would. It was beautiful. It made her heart ache and pooled tears in her eyes in a way that little else could.

There was a reason she shouldn't take vacations. They reminded her how much of life she was missing out on. The sooner this wedding ended, the sooner she could get back to her work, the one place she knew her purpose and could make a difference.

She forced herself to focus on the present and scanned the perimeter from her spot in the back row, but she couldn't find any source of concern. The ceremony seemed as safe as the mountain vista was peaceful.

The officiant's head bowed, and a quick glance around her showed that everyone else followed his example.

Dear Father. His prayer began.

It was the same way Mr. Colbert had started his prayer for

Kaley a short time ago. The idea of God as Father made her bristle. Fathers couldn't be trusted, so how could God?

Avery rubbed her arms. These people were getting under her skin. The sooner she could get back to Tampa and her normal routine, the better.

Movement beside her made her spin, but Avery relaxed when she recognized Jayna. Her flushed cheeks indicated she had been hurrying.

"What'd I miss?" she whispered.

"Not much, the officiant is praying," Avery said.

"Oh, good. The cake is baking back in our cabin. I have to leave in twenty-five minutes to make sure I don't burn it, but I had to come. This moment is too precious to miss." Jayna dabbed at her eyes. "Look at Kaley. She's beautiful."

Avery nodded but didn't want to encourage Jayna to start babbling.

"And look at him. I don't think I've ever seen Reef cry before, but his cheeks are wet." Jayna's clasped her hands. "He loves her so much."

"Shh, they're praying." She could care less about the prayer, but if it saved her from Jayna's gushy commentary, the officiant could pray for as long as he wanted.

"Sorry, I'm just so happy."

Avery resisted the urge to eye roll. Happiness was fleeting. Jayna knew that better than anyone after her history of broken relationships. Still, Avery couldn't deny that Jayna had changed since her ordeal in the Bahamas. She seemed to be in a smart relationship with Liam now, but even with a man as dependable as Liam, he was bound to disappoint her at some point.

She would suspend her relational sarcasm for today, though. This was a wedding, and the way Jayna kept smiling at Liam on the platform, the woman was probably dreaming of her own.

Good grief. How had Avery landed in a group of such hopeless romantics? Had everyone forgotten that men like Big Eddie roamed free? The world was not safe, people were not trustworthy, and fathers—in her experience—were not good.

Those were the hard, ugly facts.

The vows had been said. The cake eaten. The bubbles blown. The send-off complete.

Everyone was alive, and Jayna's cake had looked better than the one he and Avery had initially picked up. No doubt it tasted better too, but Avery had forbidden anyone from so much as swiping icing off the original cake in case it had been tampered with. Jayna had saved a sample for Avery and trashed the rest.

As daylight faded, Ethan tugged his tie loose while the last of the guests drove off, leaving only him, Avery, Liam, and Jayna in the parking lot with his car and Reef's. They were waiting for the tow truck before they all crammed into his rental to head back to the Airbnb for one final night.

"Exactly how are we getting home tomorrow?" Jayna yawned and leaned against Liam's shoulder.

Liam tugged her into a side hug. "The hope is that we can get a mechanic to fix Reef's car in the morning, and then we'll meet up with Reef and swap his SUV for yours."

"So we'll drive home to Tampa with the words *Just Married* painted on the back window?" Jayna smirked.

"Please tell me we'll visit a car wash first, or we'll be getting honked at all the way," Avery groaned. She was once again shoeless. In one hand, she held both heels, and in the other, the cake sample in a triple zip-locked bag.

Ethan stifled a laugh. She looked such a far stretch from the no-nonsense agent she was.

Avery glared at him. "What's so funny?"

"We are."

She made a sweeping gesture with her hands to Reef's Subaru and the cake sample. "This—is not funny. People could have been seriously hurt. The wedding could have been a funeral, and poor Jayna is about to pass out from the exhaustion of whipping together a wedding cake in record time."

"But it tasted good." Liam kissed her cheek. "Mmm, you taste good."

Jayna giggled and swatted him away.

Avery looked as if she had swallowed a bag of sour gummy worms. "C'mon, you two, I just sat through a wedding. My threshold for romance is maxed out."

"Weddings have the opposite effect on me." Jayna shivered closer to Liam once more in the cool evening air. "It makes a girl dream."

"Obviously," Avery muttered and turned toward the sound of tires on the gravel. "The tow truck is here. What a mercy."

"You and Jayna can wait with Ethan inside his car if you want," Liam said. "I know it's getting cold out here, and you gals aren't dressed for it. I should only be a few minutes with the tow truck guy, and then we can leave."

Ethan pulled the key fob from his pocket. "Yeah, let me turn on the engine and heat for you."

Avery hesitated for a moment before she trailed Jayna toward his parked rental. She might not admit it, but she had to be cold and tired like the rest of them.

Jayna climbed in the back seat with Avery and sighed with relief when he shared where she could turn on the seat warmers. "Oh, that's heavenly," she murmured.

"They are pretty sweet," he agreed and switched on his seat warmer while keeping an eye on Liam in the rearview mirror.

"What do you do again?" Jayna asked. "I know you, Kaley, and Reef are all friends, but I don't know how you are connected."

Either the warmth from the seat or the realization that Avery already distrusted him coaxed out the truth. "Kaley is my therapist. I met Reef through her, and long story short, he and I became good friends."

"Oh," Jayna said. She was at least polite enough not to pry.

"Professionally, I'm part of Semper Security. It's a security team of Coast Guard vets, and we all have each other's backs." He paused. "I couldn't ask for a better group to work with."

"That's so cool you're all Coast Guard veterans," Jayna said, "and your security experience has been such a help here at the wedding with some of the scares Kaley and Reef have had. What a blessing you came."

Ethan chanced a glance in the rearview mirror at Avery who was busy on her phone. Fat chance she saw his presence as anything but a curse.

"How do you know Reef and Kaley?" he asked.

"It's a complicated story," Jayna said, "but the short version is that I was engaged to a Bimini resort owner who was working with a drug runner—to be clear, I didn't know that when I accepted the ring. Avery and Liam were investigating this covert group's operations and ended up going undercover in Bimini. They helped me find the courage to get out."

"You're the one who helped us," Avery said. "Liam would be dead if not for you."

The air in his rental stilled until Jayna whispered, "We helped each other."

Ethan whistled. "Whew, that's quite the story, but how do Reef and Kaley fit into that?"

"They happened to be in Miami buying a boat for Reef's business when all this was going down. I had met them on a church trip right here to Beech Mountain and called them because I was desperate for help. They dropped everything and boated over to Bimini. They were with us when we found Liam, who had been taken by the drug runner, and when—" Jayna choked and didn't finish.

Ethan's stomach clenched. What had happened that she didn't want to talk about? Everyone she had mentioned was at the wedding today, so things must have turned out okay.

"You did everything you could for Mario." Avery broke the silence. Her tone was so gentle Ethan almost didn't recognize it.

Jayna sniffed. "I should have done more. I wish I could have kept him from dying."

The pieces started to connect for him. "Jayna, was this Mario your ex-fiancé?"

"Yes, and he died taking a bullet for me."

Ethan spun to look at Jayna in the back seat. "I'm sorry. That's heavy stuff."

"Yeah, and like an idiot, I made a promise to him I don't know how to begin to keep," Avery lowered her gaze.

"What promise?"

Avery's eyes flashed his direction. "I don't want to talk about it."

Ethan held up his hands. "Got it. Can I give you a piece of advice though?"

Avery's lips pressed into a thin line. "Sure, whatever."

He forced a smile anyway. The woman could use fewer scowls in her life. "The best way to get over your past is to help others. Take it from a guy who worked in Guantanamo. I saw what living under a Communist regime is like, and I want to help the people of Cuba any way I can. There's this place where I volunteer, and we ship supplies to Cuba."

"That is wonderful, Ethan," Jayna said, "but the best way to get over your past is to ask Jesus to redeem it. Trust it from a girl who's made a lot of mistakes."

Interesting. Jayna was into Jesus like Kaley, like Reef, like most of this crazy wedding party. Were they all delusional, or was there something more to this Jesus stuff than a hokey religion?

He cast a look in the rearview mirror at Avery, but she had diverted her attention to the side window. "Looks like Liam is finishing with the tow truck. I'll be so glad to get out of here—"

The blast of a gun cut her off.

"Get down!" Ethan cried but cast a glance out the back side window. The tow truck driver dashed to his vehicle and slammed the door.

Liam lay motionless on the ground.

Chapter Fifteen

Who would be next?

Avery held her head with her hands as the thought pounded against her skull. The waiting room at the closest hospital was virtually empty except for her and Ethan, who had left to go find a vending machine.

Most waiting rooms should be empty at one o'clock in the morning.

A nurse had taken Jayna back to the post-surgery room where Liam was resting. Only one person was allowed in the room, and she was his girlfriend. Avery had wanted to argue that she was his boss, but she held her tongue. Jayna had sobbed on and off the whole time Liam was in surgery. Hopefully her state of mind was clear enough now to convey whatever the doctor told her.

What a mess. They had to connect with Reef at some point to swap vehicles, assuming his SUV could be fixed tomorrow morning. She had wanted to call Reef right away and tell him about the shooting, but both Jayna and Ethan insisted they wait until morning. Those two softies didn't have the heart to spoil his wedding night.

She hoped the newlyweds would choose somewhere safe to stay tonight. If not, everything they had done to keep them from harm would be for nothing.

"You doing okay?" Ethan's quiet voice startled her, and she jerked her head up. He still wore his suit, but his tie hung loosely around his neck, and he'd unbuttoned the top few holes of his white shirt. In one hand, he held some kind of soda, and in the other, he extended a water toward her.

It made him seem remarkably accessible and— She snipped the thought.

"No one is ever okay in a hospital waiting room." She set the water on the table beside her and rubbed her arms. "And this place is freezing."

"Here." He retracted one arm, then the next from his suit jacket before she could protest. "Wear this. Hopefully we'll get word soon."

Her pride resisted the jacket, but she risked losing feeling in her hands. She nodded instead. "Thank you and thanks for the water."

"You're welcome." He chose the chair across from hers. "Remind me to decline the next wedding invitation I get unless it's from my sister."

"You have a sister?" The words slipped from her mouth before she could plug them. Man, she was tired if she was encouraging conversation with the crazy security officer.

"Two, actually." Ethan took a gulp of his soda. "The older one told me she's dating someone, though I haven't met him. The younger one is nineteen so she'd better not be."

Avery snorted. "You never know."

"You have siblings?" Ethan capped his bottle.

"Nope."

"Lucky," he laughed.

Her pulse roiled. Lucky to have no one? No one to annoy you? To get you in trouble? To boss you around? To care about you? To call you?

Avery once more had to cut her train of thought before it got out of hand. She snatched the water off the table and chugged several mouthfuls to avoid saying something she would regret.

She could feel Ethan's gaze on her. "I mean, they're a real pain, but I do love them." His tone was softer.

Jayna's reappearance saved her the trouble of a response. Her mascara streaked her cheeks, but a wobbly smile on her lips gave Avery hope. She rose and stepped toward her. "Well?"

"He's going to be okay," she blubbered and ran straight into her arms.

Avery sighed and awkwardly patted the sobbing woman on the back. "What does that mean? What did the doctor say?"

Ethan held a finger to his lips and shook his head. "All that matters is that he's going to be okay."

Jayna pulled away and wiped her eyes with Ethan's jacket sleeve. He'd need to get that dry cleaned.

"The doctor said he should wake up in the next hour or two," Jayna said. "I want to be here then, so I'm going to spend the night. You two should go back to the cabin though. Could you please bring me my bag in the morning though? I'm pretty sure we have to check out of the Airbnb mid-morning anyway."

"Sure, we'll drop it off tomorrow." Ethan ran a hand over his face. "I'm guessing Liam will be here for a few days."

Jayna yawned. From the strain and the long day, she looked about ready to pass out. "I think so. The doctor said the bullet didn't do any major damage. It missed his heart by a few millimeters."

Relief washed over Avery. "Lucky guy."

"God was watching over him," Jayna said. "Anyway, I'm going back to his room. I'll text you updates when I get them."

"Sounds good." Avery would probably learn more via text message than in person, at this rate.

All that mattered was that Liam was in the clear. The shooter must have been sloppy. Next time, they might not be so lucky.

The next morning, Ethan pressed the key fob to unlock Jayna's SUV, yanked open the door, and swung inside. Somewhere behind him in the parking lot, Reef drove off with his repaired Subaru. As for Avery—

Ethan glanced in the rearview mirror just as she hopped into *his* rental car.

That woman.

"It looks like a fun car to drive," she had said and held out her hand for the keys.

He had seen right through her. His sedan was just an ordinary rental, but the woman wouldn't be seen dead in an SUV with phrases like "Just married" and "Honk for a kiss" scrawled all over the windows. Whatever had caused her to have such a giant chip on her shoulder when it came to relationships was beyond him.

Whatever. They had to drop the SUV off at the hospital for Jayna. Then, she and Liam would drive it home whenever he was well enough to be released.

That left Avery stuck riding all the way back home to Tampa with him.

Ethan grinned at the memory of that conversation as he pulled out of the shopping plaza onto the main road. Avery had looked none too pleased, but her other choices were waiting to ride back with Jayna and Liam in a few days or spend money on a rental or plane ticket.

She had muttered something about work, and that yes, she would ride back with him. He said that was fine, as long as she agreed to drive fifty percent of the time—to give his poor ribs a break.

The mention of his ribs had earned him another glare.

Someone laid on the horn behind him, and he jerked his head to the rearview mirror. It was Avery in his rental—though she was two cars back. They had stopped at a red smalltown traffic light. What was her problem?

Oh wait. *Honk for a kiss.* Now who was being funny—

Movement in his peripheral made him glance sideways and then immediately step his foot on the gas to run the red light.

A giant tractor was barreling down a hill straight for him.

Avery slammed her palm on the horn. Ethan had to stop daydreaming and move. The tractor raging their way gave them only seconds to get clear.

At least the car behind her clearly saw it and pulled onto the shoulder, giving her enough room to shift to reverse and accelerate backwards far enough to hopefully avoid a collision if the tractor turned her way.

But it seemed razer-focused on Jayna's SUV.

She screamed in frustration and blared her horn again.

The SUV jolted in front of her. Finally!

But Ethan wasn't in the clear yet. He was about to run the red light. She couldn't see from her position what vehicles might ram him.

Like an angry bull without brakes, the tractor plowed across the road in front of her and careened into a ditch adjacent to the road. She didn't see anyone inside, but a blur of letters covered one of the windows. She couldn't read what it said, but she wasn't taking chances. Yanking out her phone, she dialed 9-1-1 and yanked open her door.

Her hammering heart pulsed in her ears. Ethan had made it through the intersection. Horns blared, and tires squealed, but no one crashed.

The driver behind her had also jumped out. "Are you okay?" A middle-aged woman called.

"I'm fine." Avery ran to the edge of the shoulder. "Did you see anyone inside?"

The woman shook her head and strode toward the end of the pavement for a look herself. "I was too far away, but I called the police. Help should be here soon."

The tractor had flipped several times and come to a stop on its side. The windows somehow hadn't broken, and now, Avery could read the words.

Her throat tightened. No, it couldn't be—

"I'm coming for you." The woman next to her turned to face Avery. "What a strange message. What does it mean?"

Avery didn't respond.

That tractor hadn't been meant for Ethan.

It had been meant for her.

Chapter Sixteen

The hospital's sliding doors closed behind them, and the cloudless sky of another stunning mountain morning made Ethan wish he hadn't forgotten his sunglasses in the car. Given the close call with the tractor, another police report, and Avery's tight-lipped answers to all his questions, he was lucky he hadn't forgotten his keys.

"You want to drive or want me to?"

Avery silenced him with an outstretched palm. "I'll drive, but please, no more questions about this morning." The strain in Avery's tone and creases in her forehead told him that even this woman, a Captain Marvel in the flesh, had her breaking point.

At least she had said *please*.

Ethan tossed her his keys and circled around the car to the passenger side. "Fine. But I don't believe you for a minute if you say those red letters on that tractor weren't a message intended for you. Remember, you should have been the one driving Jayna's SUV, not me."

Avery yanked the driver's door closed and then checked her mirrors. "I don't care what you believe. I just want to get home in one piece."

"Yeah, and someone else is doing their best to stop that."

They pulled out of the hospital parking lot. They had managed to drop off Jayna's SUV without further incident, but Ethan kept checking the side mirrors. What would come charging after them this time?

The road, however, seemed eerily quiet, much like the woman next to him.

He cleared his throat. "I got a text from Reef who wanted to check on Liam. He and Kaley have changed their honeymoon plans and re-booked under a friend's name. Hopefully they can stay under the radar."

"Smart," Avery said.

"What are you doing to stay under the radar?"

She peeled her gaze off the windshield for a moment. Those fiery blue eyes would be beautiful if they didn't always look so angry. "My job is not to hide. My job is to protect innocent people and hunt down perpetrators. That's what I'm going to do."

"What if the perpetrator is hunting you?"

"All the better." She pressed her lips into a thin line and resumed her hard stare out of the windshield. "I have to stay one step ahead of him."

"Your colleague Liam won't be able to report for duty for a while. Who's watching your back till then?"

Avery's chin tilted. "I have a team, and sometimes, I work alone."

This woman was impossibly proud. "You can't watch your own back."

Her hands gripped the wheel, but this time, she didn't acknowledge him with a look. "Why not? I've been doing it all my life."

Avery's tone was like a gut punch, but hard as it was, it revealed a chink in her armor. "Even the strongest need help sometimes. My agency could—."

She sucked in a deep breath and reached for the radio. "You can help me with one thing."

The edge to her voice had gotten sharper. He hesitated. "What's that?"

"Less talking."

Her apartment had never looked more wonderful.

Or more lonely.

Avery dropped her duffle on the kitchen floor and tossed her mail on the counter. What was wrong with her? The eleven-hour ride home with Ethan should have cured any immediate need for companionship. Solitude should have seemed like bliss.

Well, the solitude she shared with Bob, her betta fish. She tapped on his bowl. His blue tail drooped. Poor guy had been on a fast for a few days, because with Bella out of town, she didn't have anyone to feed him. As she tapped his food into the bowl, she glanced at her fridge. She probably didn't have any food herself.

It was almost midnight, but her stomach growled. She could go out to a bar and get some food, but Ethan's chiding voice ruined that idea. He had lectured her about being a target, needing security, and not taking risks. Going out at midnight would fit his definition of a risk. Getting a late-night take-out delivery would be better. Chinese sounded good.

As she tapped in an order on her phone, she paused. Since when did she care what he thought? She had skirted his questions about the underworld she was investigating—that was for his own good. The last thing he needed was to get added to the hit list.

His questions that rubbed her the worst were the ones about God. Ethan seemed to be genuinely "searching" as some would call it, and she was the last person he should be talking to.

He should talk to Reef, Kaley, Liam, or Jayna. They would all be happy to ramble on about their faith.

She didn't have any. What did that make her? An atheist? Her order complete, she tossed her phone onto the couch, collapsed next to it, and kicked off her shoes.

A few of her colleagues touted that title with pride and enjoyed verbal sparring matches with people of faith. That wasn't her thing. Her logic wasn't complicated, and she didn't need to argue it with anyone. She didn't believe in God because if He didn't show up for little girls, He wasn't going to show up for big ones.

To get Ethan to quit with his questions and conversation in general, though, she had made a promise, the second one she regretted. Maybe, just maybe, volunteering a few hours to help provide supplies to the people of Cuba would somehow ease her conscience about the first one.

Minutes later, a knock on the door pulled her from her thoughts. Swinging her legs off the couch, she checked the peephole.

No one was there. Odd.

Cracking open the door, she scanned the vicinity for her delivery person. No one was in sight, but a plastic bag sat on her doorstep.

A chill ran down her spine as she bolted the door and placed the bag on the counter. This was her Chinese, wasn't it?

Her growling stomach reminded her she needed to eat, but her stomach twisted in knots as she unpackaged the bag. Just as she had ordered, there was a box of rice, a plastic container with her sesame chicken, and—

Her breath hitched. A pile of crumbs—what must have been fortune cookies at one time—were scattered along the bottom of the bag. A handwritten message lay in the middle of the crushed cookies.

I always collect my debts.

Chapter Seventeen

Keeping his hands on the golf cart steering wheel, Ethan shrugged a shoulder, hoping his shirt would catch the perspiration trickling down his neck. Too bad Florida didn't take its cues from Beech Mountain's autumn temperatures.

The little fan in the golf cart was no match for the warm afternoon combined with pavement, but security was security. For another hour, he would monitor the parking lot while the minor league hockey game concluded, and then he would help direct traffic. It wasn't a hard job, and he was grateful his boss was reserving the more technical jobs for his colleagues who didn't have bruised ribs.

In his pocket, his phone vibrated. Did his boss need something? Retracting his phone, he glanced at the screen.

Avery.

He frowned and tucked his phone back in his pocket. Texting on the job was taboo in his field, a distraction he couldn't afford.

She was probably calling to back out of joining him tonight at Ayuda Para Cuba (APC), a local mission group led and organized by the Cuban diaspora in Florida to help their family and friends still in Cuba.

His phone continued to vibrate. The parking lot was dead, and he was allowed a ten-minute break to use the restroom or get a snack. Pulling the golf cart to a stop outside the outdoor facilities, he retracted his phone once more.

Three missed calls and one text message.

You were right. I need help.

Good thing he was sitting down. Avery—admitting she needed help? To him? Something must have scared her and scared her badly.

He texted back. *On a job right now. Is this urgent, or can I call you in an hour?*

The dots on his phone told him she was texting back.

An hour is fine. Call when you can.

He sighed in relief. An hour meant she was safe for now, but he had no doubt someone had her in his crosshairs. *I'll call when I get off. You want me to pick you up before APC? I can grab us dinner to go.*

She texted back. *Yes. Thanks.*

Wow, reaching out and accepting his help. Maybe God could work miracles.

At least there was no emergency for now. He might as well take a break since he had already parked.

After a quick trip to the bathroom, Ethan shoved some spare change in a vending machine to get a soda. As he reached for the beverage, something moved in his peripheral. He spun.

No one was there.

He blinked. Something or someone had moved in the direction of his golf cart beyond the sidewalk. "Hello?" he called with one hand poised on his radio and another on the concealed carry in his belt.

Scanning from side to side, he started toward his golf cart. Stripes of red on the windshield and a hissing noise heightened his sense. He pressed his radio. "Ethan Bridger, requesting immediate backup in the parking lot. Over."

His colleague responded a second later. "What's your situation? Over."

The red letters glared at him as the remaining air fizzed out of his slashed tires. "Vandals."

"Roger that. How many?"

Whoever had done the job had made quick work getting in and out. The surrounding area was silent, though the culprit couldn't be far.

"I don't have a visual. Over."

The one visual he had was of his windshield and the message that read loud and clear. *Stay Away from Avery.*

The blue Dodge Ram in the parking lot flashed its lights, directing Avery its way. For some reason, she had been looking for the black sedan, but that had been a rental.

Had it only been a week ago Ethan had swooped in to her "rescue" in this giant of a truck? She had never wanted to see him again, and yet here she was, accepting dinner and a ride from him—and wanting to hire him for security.

She must be losing her edge.

He jumped out and rounded the hood to get her door, but she waved him off and reached for the handle. "Not necessary."

Ethan grabbed it anyway and swung open her door. "Yes, necessary." He scanned the parking lot of her apartment complex. "Please get in. We need to talk."

His tone suggested no room for argument, so she climbed inside and let him close the door firmly behind her. When was the last time a man had gotten her door? Probably some date in her twenties that she had ended before giving the poor guy a chance.

She shook her head as Ethan hopped in the driver's seat and started the engine. His pressed black polo and damp hair suggested he'd managed to change and shower after his shift, as did the subtle spicy fragrance of his cologne.

What was wrong with her? Ethan was not a date. He was a professional, like her. He certainly had his issues, but at least she knew what they were.

His gray eyes glanced her way. They softened and lingered long enough on her face to make her stomach do a strange flip-flop she hadn't felt in years. "You look nice for just volunteering at the mission."

Avery dropped her gaze to her lap. She'd worn a dressy black tank-top and her dark-washed jeans. "I didn't know what to expect and figured I should make a good impression in case my direct personality rubs someone the wrong way."

Ethan chuckled. "At least you're aware. In that case, you should have worn the green number from Kaley and Reef's wedding. That would definitely impress."

She tried to glare but felt her lips curling into a half-smile. "I won't break out that thing again until the next wedding or funeral I have to attend."

His face puckered in a frown. "Not a funeral."

Avery shrugged. "They're pretty much the same thing."

"You should add cynic to your resume."

"It's already on it," she shot back.

He held up a hand and then motioned to a brown bag on the console between them. "Help yourself. Hope you like Chinese."

Now her stomach felt queasy. "Funny choice. It's what I ordered last night and then someone tampered with it."

His eyes flashed her way. "What? You'd better back up and start from the beginning. All you told me on the phone was that someone had threatened you at your apartment and you wanted to hire my agency for security. I need to talk to you about that, but you go first."

"There's not much to tell." She had to keep her voice steady. He couldn't know how much a direct threat at her home had shaken her. "I ordered Chinese. When I unpacked it, I found that someone had opened the fortune cookies, crushed them, and scattered them in the bottom along with a hand-written fortune that read, 'I always collect my debts.'"

"So whoever was targeting Reef, Kaley, and Liam is also after you," Ethan said. "I hate that I was right."

At least he wasn't rubbing in that fact. Avery helped herself to one of the two chicken and noodle bowls and popped off the lid. "On the bright side, I never got to eat that Chinese, so this is great."

"I like orange chicken, so I got the same for you. Hope that's okay," Ethan said.

"No complaints." Avery chewed a bite. "Now what do you need to tell me?"

Ethan's hands seemed to grip the steering wheel more tightly. "Someone told me to stay away from you today. Clearly, I don't plan on it. I already called my boss and told him about the threat and your request. He's free to meet with us first thing tomorrow, set up the terms of service based on your needs, and then we'll get you a quote. If you accept, we'll have the contract ready and can start providing security immediately."

Her throat tightened around a bite that might have been too big. She had forgotten about lunch at the office today, but more than that, a new fear tugged at the back of her mind. "I like to work with people I trust. You've proven yourself trustworthy. What about your other colleagues?"

Ethan stiffened but nodded. "I get it, but we are a tight-knit group, and I've worked with each of my colleagues. All of them are Coast Guard vets like me, and we each have our own battles we're fighting. We don't let those interfere with our work—or we make sure someone can cover for us. But you won't have to take my word. We'll provide you plenty of references so you can cross-check us."

She twisted her plastic fork around more noodles. "I trust you. Anyone who takes a threat for someone who's not a client and isn't scared off has my vote."

Ethan chuckled. "I've had my share of threats before, but the ones aimed at you aren't empty. Liam's in the hospital, my golf cart is in the repair shop, and someone probably poisoned your Chinese."

"Hopefully not this one though," Avery poked at her chicken. "At least it tastes good."

"You're welcome," Ethan smirked. "I'll eat mine when we get to APC. So tomorrow morning works for you to meet my boss?"

"Yep—text me the time, and I'll be there."

"Good. Now let's talk about APC. You mentioned a promise you don't know how to keep when you agreed to come." Ethan grinned. "I'm guessing you showing up has more to do with that promise and not my personality."

Avery finished the last of her bowl. "Correct." She wouldn't admit to him that his personality was slowly—very slowly—growing on her.

"Ha, I figured. So then—" Ethan tapped the wheel for her to continue.

She huffed out a breath. "Jayna already told you about her ex-fiancé who died taking a bullet for her. One of the drug runner's men had knocked me out cold, and unfortunately, I didn't wake up soon enough to prevent Mario from being shot. But I did manage to take out Mario's shooter before he could refocus his sights on Jayna.

"Anyway, all that to say I found Mario with Jayna right before he died. He was begging for us to help his cousins. Watching a man bleed out, I wanted to give him some sense of peace, so I told him I'd help, not really knowing what I was agreeing to. Only afterwards did Jayna tell me he was asking for his cousins in Cuba who want to immigrate to the United States. Mario had worked with the drug runner to get the money he needed to bribe their way out."

"I've heard rumors about bribing your way to the front of the list," Ethan said. "Of course, any official you talk to will absolutely deny that, but I don't doubt it happens. Still, I'm guessing you figured out quickly how hard winning the lottery to immigrate legally is."

"Try virtually impossible," Avery sighed. "Winning that lottery is like finding a needle in a haystack."

"Well, volunteering at APC won't change that, but you will be helping the people of Cuba." Ethan tugged the wheel and turned onto a road and past a sign that read, "Ayuda Para Cuba" with an arrow pointing right. "If you give me the names of the men you're hoping to find, I can ask my contacts to put out feelers for them. Maybe you can at least send them word that their cousin died trying to help them."

"Small comfort that will be." Avery stared out the window as a pair of large warehouses came into view.

Ethan pulled into a parking space and turned off his truck. "Small is better than none. Who knows? Maybe a miracle will happen and you'll be able to keep your word."

Avery reached for her door handle. "You believe in miracles now? I thought that was just our religious friends."

He offered her a half-smile and hopped out. "I'm starting to think there might be something to their faith talk."

She slid to the pavement and met him at the back of the truck.

"If their God can help me keep my promise and stop the maniac I'm trying to catch, then I'll give Him an audience."

"I don't think it works that way," Ethan frowned. "Not that I'm an expert or anything."

Avery shrugged. She didn't want to start an argument. "That's because faith is make-believe, but if it helps you feel better about yourself, I'm not going to judge."

Ethan opened his mouth as if to disagree but instead motioned her forward. "Let me introduce you to the workers of APC. There's some pretty faith-filled folk among them who believe they're God's hands and feet. Whether you agree with them or not, I think you'll like them."

She forced a smile to hide her skepticism that this wasn't all a waste of time, but only time would tell. On both counts.

Chapter Eighteen

To an outsider, the warehouse tables covered with boxes and supplies looked like pure chaos. From his time working at APC the last two years, Ethan knew better.

Today's task was compiling first aid kits. Various vendors had donated close-to-expiration salves, ibuprofen, and cleansing packets, while other donors had supplied bandages and other basic items any American took for granted in his medicine cabinet. Some clever seamstresses had designed nylon bags to store the kits, and the goal was to package a few hundred to stuff in two large suitcases for Miss Martha to take with her on a flight tomorrow.

Ethan smiled as the older lady moved to his table. Though he guessed she must be in her early seventies, she remained trim and in better shape than many women decades younger. A self-starting entrepreneur who had emigrated from Cuba, Miss Martha was rumored to have millions in the bank which she funneled liberally into APC, the nonprofit she had founded, and in the monthly airplane tickets she purchased to Cuba to move supplies there.

She still had relatives there, but it wasn't just her family she helped. She, along with other members of the Cuba diaspora, worked tirelessly to help provide basic supplies that simply weren't available in Communist Cuba. Her Cuban contacts organized a list of prescriptions and other medical supplies that people there needed, and Miss Martha rallied her troops to acquire them.

He came once a month to help with sorting and packaging. They were the ones petitioning vendors, accumulating donations, and purchasing the balance of the requested items.

Barely five feet tall, Miss Martha reached up to pat his shoulder. "Good to see you again, Ethan." Her gray curly hair framed her wrinkled face, but her dark black eyes held a vibrant twinkle.

"Good to see you too, Miss Martha," Ethan leaned down to give her a side-hug.

She snapped on some disposable gloves. "Still fighting your battles?"

He sighed and reached for a new nylon bag to fill. "Always."

Miss Martha poked a finger at him. "You know you wouldn't have to fight so hard if you'd let God do the heavy lifting for you."

"So you've told me."

"And I'll keep telling you until you start listening."

Ethan tried to hide a smile. Perhaps when someone reached seventy, she earned the right to say whatever she wanted without a filter. Miss Martha meant well, and after talking with Reef and Kaley, he was warming up to the possibility she was right.

"Does your girlfriend believe in the good Lord, or do I need to work on her too?" Miss Martha offered a sly grin.

He choked on a laugh. "She needs even more work than I do."

"Heaven, help us. Where are all the good Christian girls these days?"

"They're hanging out with good Christian guys—not mess-ups like me."

Miss Martha narrowed her eyes. "Now you listen to old Martha, Ethan Bridger. You are not a mess-up. You are made in God's image, and He's got good plans for you."

A retort rose in his throat, but he swallowed it. "I don't want to argue with you, Miss Martha, but I'm not seeing much good in any plans for me right now."

"That's because you aren't seeing the way He sees. You see a mess. He sees raw material." Miss Martha held up a bottle of ibuprofen. "Take these pain pills. To the American manufacturer, they're a liability because they expire soon. To my Cuban friends, they are priceless for the relief they will bring."

Ethan paused to study the bottle he had placed in the bag. He sure felt like expired goods. Could God have a purpose for him now?

"You're a wise woman, Miss Martha," he said.

"Wisdom doesn't do any good unless you take it to heart."

He gulped in relief as Avery walked their way. "Hey, we're all out of fabric bandages at my table. Do we have more of those?"

"We've got fabric bandages in droves—but we've also got some heart medicine." Miss Martha reached into a large box behind her and pulled out two small books a little larger than a smartphone.

Avery's brow furrowed. "That's a New Testament—not Advil."

Miss Martha extended one copy to Avery and another to him. "It's a lot longer lasting than an Advil, and you both need a healthy dose of it."

Ethan coughed to cover a laugh. He'd never seen Avery so bewildered. She was kind of cute when she didn't know what to say.

"I'm sorry, but do I know you?" Avery accepted the book, probably to keep from being rude to the older lady.

"You do now. Most people call me Miss Martha. From what your boyfriend was telling me, you both need to read more of the good Lord's Word. It will be health to your flesh and strength to your bones."

Avery's mouth hung open.

Miss Martha winked. "That's from Proverbs in the Old Testament."

She clamped her mouth shut and glared at Ethan. "Very interesting—but Mr. Bridger here is not my boyfriend."

The sweet lady nodded in approval. "Well, that's good news at least. You both need to get right with the Lord before pursuing a relationship."

Avery's eyebrows shot up to the sky. "Um, okay. I'll just take this box that says bandages and get back to work."

"I'm so glad you came to help." Miss Martha scooped an armful of New Testaments into a bag and then handed it to Avery. "Be sure to add these books to your first aid kits too. They will probably bring more comfort than any medicine will."

Ethan stared at the copy Miss Martha had handed him. When was the last time he had read the Bible?

He chanced a glance at Avery. She was about to put her copy in the bag with the others.

"No, no, dear, you promise Miss Martha you'll keep that one and read it too. You can't call me a crazy old lady until you've read it. Once you read it, you can call me anything you want."

Color crept into Avery's cheeks. "Ma'am, I would never—"

Miss Martha shook a finger at her. "Say you'll read it, and I'll leave you alone."

Avery cast a helpless look his way. He shrugged. "I'll read it. What about you, Avery?"

Her silent plea turned into a thanks-for-throwing-me-under-the-bus scowl. "Fine. I'll see what it says." With that, she snatched up the box of bandages and the bag of Bibles and retreated to her table.

Miss Martha stared after her with a triumphant smile on her face. "She strikes me as a girl of her word. I think she'll keep her promise."

Ethan tucked his copy in his pocket. Poor Avery had come here to find a way to keep the last promise she made, and now here she was, making another one that made her uncomfortable.

Would reading a New Testament offer any hope for either of them?

A grin tugged at his lips. Only time would tell. Either way, it would give him a chance to pester Avery.

He would just have to make sure he read his copy first.

Chapter Nineteen

Bella's text came as Avery sat in a drive-thru for a late morning coffee. She had just left Semper Security where she had signed a contract with them. As much as she didn't want to take on more expense, the safety of her team came first. With Liam recovering in the hospital, she couldn't afford to let another team member take a hit.

How did the wedding go? Bella's question was innocent enough, but Avery knew it was a soft opener. Her former foster sister wanted an update now that she had returned from vacation, and Avery was grasping at straws.

Still, she had one small lead. Avery had arranged a video visit with Russo. Now that the woman was sitting in a cell with a life sentence, maybe she would be more communicative.

Good. Avery texted back and chewed her lip. The bride and groom almost being killed and her colleague being shot were not good, but the wedding itself was fine as far as weddings go. *How was Cancun?*

Bella answered with a picture of her, her husband, and Gianna snorkeling in clear blue water. It reminded Avery of Bimini, minus all the drama of that trip.

Looks fun. Avery texted. *I've got a meeting with Russo this afternoon. I'll fill you in after.*

How about lunch tomorrow downtown? Bella texted a pin to a café in downtown Tampa, and Avery gave her a thumbs up.

If she believed in prayer, she would pray for good news to give Bella.

"What can I get started for you?" The drive-through's speakers pulled Avery to the present. Though Florida's fall weather involved a heavy blanket of humidity, the cool weather of the mountains clung to her memory.

"Black coffee with a splash of pumpkin," Avery said. That was about as festive as her order ever got, but she needed a dose of happy before she returned to her office to conduct the professional video visitation she had scheduled with Russo.

The last time she had seen the woman was when her team arrested her in Oaklawn Cemetery. The Hollywood director had no doubt expected a slap on the wrist—not a life sentence. But kidnapping, physical assault, fraud, and accomplice to murder were no minor matters, and not even her iconic status could rescue Russo from her penalty.

Would the sentence soften her or make her even more clammed up about her involvement with Big Eddie? No doubt Russo knew how to find him. She could provide the information Avery and the Hillsborough Sherriff's Department needed to break the backbone of his underground network—and bring the criminal mastermind to justice.

But would she?

Ethan pushed back in his desk chair to stretch. His ribs were less sore, but his muscles remained tense as he rotated his shoulders and blinked to give his eyes a screen break.

The cubicle he called an office lacked the familiar mementos that graced some of his teammates' desks. There were no family pictures, only a calendar of white-tailed deer that one of his baby sisters, now in college, had given him last Christmas. Somewhere he had a family picture, but he wasn't about to put it on his desk. No way would he put Chloe and Tori in harm's way due to his line of work.

Besides, most people had pictures of their spouses and kids, not little sisters, even if they weren't so little anymore. He stared at the empty shelf above his desk, and his thoughts flipped to Avery. Would she ever let herself be the woman in a guy's picture frame?

He shook his head and turned back to his laptop to finish the incident report on yesterday's hockey game. Avery kept invading his thoughts, and it had to stop. She was a client now, and their relationship must remain strictly professional.

His work cell vibrated, and Jake's name flashed on the screen. He had spoken with his boss earlier this morning when Avery had come in to sign her contract. Something else must be on his mind.

Swiping to unlock the screen, Ethan read the text. *Stop by my office when you have a sec?*

There was no reason to waste time wondering. He texted back a quick reply and saved his report before locking his screen. Even in a secure environment, the privacy of their clients was something he didn't take lightly.

He strode toward his boss's office, a few paces down from his cubicle, and tapped on the open door. "You wanted to see me?" Ethan asked as Jake flicked his gaze toward him.

"Yes, please, come in."

Ethan's stomach squeezed. He had no reason to be nervous. Jake was his boss but also his mentor. Still, there seemed a hesitation in his mannerisms that didn't make sense.

Settling into the chair opposite Jake's desk, Ethan waited for his boss to explain. Ethan's gaze rested on the small wooden plaque next to Jake's business cards on the edge of his desk. Ethan had never paid much attention to it before, but now, he realized there was a hidden word in the markings: *Jesus*. Huh, he had never pegged his boss as a man of faith.

Jake, maybe a decade older than him, had a head of full, white hair and penetrating gray eyes. He had done search and rescue for the Coast Guard before his honorable, medical discharge. Although his boss didn't show it, he had scars like Ethan that were below the skin and ran deep.

Jake leaned forward. "I wanted to ask you about Avery."

Ethan frowned. "What about her? Is everything okay with her contract?"

His boss waved off the question. "Yes, all the paperwork is fine, and I'm glad our agency can help her, but she specifically asked for you to manage her security detail. Before I agree to that, I need to know you two aren't involved."

Ethan blinked. "Involved? With Avery? The woman is a lock box. I earned her trust because of the situation she told you about that happened at our mutual friends' wedding. Other than that, she could care less about me. It's convenient I happen to work for a security agency, and she's in need of our services."

"Hmm, I will take your word for it," Jake said, "but I have an eye for these things. If at any time you feel emotionally attached or compromised, promise you will tell me, and I will put you on another assignment."

"Understood."

"That's all for now. Thanks."

Ethan took the long way back to his cubicle and stopped at the vending machine in the break room. As he stuffed in enough pocket change to buy a soda, he mulled over the conversation with his boss. Jake thought Avery liked him. That revelation made him smile wider than he had in a very long time.

Perhaps he was more emotionally invested than he cared to admit.

Chapter Twenty

The prison jumpsuit did not complement Russo's faded tan. The harsh orange combined with the absence of her Hollywood-ready makeup aged her a good ten years.

What hadn't aged was the sauciness of her smile.

Avery sat up straighter in her desk chair and blessed herself for remembering to use a virtual background instead of showing Russo how basic her office was.

But the point of this conversation was not to let the woman gnaw at her insecurities. The point was to get Russo to talk. Avery had at best forty minutes to do so before their virtual connection would end.

She tucked the flyer about Gianna's Friday recital out of sight behind her desk calendar, folded her hands, and began. "I heard about your life sentence last week and thought you might be more interested in talking with me now. If you cooperate, there's a chance we can moderate it."

Val laughed. "How good a chance?"

Avery arched an eyebrow. "At this point, my odds are better than the ones you're facing. You won't be able to work on your tan while serving life in prison."

The smirk on her face widened. "Oh, that setback is temporary."

"Then tell me how to find Big Eddie."

Val leaned her face closer to the screen. "Darling, if I did that, my life would be temporary."

Avery took a breath to pause. "I can understand your fear of the man, but you're in a state penitentiary. We can protect you."

Her cheeky grin vanished. "You're a fool to think that. His reach can extend anywhere." She leaned back in her seat. "Besides, if I told you what you wanted to know and if you managed to reduce my sentence, you better believe it would do me no good. I'd be dead the moment I stepped out of this place."

Avery's pulse raced. This conversation was not going at all how she had hoped. "He would never know. We could put you in a safe house. There are options, but there's no point discussing them unless you cooperate."

Val pressed a finger into the screen. "For a detective, you're a terrible listener. But you'd better listen up, because I do have a message for you—from Big Eddie himself, no less."

Her mind raced. Big Eddie must have contacted Val using video visitation. Perhaps she could request a log of her recent visits. More than likely, he used an intermediary, but the videos might give her a lead.

"I'm listening."

"About time," Val snorted. "Big Eddie says to watch your back, because there's a target on it."

Avery chuckled. "That's it? That's the message?"

Val's eyes flashed. "Don't believe me? Look at your boy Liam. If he recovers, there are more bullets where the last one came from. You think your precious Kaley and her new hubby will ever celebrate their first anniversary? And I would start cooking more at home if I were you. Not that it will matter. Big Eddie is coming for anyone who's messed with his hood."

"As if he's some sort of saintly godfather," Avery spat. "The man is responsible for murder, fraud, prostitution—and that's the short list. I will stop him with or without your help."

Val threw back her head and clapped her hands. "Bravo! Brave speech. Really, that was poetic. I should write it down to use in a script someday, because that's the only place it belongs— fiction. The real world doesn't work that way. The good guys don't win in real life.

"Oh, and another thing," Val hurried on. "Stop obsessing over Anthony Casale. He may have been your foster brother, but he was rotten and a rat. My advice is to stop poking your nose where it doesn't belong, buy a sailboat, and live on it for the rest of your life. Maybe you'll get lucky, and Big Eddie will bore of hunting you."

Avery's mouth went dry. How did Val know all this information—about Liam, Kaley and Reef, and Anthony being her foster brother? Did that mean Bella wasn't safe?

No, Val knew a lot, but she didn't know everything. "I'd worry about yourself if I were you. I live in a free world where good guys do win. You living in a penitentiary for the rest of your life is proof."

Val lowered her gaze and picked at her nails. "Don't you worry about me. I'll be working on my tan soon enough. For now, I've joined a lifers' club for hoots—though again, I don't plan to be here over a year—and, get this, I even agreed to participate in a prison preventers program to teach high schoolers all about the unglamorous nature of prison life. I'm going to have way more fun with that than I should.

"But enough about me. I'd worry about you, sweetcakes." She exaggerated a yawn. "I'm bored of this conversation. I've delivered my message, so I think I'll go rent a movie on my tablet. Cheers."

The video call ended.

Avery slapped her laptop shut and spun in her chair. Prison hadn't mellowed Val at all. The woman was as cocky and condescending as she had always been.

At least in a small way, the conversation had been a success. First, Val had finally talked with her, the first time since she'd entered the prison system. Second, Val revealed that Big Eddie had been in contact with her, a possible lead she could research. Third, it told her that hiring Semper Security was the right move, and she also needed to look into protection options for Liam, Jayna, Kaley, and Reef when they returned to Tampa.

She glanced at her phone. It was just before five o'clock. She had to send a quick memo to her team, check in on Liam, reach out to Reef, request the court's permission to view the logs of Russo's video visits since her sentence, and find something for dinner.

Dinner. Val's words lingered in her mind. Maybe she would pop open a can of soup in her pantry and call it a night.

Chapter Twenty-One

His phone buzzed on his bed stand, jolting Ethan awake. He fumbled to find the off button. It took five tries because he was out of practice.

Wow, he had slept until his alarm. Rubbing a hand over his face, Ethan lay back against his pillow and sighed, savoring the fact he'd enjoyed four hours of uninterrupted sleep. But then he remembered why he set the alarm for eight o'clock in the evening and rolled to his feet. His shift to monitor Avery's apartment started in an hour. He needed to eat something, and he wanted to shower to rinse off any mental cobwebs.

And maybe to look fresh in case he happened to see Avery.

He shook off the thought. No, he didn't want to see Avery tonight. Seeing Avery would mean she was in trouble, and he hoped the threats piling up against her wouldn't translate into anything more that–empty threats.

After tossing a frozen meal in the microwave for five minutes, he jumped in the shower and then donned his undercover uniform: dark wash jeans, black shirt, long sleeve black jacket to conceal his sidearm, and matching—he grinned—black baseball cap. The microwave beeped right as he finished.

He'd eat in the car. Traffic shouldn't be bad this time of evening, but Avery's apartment was a good forty-minute drive, and he preferred reaching his assignments early.

After locking up his apartment, he headed for his truck, parked in the well-lit lot. A quick scan revealed a few neighbors going about their day, nothing out of the ordinary. Even though his complex was gated with a security guard, he always did his own perimeter checks.

Something on his windshield caught his attention. It was a flyer, like the one some solicitor might leave in a retail parking lot.

He frowned as he popped open his door and placed his dinner on the console. This wasn't a retail lot. Solicitors weren't allowed. Maybe one of his neighbor's kids was selling Girl Scout cookies? That was probably it.

Snatching the flyer, he was about to toss it on the passenger seat when a picture caught his eye.

There were actually two pictures.

His chest clenched. He yanked his door shut, pressed the lock button, and started to drive as if nothing were out of the ordinary.

Whoever had left that flyer was no doubt watching him for a reaction.

He couldn't let them know that they had hit their target. But what about Avery? What would she think of him?

Maybe she would call him a coward. Maybe he was. But he had promised himself never to let someone he loved get hurt again.

He speed-dialed his boss the minute he left the complex.

"Ethan? Is everything all right?" Jake answered.

He paused to steady his breathing. "Please take me off Avery's detail." Saying the words felt like failure.

"Do you mean—"

"No, it's not what you said earlier." Ethan braked at a red light and closed his eyes for a split second.

The pictures of his sisters splayed across his memory.

"I received a threat against my family. I can take personal threats all day long, but them, you know I can't."

Jake sighed. "Yes, I understand, and I'm sorry. Were you heading to Reynold's place now?"

"Yes, can you get someone this last minute?"

"Always."

"I'm sorry."

"Don't apologize. Stand by. I might need you to sub somewhere else."

"I'll wait for your instructions."

His boss ended the call, and Ethan turned into a fast-food drive thru. He didn't need anything to eat. He hadn't eaten his original dinner, now cold in the passenger seat, but he did need a place to think. This long drive-thru line would work fine for now.

He gripped his wheel in frustration. This Big Eddie character had found out all he needed to cripple Ethan from effectively helping Avery. The man had placed him in check mate before Ethan had even started playing.

His sisters were in college on opposite ends of the United States. He couldn't protect both of them, and he wasn't about to choose one—or ask them to leave their college careers so he could hide them in some safe house until his work with Avery was done.

Would she understand, or would she think he was a coward?

His phone pinged with a message from his boss. *Phil is en route to Reynold's place. I need you to take his security shift that starts in an hour. It's an all-nighter.*

He texted to confirm and that he'd wait for those instructions. He hoped this shift was for a game or something with activity, because another quiet detail like Avery's would leave him with too much time alone with his thoughts.

A rap on his window reminded him he was in a drive-thru line. A teenager peered at him with a questioning smile. "What can I get you?"

Ethan handed him a credit card and sighed. "The strongest coffee you have."

Chapter Twenty-Two

Her can of chicken noodle soup left something to be desired. Maybe she would bake cookies. Cooking wasn't her thing, but she liked to think baking made up for it. If she baked cookies, she could text Ethan and see if he wanted any on his shift.

The thought made her face flush. He was a professional on a job, and she wasn't supposed to contact him unless she had a concern. But he had gone out of his way for her and paved the way for her relationship with Semper Security. The least she could do was show him her appreciation. Besides, she could give some to Bella for Gianna tomorrow during lunch.

She swung open her pantry, confident she had the ingredients for chocolate chip. Soon, her counters were messy, and her cookie sheets were full. The sweet aroma of baking cookies filled the space.

While waiting, she made herself a decaf espresso and curled up on her couch. A glance out her window revealed the lit sidewalk where a couple walked their dog. It was something she saw all the time, but usually she was hurrying off somewhere for work. The stillness of this moment reminded her how alone she was.

She was alone by choice. Besides, she had Bella. Gianna was her goddaughter, so in a way, she did have family.

What would it be like to matter to someone, to start her own family? No, men often walked out, and if something happened to her, she would never want a child to endure the foster system like she did.

Being alone was safer, but it was lonely.

She could get a dog.

No, she wasn't home enough to take care of it. She was barely home enough to feed her betta fish.

Avery reached for Bob's fish food and tapped some in the

bowl. He swam toward it as if he hadn't eaten in days.

"It's you and me, buddy," she sighed and replaced the food dispenser on the end table. That's when she noticed the small book on the edge. Right, it was the Bible the woman at APC had given her.

It would have been rude to refuse her, but why had the woman made her promise to read it?

Well, she had promised, but she hadn't said how much. Avery would give the woman until her timer dinged.

With a grunt, she reached for the book and opened to the beginning. She needed to find a short book. Flipping to the end, she stopped on one called I John. Perfect, it had five short chapters.

She started skimming, and the words didn't seem to make sense.

Fellowship.

That word made her pause, and she went back to reading. ... *³that which we have seen and heard we declare to you, that you also may have fellowship with us; and truly our fellowship is with the Father and with His Son Jesus Christ.*

Her chest squeezed. The words felt like an invitation to be less lonely.

She glanced around the room. Her betta fish couldn't judge her for wanting more company than him. This was probably nonsense anyway, but she kept reading.

⁵This is the message which we have heard from Him and declare to you, that God is light and in Him is no darkness at all.

Avery paused. At least God was for the good guys. Maybe He appreciated that she was working against the dark. She hurried on and rested on verse seven. *⁷But if we walk in the light as He is in the light, we have fellowship one with another, and the blood of Jesus Christ His Son cleanses us from all sin.*

Wait, she was already "in the light" or on the good guys' side. If that was the case, why wasn't she experiencing this so-called fellowship? Why did she still feel so alone?

With a frown, she read on. *⁸If we say that we have no sin, we deceive ourselves, and the truth is not in us. ⁹If we confess our sins,*

He is faithful and just to forgive us our sins and to cleanse us from all unrighteousness.

The words felt as if someone had punched her in the gut. Was she deceived? Was she a liar? What sins did she have to confess?

She was the one who had been wronged. People had hurt her, disappointed her. They had lied and said they were coming back when they didn't. Why hadn't God done something about that?

Her timer dinged, and she slapped the book shut. She had been silly to think the Bible had anything to offer her.

As she pulled the cookies from the oven and set them to cool on the rack, she also felt silly for making them in the first place. Whatever. She couldn't eat them all alone, so she might as well offer some to Ethan.

After shooting off a quick text, she scooped the remaining batter onto the cookie tray for her second batch. She had no sooner set the timer for it than her phone pinged.

With a smile, she reached for it, but the text wasn't from Ethan. It wasn't a number in her contacts.

Hi, Avery, this is Jake from Semper Security. I had to take Ethan off your detail, but his replacement has arrived and is monitoring your premises and the video surveillance at your office. All clear so far. Have a good night.

She wanted to ask what had happened with Ethan, but that wouldn't sound professional. Instead, she gave him a thumb's up and scrolled back to her text thread with Ethan. Maybe he was sick, but he had seemed fine earlier. Maybe he had car trouble.

Hey, what's up? Your boss said you're not coming.

The silence that met her question seemed to answer for him. Like so many before him, he must have decided to walk out of her life too.

She stuffed one cookie in her mouth and left the rest to cool on the baking sheet. She'd give them to Bella for Gianna—and then not bother baking again for a very long time.

"At least betta fish don't disappoint you," she muttered and strode past his bowl to her bathroom.

She glared at the small book on the end table. So much for

light and fellowship. She'd keep fighting for the good guys, by herself if she had to.

The way she always had.

Avery started her day at the office at six the next morning and spent the first three hours watching Russo's video visitations, thanks to the court granting her request and the prison authorities promptly cooperating.

The bad news was that she had nothing to show for it but dry eyes and a queasy stomach.

Avery reached for her coffee mug but found it empty. Empty like every single lead she'd gotten on this wretched case.

Something didn't add up though. How could Russo know so much about her situation and Liam's? How was she getting her intel? The logs the detective had given her showed she hadn't had any in-person visits, just video ones. Those were mostly from a girlfriend whose useless prattle she would now have forever engrained in her skull.

She was missing something. Maybe a call to her former boss would help, though the odds of her getting to speak with him were slim, and she wasn't about to call his cell. His direct office line would do.

The familiar "please leave your message …" sounded in her ears, and she waited for the recording to end.

"Sheriff Hannaford, this is Avery Reynolds. I wanted to run a few updates by you on the Big Eddie investigation. When you have a chance, please call my cell. Thanks."

Leaving the message made her feel better, but also filled her with old doubts. Had she been wrong to leave the force in the first place? Maybe her goal of using her own private investigator business to solve her foster brother's murder and jump start her own career had been premature.

So far, her agency had helped other people but not the one who gave her whole operation purpose.

Bella.

Noon was a little over two hours away. She needed an update for her foster sister, and more than that, she needed to find Big Eddie.

All-nighters in his early thirties were very different from all-nighters in his twenties. Ethan felt older than his thirty-three years when he finally unlocked his truck at six in the morning. All he wanted was breakfast and his bed.

Peace of mind would be nice too.

He looked at his personal phone for the first time since his shift had ended and held his breath. There were two missed texts from his sisters and one from Avery.

Ethan scanned the ones from his sisters first. They were talking about flying to their parents' place for Thanksgiving and asked if he'd mind them bringing some friends home with them. Reading between the lines, he guessed they meant boys.

No one would be good enough for his sisters, but he might as well vet these guys. His parents wouldn't mind the extra mouths. They would be as eager as him to get to know their "friends."

A decade ago, he had been the one bringing his girlfriend home. No doubt his parents had hoped he'd find the right one, settle down, and have some kids they could dote on.

His chance had come and gone, but he sure hoped his sisters would have normal lives even if he never could. They might not if he put them in harms' way.

After shooting off a quick text back to them, saying he'd be glad to meet their friends, he moved on to Avery's text.

The disappointment in her words ripped through him. He had let her down, the last thing he wanted to do.

Texting *sorry* didn't seem enough. He wanted to see her in person, to explain. But what if someone were watching him or monitoring Avery's movements? If he met her, he needed it to be in a casual place no one would suspect.

A memory tugged at the back of his mind. Kaley and Reef's young professional group had a worship and prayer service one Thursday a month at their church. He had gone once or twice, and it had been a nice enough time. What were the odds this Thursday was that night?

He wasn't about to text either of them on their honeymoon to find out, so he did a quick search for Crossroads Christian Church and pulled up the events page. Sure enough, the meeting was tonight at six o'clock.

Snapping a print screen of the page, he texted it to Avery. *I'm sorry I let you down. Let me explain? I can meet you tonight at this event.*

There, he was offering an olive branch. If she wanted to know and wanted to still be friends, she'd come. If not, he had at least tried.

As he backed out of the parking lot, his phone pinged, and his pulse quickened. Could that be Avery? He shifted back to park before checking his phone.

No, it was Chloe. *Is there anyone you'd like us to meet this Thanksgiving? Winkey face.*

He sighed. If only there were. His sisters didn't understand and would never understand. They knew he'd gotten a medical discharge, but they didn't know about his best friend's tragedy or his ongoing PTSD.

Kaley's words rang in his memory. Maybe he was wrong not to tell them the whole truth, but then, he couldn't protect them from the ugliness of it all.

He started to type a reply when another text came through.

Avery.

There were no words, just a thumb's up.

Ethan grinned and started driving toward the lot's exit. It wasn't a yes, but it wasn't a no.

From Avery, that was the best he could expect.

Chapter Twenty-Three

Downtown Tampa seemed more crowded than usual at lunchtime, and Avery had to park farther away than expected. She all but sprinted to Bella's favorite café to make it before noon.

Her heart fell when she spotted Bella at an outside table. She wore a wide brim black hat, her trademark designer sunglasses, and a velvety red dress. She looked ready to step into a magazine cover shoot.

Subtle, Bella was not.

Avery could only hope she wasn't a target, because anyone looking for her could spot her a mile away.

Bella rose and greeted her with a hug. "You look rested, Avery. I think some time away is what we both needed."

Rested wasn't the word that came to mind after Reef and Kaley's wedding, but Avery didn't want to go into detail about Liam's shooting or her mixed-bag experience with Ethan. "It was good to have a change of scenery." Avery chose a seat at the table that gave her the best view of the road. "You enjoyed Cancun?"

"It was gorgeous, and Gianna loved all the water excursions." Bella sipped an iced beverage. "I got a water for you and told the waiter to come back in a few, though I already know what I'm getting."

Avery shook her head. "You always order the same thing."

"And you don't?" Bella tweaked an eyebrow.

"No, I can't be too predictable in my line of work."

Bella laughed. "I'm pretty sure that at least with your menu, you're allowed to be predictable."

A tan sedan idled by, and Avery trailed it with her gaze until it disappeared around the corner.

When she felt Bella's gaze on her, she turned to find her friend studying her. "What's wrong, Avery?"

Avery sighed and leaned forward. She needed to level with her. "Bella, you should be careful. People associated with the Big Eddie case are receiving threats. One of my team members has been shot. Other attempts have been made."

Bella squinted at her. "Threats against you?"

"It's not me I'm worried about. I don't think you're in danger since we have been discreet about you hiring me, but you must be careful just the same."

Pursing her lips, Bella nodded. "I will be. Is your associate okay?"

"He's expected to make a full recovery."

The waitress appeared to take their order, and then Bella turned her focus back to Avery. "Does all this—danger—mean you're on to something? Big Eddie is worried you're getting close?"

Avery paused. Her getting close? She had never felt farther away from finding Tampa's underlord.

"I'm not sure, but our efforts must have made him uncomfortable. As far as updates go, Russo received her sentence—life in prison. In that sense, we've permanently put one of his accomplices and backers behind bars. He's not too happy about that."

"I can imagine," Bella said.

A cyclist paused outside the dining area for a swig of water before continuing down the street, while a pair of dog walkers took advantage of the watering bowl for pets the café had set out beside the entrance.

Had she imagined they had glanced her way?

Avery sipped her water and then continued. "I spoke with Russo, thinking she might be more willing to talk, but the woman is as stubborn and arrogant as ever. I have a conference call with the sheriff—my former boss—this afternoon to discuss some questions I have for him after my chat with Russo. He said he has an opportunity for me at the next Buc's game this Sunday, so we'll be talking about that too."

She paused as the waitress returned with their food. After thanking her, Bella prayed over the meal. Avery had assumed it was merely a habit Mama Casale had taught her, but maybe it meant more. She tucked that thought away for later.

"Anyway, I'm sorry I don't have something more concrete, but I will not leave any rock unturned in this case—"

Movement in her peripheral caused Avery to jerk sideways in time to see the same tan sedan creeping toward their seating area. This time, the back passenger window was open a notch, and a gun's muzzle rested on it.

"Down!" Avery dove on top of Bella, sending them both crashing to the pavement, as glass shattered inches away. The shooter must have used a silencer. Other patrons screamed as the sedan's tires squealed during its hasty retreat.

Avery jumped to her feet but couldn't glimpse the license plate number in time. She then knelt next to Bella. "Are you okay?"

Her friend was visibly shaking. "I'm—fine. That was—too close. Were they shooting at you—or me?"

Police sirens wailed in the distance, probably responding to a witness's 9-1-1 call. "I was likely the target," Avery assured her. But fear for Bella doubled in her gut.

What if they were both the target?

Avenging Anthony's murder was one matter, but Avery could not risk anything happening to her beloved Bella.

"As a precaution, I'll arrange security for you and your family."

Bella hugged her. "Thank you. I—I don't know what I'd do without you."

She didn't deserve Bella's praise, not until Avery stopped Big Eddie once and for all.

By the time she made her statement to the police, ensured Bella was safely home, and arranged security for her, Avery barely had time to return to her office before her call with Sheriff Hannaford.

"I hear you've had quite the day," Hannaford said after his receptionist transferred her call.

Avery sighed and kicked off her shoes underneath her desk. The privacy of her office offered her the chance to unwind even while working. "Word travels fast," she said.

"I could read the report, but I'd like to hear your take on the incident," Hannaford said. "Then, we can talk about Russo and the Buc's game."

"I'm still wondering who the target was," Avery said, "but it could have been both of us." She filled Hannaford in on the threats and shooting in Beech Mountain. "Basically, it seems as though anyone linked to putting Russo behind bars or thwarting the drug trafficking operation is now in danger. Big Eddie seems to have a pin on each one of us, and it's driving me crazy that I haven't been able to move closer to exposing him—or figuring out his real identity."

"Don't sell yourself short. The fact you've taken out Russo and blocked a revenue source are successes."

"I'd like to ask your opinion on Russo." Avery skirted his praise. "She knows about my colleague being shot and details she has no business knowing unless someone from Big Eddie's team told her. However, I watched hours of her video visit recordings, and there was nothing to suggest any type of communication. How is she getting her intel?"

"It could be word of mouth through other inmates," Hannaford said.

Avery hesitated. "I tried to coax her to reveal what she knows about Big Eddie, but she said that if she did, there would be no point to leaving prison, because she'd be as good as dead. Then she boasted that she'll be out of prison soon enough."

"She's bluffing." Hannaford's tone held disbelief. "People don't break out of prison these days."

"I wish she would cooperate. She is the missing key to

finding and taking this Big Eddie character down.”

“Give her time. As her life sentence starts to sink in, she might be more cooperative.”

Time. It was exactly what Avery didn’t have.

“Meanwhile, we run our own offensive,” Hannaford said. “We’ve got a new lead. Bradley Weber is a name that doesn’t mean anything to you now, but one of the few arrests we made in the sting operation worked for his signage company. There’s no crime in unknowingly hiring a pervert, but Weber only suspended him after learning of his new criminal record. Turns out, the man is already back at work even though the suspension period hasn’t expired.”

Avery scribbled Weber’s name on a sticky note. “How do you know that?”

“My office checked in with his HR department. HR admitted it seemed strange, but said there were extenuating circumstances they were not able to discuss.”

“Sounds like code for—I’m just following the boss’ orders,” Avery muttered.

“My thoughts exactly,” Hannaford said. “Anyway, Weber rents a suite at Raymond James Stadium and has invited distributors to join him for Sunday’s game. Long story short, I contacted a friend of mine who does sales for a major distributor. He agreed I could send someone undercover posing as his merchandising specialist. I’d like to outsource the job, and you came to mind. You want in? It will involve a lot of boring research, and you can leave your hooker costume in the closet where it belongs.”

She deserved that dig but recognized this second chance. “I’m in. Boring research is my jam. For the record, I burned the hooker costume.”

Hannaford chuckled. “Good, I’ll send you what I have on Weber and his company so you can get started, and then I’ll connect you with the rep you’ll be working with. I’ve got another call in a minute, but we’ll talk again soon.”

Avery set down her phone and rubbed her eyes. She had a conference meeting with her team about their other clients in fifteen minutes and needed to check in with Liam after that.

Would she even have the energy to meet up with Ethan tonight? She should forget him. Undependable people weren't worth her time.

But something in her gut told her he had a reason for not showing up, and she needed to know what it was.

Chapter Twenty-Four

Avery braked for her turn after the Crossroads Christian Church sign and scanned the campus. It was larger than she expected, but another directional sign guided her to the youth building, where the young professional's event was being held.

She smirked. How many times had Liam invited her, and she had turned him down? He had insisted that she would fit in with this group that mixed "young" adults in both their twenties and thirties. Not that it mattered to her. Meeting Ethan here was a one-time thing, simply because the church posed as an innocent gathering place.

Hearing Liam's voice had been a relief today. He sounded like himself, and the doctors had discharged him earlier in the day. He and Jayna had driven to a friend's cabin in South Carolina where he could rest a few more days before the long drive home.

He had been sure to point out their friend was staying at the cabin with him, so he and Jayna weren't unchaperoned.

Not that she cared. Who needed chaperones when you were adults? Given Jayna's past, it seemed unnecessary, but still, she admired Liam's chivalry. Maybe he was going out of his way to make a point that Jayna was different now.

Avery locked her car and strode toward the building's entrance. A few people milled about outside the glass doors. They looked to be twenty-somethings, a bit younger than her. Their ripped jeans, casual dresses, and board shorts made her hesitate. Perhaps her dress pants, heels, and fitted black sweater weren't the right choice.

She'd never been good at blending in, perhaps because she had never fit in. Jumping around schools due to foster care had seen to that. Mama Casale had once told her, "The only place you need to be comfortable is in your own skin. Be yourself, Avery."

Mama Casale. How she missed that woman.

How much she wanted to honor her by giving her son's killer the justice he deserved. How far short she kept falling in her work to do so.

"Avery! It's good to see you." A curly-haired woman waved at her.

Avery blanked. Had she been at Kaley's wedding?

"I'm Olivia," she smiled. "You probably don't recognize me without all the fluff and fanfare, but I was Kaley's maid of honor."

"Oh yes, sorry. That day was a blur."

"No joke." Olivia walked with her inside and motioned down a hall. "I didn't know you came to our worship night. I've had to miss a few months because of work."

"I don't come." That sounded too harsh. "I mean, I haven't come before. I'm here to meet someone tonight."

"Oh?" Olivia's arched eyebrows indicated her budding curiosity.

"Just a colleague," Avery hurried on.

"Heard that one before," Olivia laughed but must have detected Avery's lack of amusement. "Sorry, I'm a matchmaker. Can't help it. I called Reef and Kaley an item before Kaley had a clue."

Avery glanced at Olivia's left hand. No ring. Interesting. A matchmaker with no match of her own.

But she didn't want to encourage this conversation. They reached a comfortably large room with two rows of chairs and a stage up front. A few people mingled, but there was no sign of Ethan.

"I need to help out in the sound booth, but it was good seeing you." Olivia parted from her side to slip inside the booth at the back of the room where a dark-haired man sat on a stool monitoring a sound board. He glanced up when he spotted Olivia, and his face broke into a lopsided smile.

Maybe there was a match for the matchmaker after all.

But where was Ethan?

There was no missing his six-foot frame. A quick scan of the room confirmed he wasn't here.

She slid into a chair in a back row that gave her a full view of the doorway—and easy access to it if he failed to show up.

The thought burned her cheeks. What if he were wasting her time?

Her phone pinged as a guitarist and keyboard player took their places on stage.

It was Ethan. The tightness in her chest relaxed as she scanned his message. *Just parked. Save me a seat.*

The room was starting to fill up as the music started. The leader invited everyone to stand and sing, so she rose along with the others. The music was upbeat and nice enough, but she wasn't paying attention.

Her gaze kept drifting to the door.

Someone tapped her shoulder, and she spun. Ethan offered a tilted grin. "Surprised you weren't paying attention to all the entrances."

Avery flushed. "I assumed you church people followed rules. That's the main entrance."

"Ah, you know we have to always keep the element of surprise in our work," Ethan said. "Thanks for meeting me here."

"Why did you quit?" The words rushed out before she could tame them. "You were the one who suggested your security agency. I mean, you don't seem like a guy to back down."

Ethan's shoulders tensed. "Yeah, fair question. It's rude to talk during service though."

Avery bit her tongue. They were in the back row of a quasi-church service. Surely no one would care.

But Ethan seemed to care. He directed his gaze toward the front, and to her surprise, started singing as the leader transitioned to a slow, pensive song.

She stuffed her hands in her jacket and peeked at Ethan. His low baritone was rather nice, but suddenly, it wasn't his voice that had her attention.

It was the lyrics.

"Just as I am though toss'd about, with many a conflict, many a doubt …"

Avery blinked. That was her. Her path seemed littered with conflicts, problems, and more questions than answers.

"Fightings and fears within, without, O Lamb of God, I come!"

Lamb of God? She had never understood all the strange religious metaphors, but something to the lyrics pulled her in and made her want to listen.

"Just as I am Thou wilt receive, wilt welcome, pardon, cleanse, relieve; because Thy promise I believe, O Lamb of God, I come!"

Pardon. Her reading in I John jumped back into her mind, but she didn't need pardon. She hadn't done anything wrong.

The musicians ended the song, and someone named Pastor TJ took the stage. Great, how long was this lecture going to take before she got answers from Ethan?

Ethan, however, seemed to be in no hurry. In fact, he pulled a small Bible from his jacket pocket. It looked like the one the woman at APC had shoved into their hands.

"You start reading yours yet?" he whispered.

"A little," she muttered. What did it matter?

"Interesting stuff, right?" His piercing gray eyes didn't seem to be jesting. They searched her face as if trying to read her.

"Yeah, interesting." She crossed her legs and settled back in the seat. "How long is this service anyway?"

Ethan shrugged. "Not long. At least, it doesn't feel long to someone who doesn't sleep and has nowhere else to be."

His words made her wince. She didn't have anywhere else to be, and frankly, she hadn't been sleeping well either. How did she have so much in common with a PTSD vet?

"Just as I am—just as you are," the pastor began. "That's where we start, but that's not where we stay."

Ethan leaned forward, as if hanging on the pastor's every word.

Avery sighed and slouched against the padded chair. This was where they differed. Ethan was desperate for something, anything, to patch up whatever wounds his past had inflicted.

Her past had left its own scars, but nothing a pastor said could even begin to help. God had never solved her problems, and He wasn't about to start now.

Righting wrongs was up to her, and she wouldn't fail. She couldn't.

Chapter Twenty-Five

Just as I am. That phrase continued to play in Ethan's mind as the pastor closed in prayer. Ethan leaned his palms against the seat in front of him and glanced around the room. Most people had their heads bowed, including Avery, though he guessed the reason was simply that Pastor TJ had instructed everyone to do so. If she was anything, Avery was a rule follower.

Soft keyboard music gently emphasized the melody for the words running through his mind. His broken life, his painful past didn't exclude him from God's love. He could accept God's grace and forgiveness just as he was and trust God to make something meaningful out of his mess.

That's what the pastor had said. It seemed too good to be true, but the tug he felt deep inside was undeniable. Here was the first glimmer of hope he'd found since Troy's death.

"If you want God to change your life," Pastor TJ was saying, "all you have to do is admit you're a sinner, believe that Jesus died to pay for your sins, and that He rose so that you can live forever with Him. You can do that right where you're standing, or you can come up here, and I'll be glad to pray with you."

Ethan's pulse quickened. He wanted to believe. He wanted this hope. He had nothing to lose, except maybe Avery's respect, but had he ever had that anyway? She had loathed him at the start, and now, she was only here out of desperation.

He chanced a look at her. She bowed her head dutifully, but her boots tapped ever so slightly. She was impatient, ready for this service to end. Why hadn't the pastor's words touched her the way they had him?

Ethan directed his gaze ahead. He didn't know, but now was

his chance. No matter what Avery might think of him, he needed to take it.

Moving past her into the aisle, he strode forward. With each step, his heart felt lighter. Pastor TJ extended a hand toward him, and it felt like a lifeline.

"I recognize you. You were at Reef and Kaley's wedding, right?" Pastor TJ asked. "Sorry, I don't remember your name."

"It's Ethan, sir."

"Call me TJ," the pastor said. "What's on your heart?"

Ethan swallowed. No turning back. "I'm a sinner, and I want God's second chance."

TJ's face lit up in a smile. "God's saving grace is free for the asking. You want to pray with me?"

Ethan glanced around. "Right here?"

TJ led him to an empty seat on the front row. "Right here if that works for you."

"Okay. Sure." Ethan sat on the edge of the seat. "I don't know what to say though."

"Tell God what you told me. No special words required."

Ethan pressed his eyes shut and gripped his knees. "Okay, well, God, you know my scars, my sins. I've tried, and I can't make them right. I ask that You would take me just as I am. I believe You can save a mess like me."

Emotion rose in his throat, and he couldn't go on. Saying the words out loud felt so freeing.

"Amen." TJ squeezed his shoulder. "Welcome to the family of God, brother."

Ethan looked up. "Thanks, man."

"I wish Reef and Kaley could be here to celebrate with you," TJ said. "I know they will be so happy."

Another person, a young woman, had also come forward. TJ rose. "Wait here, and we'll talk more after, okay?"

"Sure." Ethan watched as TJ greeted the woman, and the keyboard player started the umpteenth refrain of the song. The guitarist joined in with singing, and the audience followed his lead.

He sang too, because now, this was his story. He didn't understand it all, but something told him the Bible from Miss Martha and friends like TJ, Reef, and Kaley would help him find his way.

Would this song never end? Avery sighed and squinted her eyes to see if anyone up front looked about ready to wrap up this never-ending service.

They didn't.

She nudged her elbow in Ethan's direction to see if he wanted to bail but met an empty space. Now wide-eyed, she stared at the vacant seat beside her.

What? He had left her? Her gaze darted around the room and zeroed in on Ethan's broad shoulders.

In a front row seat.

Praying with the pastor.

You have got to be kidding me.

Frustration boiled inside her. She had not endured an hour-plus-long service to witness his coming-to-God moment. He had promised to explain himself, and she wanted answers, not an altar call.

The song finally ended, and when the pastor had "prayed them out"—his exact words—she marched up the aisle to Ethan and intercepted him before he could start another long conversation with the pastor.

She tapped his shoulder, and he spun in his seat. "Oh, hey, Avery!" Ethan jumped to his feet. "That was pretty awesome, right?"

Awesome was not the word that came to her mind. "Can we talk?"

A frown flitted across Ethan's face. "Uh, sure. I just need to let Pastor TJ know I'll be back."

Avery nodded to where the pastor prayed with a woman a few

seats down. "He's busy, and this won't take long."

"But Avery, they've got pizza and refreshments for everyone after the service. There's no need to rush—"

She couldn't suppress her frustration any longer. "Why did you quit?"

"Quit?" He stuffed his hands in his jeans. "You mean, why did I step away from your assignment?"

Avery folded her arms. "If that's how you want to put it."

"Look, I didn't plan to let you down. I was excited you chose to partner with Semper Security and honored you trusted me."

"But?" Avery prompted. There was always a *but*.

Ethan sighed and pulled his phone from his pocket. He scrolled to something and then flipped the screen toward her.

She squinted to study the picture of two attractive young women. Apparently, Ethan had more than one woman in his back pocket.

"Who are they?" Her tone sounded casual enough to her own ears.

"My sisters." Ethan slid the phone back in his pocket.

Tension released in her chest, but only for a moment.

"Someone stuffed their pictures inside the windshield wipers of my truck right before I was supposed to leave for my first shift at your apartment."

Her gut twisted. Big Eddie had threatened his family to keep him away from helping her, and his threat had worked.

Ethan's eyes pinched with emotion. "I already lost—I can't let anything happen to them. They're worth more to me than any job. I'm sorry."

"Then Big Eddie is winning at his game."

"Avery—"

"And what of all this?" Avery swept her arm toward the stage and toward the people huddled in prayer. "If this God is so great, can't you trust Him to protect the people you love?"

Ethan's mouth hung open, but he didn't have an answer. Her conscience warned her to stop, but she couldn't hold back the hurt and frustration.

"If your God is so great, why does He let everyone I've ever depended on exit stage right out of my life?" She bit her tongue. "You know what? Forget it. I'm glad you've got family to care about, but I've got a job to do. Excuse me."

Heat rushed to her face as she strode out the exit and past other people who were mingling and chatting happily—blissfully unaware of the evil at work in their city.

An evil she would have to keep fighting to bring down. By herself.

Chapter Twenty-Six

The pepperoni pizza would have tasted delicious, if Avery's outburst hadn't left such a bad taste in his mouth.

Ethan chewed on his crust and half-listened to the conversation around him. The lounge seating in the church's social area allowed him to be present with a cluster of other young professionals but distant enough to get lost in his thoughts.

Lately, those had revolved around the fiercely proud and independent woman who nonetheless seemed like the loneliest person he knew. Besides himself.

His sisters' picture burned in his mind. Not being able to protect them the way he hadn't been able to protect Tony—he couldn't risk it.

But Avery's sharp comment raised doubts. He believed God could save him—had saved him—and that He was the Savior of the world. He was more than able to protect anyone, but the reality was that He sometimes didn't. Ethan wasn't sure how to reconcile those two facts.

A vibration inside his pocket pulled him to the present. The screen read *Reef*.

No way, the man was on his honeymoon. "Aren't you supposed to be floating in an infinity pool somewhere?" Ethan joked into the phone.

Reef chuckled. "Yeah, that was the original plan, but we've improvised for safety. Still having a great time though."

Ethan could imagine. "So why are you calling me?"

"Pastor TJ sent me a text, and I had to call you. I'm so happy for you and want to say welcome to the family."

The genuine joy in Reef's voice was enough to make Ethan

grin. "Thanks, Reef. TJ said you would be happy."

"Dude, I'm thrilled. Being God's child is the best choice you could ever make. That's not to say life will suddenly be easy, but God will be there to help you each step you take."

A woman glanced his way, and Ethan stood to take the conversation somewhere more private. "Yeah, it's still as complicated—if not more complicated—than ever."

"Are you okay?"

The concern in Reef's tone warmed him, but Ethan hesitated to share. "C'mon, you're on your honeymoon. I'll save my problems for later."

"Kaley is reading right now. I've got time."

Ethan exhaled as he stepped into the hallway, empty except for one or two people who lingered there after the service. "I could use your advice. I connected Avery to my security agency and was planning to lead security around her apartment, but I received a threat—against my sisters. I can't let anything happen to them."

Reef was silent for a moment. "Let me guess. Avery doesn't understand."

Ethan paced the floor. "No. In fact, she came to church tonight with me to hear me explain why."

"Wait, she came to church?" Reef whistled. "Liam has been trying to get her to come for years."

"Don't congratulate me or anything. She threw in my face that if God is so powerful, why don't I trust Him to protect the people I love instead of backing down?" Ethan paused to slow his breath. His pulse was throbbing in his ears. "How am I supposed to answer that?"

The silence on the other end suggested there wasn't an easy answer. Finally, Reef spoke. "Here's the thing, Ethan. God can absolutely protect our loved ones, but we also live in a world broken because of our sin. Bad guys sometimes win on this side of eternity, but when Jesus returns, He will have the final victory over evil."

Bad guys sometimes win. That wasn't what Ethan wanted to

hear, and it sure wasn't what Avery wanted to hear.

"So what do I do?" Ethan ground his teeth. "Do I help Avery and risk the people dearest to me, or do I protect my family but leave Avery out in the cold?"

"I can't answer that," Reef said, "but I will be praying you have wisdom to know what to do. Now that you're God's child, why don't you ask Him what He wants you to do? The book of James in the Bible says that if we need wisdom, we should ask God. He will show you the way."

Ethan hadn't thought to talk to God. Good grief, he had talked to God in earnest for the first time not half an hour ago. "Why should God listen to me? I am so new at this."

"Doesn't matter to God," Reef said. "You're His child, and that makes you His priority. He's your Father. He wants you to talk to Him."

Ethan sighed. "Okay, I'll give it a try, but I could sure use some clearcut guidance."

"Keep me posted, man," Reef said. "If you need anything, I'm a phone call away."

"Thanks." Ethan ended the call and paused from his pacing to lean against the wall. Talking with Reef had been a nice surprise, but Ethan wasn't any closer to the answers he craved.

He started to return toward the room filled with his peers and pizza but hesitated at the stairwell. Aside from Reef and Kaley, he didn't know anyone, and while he would like to get to know more of this "family" as Pastor TJ called them, the problem with Avery had killed his appetite and his interest in socializing.

Taking the steps seemed the fastest way to get alone with his thoughts and with God.

"You know I'm new at this," Ethan mumbled as he reached the bottom of the stairs and exit. "You don't owe me any favors, but I could use some guidance."

There was no audible voice as he walked to his truck and started the engine, and his radio started playing. The rap music on the station jolted him. Those lyrics had never bothered him before, but now, they didn't set right. They were so opposite the music from the service.

Pecking at his phone, he did a quick search for a local Christian station and switched the channel. He didn't know the song, but he liked the tune.

His apartment wasn't far, and he really should eat more dinner. He had eaten so much drive-thru the last few days, but he wasn't a cook, and Thanksgiving with the family wasn't until next month. A burger would have to do.

Family. Chloe's and Tori's faces popped into his mind. The last time they'd been together over the summer, they had visited the self-defense gym he'd made them join back in high school. It was good to see they'd kept up with their training, and they weren't just girls with pretty faces. They were competent—and of course, he'd made sure they conceal-carried too.

However, they weren't allowed to carry firearms on campus, and even if they could, it wouldn't be enough to protect them from the long reach of Big Eddie.

"… you can depend on us to have your back, no matter how tough the job."

Ethan pulled into the burger drive thru as the voice on the radio made him do a double take. Wait, he knew that voice.

"I'm Jake Powell, owner of Semper Security, and I'm proud to be a ministry partner with UpliftedFM."

His boss was advertising on the Christian station? The memory of the Jesus plaque on Jake's desk made more sense now. That wasn't a decoration. There was a story there.

"Order when you're ready," a voice said over the restaurant's intercom.

"Uh, just a minute." Ethan cranked up the radio. Was there more to the ad?

No, another song started playing, but it was Jake's words that rang in his ears. *You can depend on us to have your back.*

He flinched. Avery hadn't been able to depend on him, and she needed someone other than Big Eddie's goons watching her back, waiting for her to misstep or drop her guard.

Chloe and Tori were capable women, and he would contact them and the security teams on their campuses. He would do everything in his power to keep them safe, and he would pray God would watch over them.

The answer he had been craving had come loud and clear over his radio. He couldn't cower to evil.

After mumbling an order, he pulled forward in the drive-thru line and pressed his boss' number. Jake worked crazy hours, and if he happened to be off, a voicemail would keep Ethan committed to his new plan and prevent anything from weakening his resolve.

He needed to ask Jake two questions.

One. What was his faith story?

Two. How soon could he rejoin Avery's security team?

Chapter Twenty-Seven

Beep. Beep. Beeeeeeppp!

With a groan, Avery rolled toward her nightstand and slapped at her phone's screen to silence the alarm. The throbbing headache and sick feeling in her stomach were not a good omen. She couldn't get a migraine this Friday. She just couldn't.

Fumbling in her drawer, she found the small pill case she kept there for mornings like this, pinched two ibuprofens between her fingers, and uncapped the water bottle also staged on her stand.

Even squinting her eyes felt like torture, but she managed to set a new alarm on her phone and shoot off a text to Tasha, letting her know she would be working remotely today. Everything she needed would be in her calendar and email which she had linked to her phone, and she never left the office without her laptop.

One more hour. Most working people didn't get up until six o'clock anyway, and today, she'd have to give her body extra grace. She had to read through the information Sheriff Hannaford had sent and brief her colleague Drew via Zoom after she'd put in several hours of research.

She'd prefer that Liam be her intel partner, but Drew would do fine, even if he didn't quite have Liam's level of finesse. Essentially, he would be ready at a text's notice to find out any information she might have forgotten in her signage research. In the meantime, she needed to brief him on what she had learned so far and give him a context for this job.

As for Liam, she needed to check in on him too. Hadn't gotten to that yesterday.

Pounding headache.

Her phone vibrated. This was too early for Tasha, unless she'd decided to take up early morning jogging.

She hadn't.

Only a fellow insomniac would text at five in the morning.
Call me when you can. I have news.
Ethan.

He had some nerve texting her after quitting and then getting all spiritual last night. He could get in line behind everything she needed to do.

The first thing was to press pause on her work, and sleep for one more hour.

Her pain medicine couldn't kick in fast enough.

An hour and a shower later, Avery propped her laptop on a pillow and set a large mug of black coffee on her end table. Sheriff Hannaford had sent her a digital file on the man he was hiring her to learn more about at Sunday's football game.

Bradley Weber. Although the man's background checks were squeaky clean, so were those of many people. In addition to the felon he employed, another red flag was a private auditor's report of his signage company receiving reoccurring payments—in the thousands of dollars—from a consulting firm called Epic Enterprises. The amounts were all slightly different in a perhaps weak attempt to suggest different services.

The kicker was that Epic Enterprises offered no clear services, per its website which was virtually unusable due to being "under construction." The ruse looked suspiciously similar to the fake LLC Avery had exposed last summer.

More interestingly, the payments all deposited to his account the Monday after every single Buc's game. A seasoned pass holder, Weber also routinely rented suites at the stadium, and this Sunday's game was no different.

Avery sipped her coffee. If Weber were one of Big Eddie's pimps, he could be running girls under their noses through his suite rentals or securing more customers for the illicit trade. Posing as a merchandising specialist for a major distributor, she would feel out Weber's character—and the characters of the others who had received invitations.

She'd already had a long chat with Hannaford's sales rep friend who had forwarded her their e-catalog to memorize. If anyone questioned who she was—since she wasn't a good old boy the crew would recognize—she would say she was a merchandising specialist filling in for the manager who couldn't attend at the last minute.

Using her open-source intelligence channels, she researched Weber's signage company, Signs-4-Success, along with its top distributors and its competitors. She started a list of rep names for the other companies who likely received an invitation, memorized the names and roles of everyone who worked at S4S, and made flash cards to quiz herself on all the sign materials and new products she might be asked about.

Time slipped away while she prepared for game day until her growling stomach warned her that the lunch hour had almost passed. She'd told Drew to plan on a Zoom conference at three, which gave her two more hours to finish preparing her brief and get food.

Her phone pinged, and she glared at it. Whatever it was, she didn't have time.

Ethan's name flashed on the screen. She definitely didn't have time for him.

Although she craved Chinese again, her close call with takeout was too fresh to make her risk another try. Instead, she dug in her freezer for some frozen fruit, tossed it in her blender with a scoop of protein powder, and settled for a smoothie. It was anything but filling, but it silenced her stomach for the moment.

She rewarded herself with some social-media intelligence research on Weber. His socials portrayed him as a family man, wife and two kids. But Avery knew well enough that the social media front often lied, and from her own experience, that a happy family was merely an illusion.

A picture of Weber with his young daughter in the front doorway of his house triggered her. How often had she hoped her father would walk back through their front door—the one he had angrily barged through to get away from an argument with her mom?

"Daddy!" Avery had screamed, but her father had charged past her into his Mustang and sped off.

Her mom's blank face refused to meet Avery's gaze. The woman who had never shown her much affection sagged against their dining room table and tilted her face away from her daughter.

Avery had tugged at her sleeve. "Mommy? Where's Daddy going?"

Her mom's hardened lips held no expression. "I don't know."

"When's he coming back?"

In response, her mom pushed her away and grabbed a beer from the fridge. "Never, I hope."

Marta Reynolds had gotten her wish. Daddy had never come home, and not one week later, her mother exited the same front door with another man on her arm—and never came back either. A neighbor found Avery digging through their trash looking for food the following week and called child protective services.

Avery shook herself and kept scrolling through Weber's feed. If he were involved with Tampa's illicit trade, he sure put up a squeaky-clean front. Most of his feed consisted of highlighting his son's baseball games and his daughter's gymnastic competitions.

Her phone vibrated with an incoming call.

Ethan. Again.

Her finger hovered over the end-call button. She had less than half an hour before her meeting with Drew, but what if he had received another threat? No, if he weren't helping her, Big Eddie's muscle should leave him alone.

What if he wanted to apologize for last night? No, she'd never met a man—besides maybe Liam—who knew how to say sorry.

Her finger pressed to accept the call anyway.

"What?" Avery forced a neutral tone.

"Avery, I'm back on your detail." Ethan's hurried voice hinted that he thought she might hang up, but after that introduction, she couldn't.

She hadn't seen this news coming. Avery clamped her unhinged jaw shut and cleared her throat. "Why?"

"Can we please talk?" Ethan's deep voice held a hopeful tone.

Avery glanced at the clock. "I've got a meeting soon."

"Dinner then. There's a quiet sushi place between where we both live. I'll send you the pin. Meet me at six-thirty?"

Her shake wouldn't last all day, and she hadn't gone grocery shopping in forever. Besides, if he were back on her detail, she needed to know what had changed. "Okay."

"Great, see you then." Ethan paused. "Hope your meeting goes well."

The smile in his voice made her stomach flop. "Um, thanks." She disconnected before he softened her to say more.

What was wrong with her? As she started her Zoom meeting, a new warmth spread through her, a dangerous feeling she hadn't felt in a long time—attraction.

She shook her head, trying to ignore the opening of her heart toward this man. This was the same Ethan who had spoiled her sting. The same Ethan who had wormed his way into her trust during the Beech Mountain trip and connected her to his security agency. The same Ethan who had then backed out on her. The same Ethan who now wanted back into her problems. Why would he do that? Only a fool would risk his safety and his family's safety for her.

Maybe the bigger question was: What was wrong with him?

Chapter Twenty-Eight

The waitress led him to a quiet booth that gave him a clear view of the entrance, side exit, and other guest tables. It was the spot he had requested when he made the reservation, and this place knew him well enough not to care about his seating requests. His reputation as a good tipper preceded him.

The modern, minimalistic décor reminded him of the woman he was supposed to meet in ten minutes. She was so different from any of the other dates he had brought here before.

Not that Avery was a date. Still, he couldn't deny that part of him wished she were. Avery was not only brilliant and beautiful, but she was also a fighter with her own scars. Even though she'd never admit it, the two of them were similar.

Maybe if he could keep her safe, she could close the case that was eating her alive and give him a chance to know her better.

Even if she never did, helping her was the right thing to do.

Ethan spotted her the minute she stepped into the restaurant wearing a classy black sweater and dark jeans. The mood lighting brought out the red hints in her light brown hair, and her intelligent eyes scanned the room.

The hostess motioned her his way, and he stood to greet her. Hugging her was out of the question, though he imagined she would feel good in his arms.

That thought made him grin.

"What?" She slid into the booth without even shaking his hand.

"Good to see you too." He chuckled. Even her icy front turned him on. Good grief, his boss had been right about her.

"I'm not sure there's anything good about the circumstances

around us meeting." Avery sipped the water he'd asked the waitress to have waiting for her.

"Maybe so, but as the saying goes, two are better than one."

Avery crossed her arms. "When it comes to surveillance and security, yes."

"And for life in general," Ethan pressed.

"I disagree," Avery said. "After all, your sisters are being threatened because of your work. When you're a loner like me, there's no one to get hurt but yourself."

"Sounds awful lonely," Ethan said. "And you're wrong. There are people who care about you."

Avery shuffled in her seat, and the waitress arrived for their orders. When she left, Avery leaned forward. "Now tell me why you changed your mind."

Ethan checked the room for any concerns and then focused his attention on the woman who was digging deeper into his heart, despite her best attempts to rebuff him. "I remembered my why. My why is to protect people, and I promised you that I would. I have warned my sisters about the threat and taken all the precautions to keep them safe that I can. Right now, you are my concern, and I want to help you finish what you started."

Her lips pressed into a fine line as if she were considering his words. "Did what happened last night have anything to do with your decision?"

He smiled at her. What would it take for her to accept Jesus the way he had? "I do have more peace now than I've ever had before. Trusting God isn't some instant cure-all to my problems, but I know I'm not facing them alone anymore."

"So you still can't sleep at night?"

He sighed. "I woke up a few times last night, but the nightmares weren't nearly as bad."

Avery snorted. "What's the point of religion if it doesn't change your pain or your past?"

Man, this woman was hurting. He leaned toward her. "The point is that it changes you. I can't bring Troy back, but I can live my life and help the people God's given me to love and protect."

Avery blinked, and her tight expression softened. "Who's Troy?"

His chest tightened. Ethan hadn't told a soul, other than his therapists over the years, about Troy and the real reason for his medical discharge. But Kaley's words rang in his memory again. *The truth is always better, Ethan, even if it is harder. The Bible says the truth sets us free.* If sharing his story could help Avery see that God could bring unexplainable peace to someone like him, then maybe she could see that He could do the same for her.

He took a deep breath and closed his eyes, visualizing the lost face of his friend. "Troy was my best friend. We met in middle school, went to high school and basic training together, and stayed in touch over Call of Duty sessions when our orders took us separate ways."

"Call of Duty—as in the video game?" Avery's face crinkled in confusion. Her phone pinged, but she ignored it.

Ethan chuckled. "Yeah, it's basically how guys catch up."

She shrugged. "Okay, whatever works for you."

"Anyway, we thought we had hit the lottery when we both ended up stationed in Guantanamo together. I was more the behind-the-scenes guy, doing ops research and analysis, while Troy was the one leading the charge in coastal security. We were working together with a team to investigate a terrorist threat when it happened."

The waitress returned with their meals, but Avery had the good taste to simply thank her and leave her fork untouched. "When what happened?" She bit her lip as if part of her didn't want to know.

He didn't blame her for that. "At first, Troy started complaining about headaches and feeling lightheaded. He told me he was hearing strange humming noises in his room at night. I thought maybe he was having nightmares and shrugged it off. Then one day, we were outside starting a routine drill when Troy face planted. I thought maybe he had tripped on something, but he complained of terrible pain in his ears and severe head pressure. He lost all sense of balance, and a few of us had to carry him to medical."

Would he be able to finish? The tightness in his throat almost made speaking impossible. Ethan sipped some water and did another security check on the restaurant exits. Avery's phone pinged again, but she kept her focus on him. "What was wrong with him?"

He could do this. He could finish. "At first, no one could figure it out. There seemed to be no reason for his sudden vertigo and head pressure. After medical discharged him, I helped him to his room, hoping he just needed rest. The next morning, the one that forever haunts me, I found him in his room having a seizure. Afterward, he couldn't get out of bed or talk. He eventually regained enough balance to walk, but it's more like an elderly shuffle. To this day, he's a shell of the man I knew. His speech remains blurred, and he requires assisted care."

Avery's brow furrowed. "I'm so sorry, but I still don't understand."

Ethan blew out a deep breath. "Have you heard of Havana Syndrome?"

Her eyes sparked with recognition. "I have heard of it, but no one knows what causes it, right?"

Maybe sushi hadn't been a smart idea for this conversation. It looked perfect, but his appetite had fled. "That's debatable. Initially, our medics thought these odd occurrences were either due to a preexisting medical or environmental condition, but Troy's onset of symptoms matches those of the Havana Syndrome victims from the embassy in Cuba. We now believe it's an intentional terrorist attack on specific individuals caused by an external source, most likely microwave energy of some kind. That would explain the loud humming sound Troy heard. I think he was getting too close to uncovering something big and was targeted to eliminate his threat."

"But surely there was nothing you could have done," Avery

said. "You can't blame yourself."

Ethan shook his head. "You don't get it. I lived in the room across the hallway from him. I should have taken his headaches and noise reports more seriously. Maybe if I had investigated, we could have protected him or moved him before his brain trauma got so severe. I lost my friend overnight to an invisible enemy, and I was helpless to protect him. It could've been me—should've been me."

Avery's blue eyes lost their iciness and seemed to melt with the closest thing to compassion he'd witnessed her express. "That doesn't make you any less of a friend. You can't condemn yourself."

Her words warmed him. If only she had been moved by something other than pity. He didn't want her pity. He wanted—

Another ping from her purse made Avery break eye contact, but like a true lady, she didn't reach for her phone. "I'm sorry you had to go through that and how it impacted you."

"Thank you." Ethan picked up his fork and pecked at his plate. "I never wanted a full medical discharge and tried to convince them to let me move to the reserves, but my onset of PTSD was too concerning for the medics to agree to it. So I had to take the full discharge."

"That's when you met Powell at Semper Security," Avery said between her first bite of sushi. "Wow, this is good."

He had to smile at her surprise. Maybe she'd start to trust his taste. "Yeah, I found Jake at the right time. He gave me hope I can make a difference in people's lives—that's why I wanted back on your detail. I failed to save one friend from an invisible enemy. I want to keep you safe so you can put a face on this Big Eddie character and keep other innocents from fates they don't deserve."

Another ping. Avery set down her fork and offered an apologetic smile. "I should see what this is about. Excuse me."

She slipped her phone from her purse and unlocked the screen. Her smile vanished, her face paled, and her hand visibly shook.

The tightness returned in his chest. "What—"

She bolted to her feet as she pressed the ear to her phone. "I have to go."

Ethan pulled a fifty from his wallet, tossed it on the table, and slid to his feet. "Then I'm coming with you. We'll take my truck."

She didn't protest or say no, just ran toward the closest exit.

A sinking feeling warned him that their invisible foe had struck again.

Chapter Twenty-Nine

"I'm on my way. Call 9-1-1." Avery croaked out the words before Bella ended the call.

Avery slammed her head against the window of Ethan's truck. How could she have forgotten? Her stupid migraine had kept her out of the office where she had left the flyer to remind her of Gianna's dance recital tonight. She had let Bella down—again.

"Talk to me." Ethan's calm but concerned voice pulled her from her negative mental spiral.

"I'm a moron. That's what." Avery glared at the map on her phone which said they still had fifteen minutes before they reached the dance studio.

"You're not a moron. You just forgot."

"You don't understand, Ethan." Avery ground her teeth. "I have done nothing but disappoint Bella with this case. The least I could do was remember my goddaughter's dance recital. Not only did I miss the recital, but there's also a fire at the studio, and Bella hasn't found Gianna yet."

"She's probably with her teacher and the other dancers," Ethan said. "Places like that have drills and procedures for emergencies."

Ethan's words offered a glimmer of hope, but the fire seemed too coincidental, given Bella's and her close call at the restaurant. If anything happened to Gianna—

"Let's focus on what we know." The steadiness in Ethan's voice helped anchor her thoughts. "There's a fire at the studio. The audience was evacuated, and parents are trying to connect with their children. The fire department is on their way. Bella will probably have found Gianna by the time we get there."

"What if she hasn't?" Avery groaned as Ethan slowed for a red light. "What if Big Eddie is behind this? What if Gianna is missing? What if she's not the last target? What if he goes after your sisters next?"

"Avery." Ethan placed a hand on her shoulder, and she jumped at his touch. It was strong but gentle. "Avery, listen to me. Even if the worst-case scenario happens, I'm not going anywhere. Big Eddie is the worst kind of bully, and we won't let him win."

"Unless it's over our dead bodies," Avery muttered.

He squeezed her shoulder before putting his hand back on the wheel. "Let's hope it doesn't come to that."

They drove in silence until they could smell the smoke and see the orange glow of the fire from the studio over the buildings. Avery shot off a text to Bella that they were almost there and hoped for an instant reply that she had found Gianna, that everything was under control.

Her phone remained silent as Ethan parked. Before he had turned off the engine, she bolted from the truck and dialed Bella. A crowd of families formed a large huddle in the parking lot, while police and firefighters maintained a perimeter around the enflamed studio. Other firefighters doused the structure in water attempting to keep the rest of the dance complex free of fire.

"Avery!" The cry came from behind her and not through her cell phone.

Avery whirled to see Bella shoving through the crowd toward her. Tears streaked through soot stains on her cheeks, and her puffy eyes were wild and bloodshot. "I've looked everywhere. I can't find Gianna. She wasn't with the other ballerinas. Her teacher is being treated for smoke inhalation and can't talk. The firefighters won't listen to me or let me through—"

She wrapped Bella in the tightest hug she had ever given. "I'm sorry I wasn't here, but I will find her."

Bella seemed to cling to her words. She nodded while choking back sobs.

Ethan's approaching form caught Avery's attention. He stood a head taller than most but somehow moved with ease through the crowd until he reached them. Glancing between Avery and Bella, he asked. "How can I help?"

Avery released Bella who continued to tremble. "Keep her

safe. I'll come back."

Bella's lip quivered. "They—they won't let you through."

"I won't be asking permission." With that, Avery darted under caution tape and ignored the protests of the officers nearby. She'd explain herself if she had to, but more than likely, the personnel had their hands too full to follow her.

She pulled her lightweight jacket's hood over her head to help protect her face from burning ash.

"Gianna!" Avery half-called, half-coughed her goddaughter's name. Did she imagine a response, or was that another siren wailing in the distance?

Charging in the direction of the studio, Avery reached the garden. The flames had found the bonsai trees, which were mere shells of their once green, manicured branches. The rose garden had been incinerated, and bits and pieces of green grass smattered the blackened earth.

But it was the fence—or rather, the flaming message on it—that froze her feet in place.

Failure. The words burned on the once-white slats and branded themselves onto her mind. They couldn't be meant for her—

Her phone vibrated. Dread gripped her chest as she swiped to read the text. A picture loaded.

Gianna. There was a gag around her mouth, and she held up a cardboard sign that read "Russo for Ricci. Don't fail. – Big E."

The flames slowly faded to black on the fence post, but the message remained loud and clear. She had failed again, and Big Eddie had scored.

One more failure would cost her goddaughter's life.

With a shaky breath, she texted back, even though she didn't have the authority to do so. "Yes, Russo for Ricci."

Somehow, she'd convince the powers that be to entrust Russo to her. How that intolerable woman would gloat at the thought of walking free—like Avery would ever let that happen.

Whatever it took, she would get Gianna back. Then she would settle the score, even if it killed her.

Avery pushed open her apartment door well after midnight. The smoke smell clung to her hair and her clothes. Every bone in her body seemed to ache, and all she wanted was to collapse into bed.

But she had to scrub the putrid smell from her skin.

After kicking off her shoes, she dropped her phone on the end table. It thudded next to the small Bible Miss Martha had given her.

She glared at it and shoved open the door to her bathroom. A lot of good reading it had done her. The problems in her life grew larger and more terrible.

The thought of Gianna spending the night away from home, a prisoner, scared—Avery splashed cold water on her face and fought the sobs threatening to shake her. Where was God? How could He let another innocent child suffer?

Unlike Gianna, Avery wasn't so innocent anymore. Even as she hurled accusations at God, her conscience pricked. *If we say that we have no sin, we deceive ourselves, and the truth is not in us.*

Despite her best efforts, Avery had failed. She had forgotten about Gianna's recital and hadn't been there for Bella. As a result, Big Eddie had stolen Gianna, and she hadn't even been present to put up a fight. Avery was no closer to avenging Bella's brother's death, and now, she had to hope she could save her daughter.

Failure.

Avery yanked on the shower and turned the dial as hot as she could handle. She might be able to wash away the smoke smell, but she couldn't erase her mistakes. If she were honest with herself, today wasn't the first time she had made them. There was also the promise she had made to honor Mario's dying wish, a promise that also seemed impossible to keep.

What was the answer? Work harder? Learn to pray?

If only it would do any good. She had never felt more haggard and hopeless. Collapsing onto her bed with her hair still wet, she set an alarm on her phone and then buried her face in a pillow.

The one redeeming spot to the night was Sheriff Hannaford who promised to request an emergency hearing with a district judge on the ransom request involving Russo for the following Monday. Their plan had to work, but there were so many hoops involved with transporting a felon—and convincing the judge her presence was necessary for the safety of the child.

Of course, they wouldn't hand Russo over to Big Eddie, but they had to make him believe they would if Gianna had a chance of surviving this ordeal.

Poor Gianna. Avery didn't fight the tears but let them wet her pillow. Her goddaughter must be so scared—and there was nothing Avery could do before the hearing she hoped would take place on Monday. Her phone remained silent, even after Avery had texted back, agreeing to Big Eddie's demand.

There was no deadline, no meet-up instructions, nothing. It was as if Big Eddie wanted her to suffer in her failure.

She still had the assignment for the Buc's game Sunday, and she would throw herself into more research about their suspect. If he were working for Big Eddie, maybe he could provide a clue where Gianna was being held.

"I'll do anything to get you back," Avery whispered.

She might even learn to pray.

Chapter Thirty

The first hints of dawn pierced one of the most moonless, dull, and boring night shifts Ethan had ever worked. As he stepped inside his truck, he thanked God for such a boring shift because it meant Avery was able to sleep safely in her apartment.

That is, if she could sleep.

When was the last time he had seen someone so tormented?

That was easy. Every morning since he'd lost Troy until yesterday, his own eyes had held that same look of terror, of utter helplessness. Ethan glanced in his rearview mirror. This morning, his eyes were tired, but there was new hope, new life in them. How much he wanted Avery to experience God too.

But she seemed so closed off and held everyone at arm's length. What would it take for God to break down her barriers?

Part of him feared the answer.

The clock in his truck read 6:07 in the morning. Ethan had already briefed the next security guard. Now, he needed some breakfast and several hours' sleep before he would be worth much to anyone. He had the rest of the day off, and he wanted to visit APC and tell Miss Martha his news. He grinned, imagining the smile on her face.

Would Avery want to join him?

He could almost see her eyes roll and hear her tell him that she had real work to do. But the truth was, today was Saturday. Although he couldn't imagine her not doing something toward helping the girl Gianna today, more than likely, there wasn't much she could do until Big Eddie sent more details about his demands and the courts opened on Monday.

Heading to APC later this afternoon. Want to join? Let me know when you can. I'm going to grab some sleep.

Done. Ethan yawned as he turned on the ignition. He needed a hot shower and sleep. Although he could practically drive the route home with his eyes closed, he shouldn't risk it. As home grew closer and his eyes grew heavier, he cranked up the radio.

The loud music muffled the sound of the revving engine until something told him to check his rear-view mirror. A tow truck barreled toward him.

With a split second to react before it rammed him, Ethan swerved to avoid another vehicle, but spun out, and veered toward the metal side rail separating him from a ditch.

All he could do was brace for impact—and pray.

Beep-beep-beep. Beep-beep-beep. What was that noise? Oh wait, that was her alarm. Avery's sleep had its share of nightmares peppered throughout, but somehow, exhaustion won out and kept her asleep a full six hours.

Snatching her phone, she silenced the alarm and scrolled first to her text messages. There were none from Bella, none from Big Eddie, and two from Ethan.

Her chest lightened, but she scolded herself. He was probably reporting on his shift. His interest in her was purely professional.

A voice nagged her. If he were strictly professional, why did he keep inviting her to this mission he was so crazy about? Before she could come up with a retort for that thought, her gaze froze on his second text message.

Got rammed. Going to the ER. I'm fine, nothing much, but I won't be going to APC after all.

Avery blinked and read the text again. Someone had tried to run Ethan off the road. His *nothing much* didn't fool her. Reading between the lines, she put together his truck must be totaled or he wasn't feeling great if he no longer planned to visit his favorite mission.

She glanced at the time stamp. The text came in ten minutes ago. He was probably still in the ambulance, and if she went through a drive-thru for breakfast, she could get there shortly after he did.

Which hospital? She texted back but wouldn't wait for a response. A drive home from her place put him in the path of one of the St. Luke's hospitals, and she'd start with that one.

As she parked in the visitor lot, Ethan's text confirmed she was in the right place. He was in a triage room in the ER, and she would have to wait to see him.

Avery took a seat in the far corner of the waiting room. The sterile smell assaulted her nose and brought back memories of Liam's recent trip to the ER in North Carolina.

She should check in on him again and shot off a text. *How are you feeling? Let me know when you're back in town.* Maybe she could take him a meal or something. Not that her cooking could hold a candle to Jayna's, but that's why there was takeout.

Then, she started a new text to Bella, but her fingers froze over the keypad. What could she say? Nothing. She could say nothing that would ease the agony of Gianna being kidnapped. *Can I get you anything?*

Avery deleted that. The only thing Bella wanted was her daughter back. Avery tried again. *Just checking in and sending hugs and hope. We will get Gianna back. I'll swing by later with coffee.* She shot off the message and set a reminder about her coffee promise.

"Avery?" The sound of her name made Avery jerk her focus from her phone. A woman stood a few paces away. Her short frame, curly hair, and broad smile were unmistakable.

"Miss Martha." Avery rose. "What are you doing here?"

"The same reason as you, I expect." She brushed a gray curl out of her face. "But you don't need to stand on my account. How is our Ethan?"

Our Ethan? Oh, right. Miss Martha had jumped to the conclusion she and Ethan were dating. Hadn't she corrected her? She couldn't remember, but now wasn't the time.

"I haven't seen him yet." Avery wasn't about to sit unless the older lady made herself comfortable. "Hopefully we'll be allowed to see him soon."

"What happened?" Miss Martha settled into the closest seat. "All he said was that he was on his way to the ER and couldn't come today like he'd promised. Not much will keep that boy from a promise, so I had to come see."

Avery smiled at the compliment to Ethan as she returned to her seat next to Miss Martha. She could only hope his accident wasn't related to her.

A nurse stepped into the waiting room. "Avery Reynolds?"

Once more, she jumped to her feet. "Yes."

"You're here to see Ethan Bridger?"

"That's right—and so is this lady." Avery motioned to Miss Martha.

"Well, the room is small, but two people can visit at a time. Come with me."

"How is Ethan?" Miss Martha strode next to the nurse. The woman sure didn't act her age.

The nurse rolled her eyes, but her cheeks pinkened. "He's not the best patient, but he sure makes up for it with charm."

"But how is he?" Avery pressed. She didn't need anyone telling her Ethan had charm, even if she pretended to be impenetrable to it.

"Lots of bruises and cuts, but nothing is broken." The nurse pulled back a curtain to the triage room where Ethan reclined in a hospital bed. "He's getting scanned for a possible concussion and should probably stay overnight for observation."

"That will not be necessary." Ethan attempted to fix the hospital gown that poorly concealed his chest.

The nurse winked. "We'll see. Anyway, I'll be back to check on you in a few."

As the nurse disappeared down the hall, Avery followed Miss Martha into the space. The hospital bed with Ethan in it took up most of the room, and Avery searched his face. He had a bruise on his cheek and butterfly stitches on his forehead.

Her throat suddenly felt tight, and the space, far too small. "You're really okay?" Her voice came out above a whisper.

"I'm fine." Ethan tapped the side of the bed impatiently. "You didn't need to come, but I mean, it is good of you to check in."

"The nurse said you might have a concussion." Miss Martha reached for his hand, the way a mother might do.

"I have a hard head." Ethan patted her hand. "Seriously, the worst part is getting more bruised ribs."

"More?" Miss Martha arched an eyebrow.

A grin snaked across Ethan's face, and he gazed toward Avery. "Let's just say a certain lady fell on top of me."

"You fell on Ethan?" Miss Martha glanced at Avery. "Did you fall off a ladder or something, and he caught you? That does sound painful, though also romantic."

Avery narrowed her eyes. "Oh, there was nothing romantic about it."

"That depends on your perspective." Ethan's eyes twinkled. His accident clearly hadn't dampened his sense of humor. "Rescuing a damsel in distress—"

Avery cut him off. "So tell us what happened. How did you end up here?"

The light in his eyes dimmed. "I was on my way home after my shift. This tow truck was suddenly on my tail and rammed me. My truck went into a ditch, which was unfortunately for me, half filled with water. I had to crawl out the window and wade out. The driver took off, and another passerby called 9-1-1. It was probably a drunk or something."

Ethan left off the part about it being his security shift at her apartment, and his comment about a drunk didn't fool her. Drunks weren't usually on the road that early in the morning. A growing sense of dread filled her. The odds were that this wasn't an accident since the driver didn't stick around to apologize.

"People these days are so rude and selfish," Miss Martha clucked her tongue. "I can't believe the driver didn't stop to help."

Ethan's smile looked forced and a little too cheery. "God was watching over me, Miss Martha. Insurance will take care of my truck, and I'll get a rental until I can get it repaired or get something else."

Her face glowed. "Ethan, hearing you say those words is music to my soul. I'm so glad you are now part of God's family. I was overjoyed at your text yesterday. I couldn't wait to see you to hear your story today, but I do wish this were under different circumstances."

"I'll be back to APC soon enough and will tell you more about it then." Ethan yawned.

Avery patted Miss Martha's arm. "He worked an all-night shift, and that nurse will be coming back for his scan. We should let him rest while he can."

Miss Martha nodded and rose. "You call me if you need anything, you understand?"

"Yes, ma'am," Ethan said. "Thank you for coming."

Avery moved toward the door as well. "Text me when you're done with your scan. If they clear you to leave, I can pick you up."

"Thanks for the offer." Ethan rubbed his jaw. "Jake said he would give me a lift though."

Heat crept up her cheeks. Of course. If she were the reason he had been shoved off the road, maybe she was the last person he wanted taking him home.

Biting her lip, she waved goodbye and followed Miss Martha out of the exit.

"You've got yourself a good man," Miss Martha said.

It was time to set the record straight again. "He's not my man."

"Oh, that's right. You both need to get right with the Lord first. So glad Ethan has." Miss Martha frowned as if lost in thought, but Avery could read her silent question: *What about you?*

"I'll pray about you two," Miss Martha finally said. "Hope to see you at the mission soon. You're welcome any time."

"Thanks." Avery parted ways and hurried to her car. The last thing she needed was Miss Martha praying her into a relationship with Ethan.

What she needed was to rescue a kidnapped child and find the mastermind behind it all who kept hurting people she cared about. For now, she would take Bella coffee and give her more hugs than she had in all of last year.

A piece of paper in her windshield caught her attention. Surely it was bad taste to advertise in a hospital parking lot?

But her fingers stilled as she read the words someone had scrawled on the paper.

You're next.

Chapter Thirty-One

Ethan scribbled a signature near the line the nurse had indicated, handed the paperwork back to her, and swung his legs off the bed. His head pounded, but the last thing he wanted was to spend the rest of the day anywhere but his own bed. The scan results showed he didn't have a concussion, so his headache was nothing some strong pain pills couldn't fix.

"You really should stay for observation." The nurse's lips were freshly coated with pink lipstick.

He didn't care for her concern and her not-so-subtle flirtatiousness. "I'm good, thanks." He patted his jeans to make sure his wallet was still there and stuffed his phone in the other pocket.

"Come back if you feel worse," she called after him.

He offered a backhand wave and showed himself out. Jake texted that he had parked right outside the exit, and his bright red SUV shouldn't be hard to miss.

A stab of guilt made his lips twitch. Avery had offered to pick him up, but he had turned her down. Though he had tried to downplay the incident with the tow truck, his gut told him it was related to his job.

More specifically, her job.

Before he could do anything else to help her, he needed to rest and make sure his head was on straight. Because every time Avery stepped into his space, his heart stuttered in a way he didn't think it ever would again.

Spotting Jake's SUV in the parking lot brought back his conversation with his boss and his concern that Avery's case was too personal. He had denied it at the time, but now, he suspected his boss was right.

His heart was invested more than he could admit, but Avery needed his help more than she would admit. She also needed Jesus, and if Jake took him off the case for good, she might associate his distance with God's distance and never listen to another word about Him.

Jake rolled down his window. "You look rough."

"Felt better." Ethan grunted and slid in the passenger side. "Thanks for picking me up."

"Always got your back." Jake started toward the hospital exit. "Sorry to hear about your truck. You need a few days off to get things squared away?"

"I'm not scheduled again until Monday," Ethan said. "That will be plenty of time to get a rental."

"And some rest."

Ethan forced a grin. "That too."

"Tell me what happened."

This was the part of the ride Ethan had been dreading, but his boss didn't waste time in getting to the heart of the matter. Ethan recounted what happened with as little detail as possible and ended with an upbeat, "Probably someone on his phone not paying attention."

Jake didn't miss a beat. "You don't believe that, and neither do I."

Ethan sighed. "You're right. I don't, but in our line of work, it isn't the first time and won't be the last time someone wants us off a job."

Jake kept his focus on the road, but Ethan read the tight lines around his mouth. "I don't know if keeping you on Avery's detail is the right move."

"Sure, it is." Ethan kept his tone level. "If not me, then someone else on the team is going to take the hits."

His boss glanced at him. "Looks like you've already taken your fair share."

"I'm not doing her detail solo," Ethan reminded him. "Maybe

give Luke a heads up to be extra sharp. The people who want to stop Avery won't think twice about stopping us too."

Jake didn't respond, and Ethan held his breath. If his boss ordered him off Avery's job, he couldn't defy him, but he couldn't let Avery down either.

Finally, his boss exhaled. "Okay, call me Sunday and let me know how you're doing. We'll make a call on Monday. Until then, I'll warn Luke to take extra precautions."

Ethan nodded and helped himself to an unopened water bottle Jake had staged in his cupholder. Jake might change his mind, but at least for now, Ethan remained on Avery's job. Somehow, he had to help her succeed in her investigation before that changed.

Sunday late afternoon, Avery pulled her hair into a high ponytail and smacked her lips together to even out the pink lip gloss. She checked her reflection in the mirror. With a lot of undereye concealer and more eyeshadow and mascara than she ever wore, she could pass for a twenty-something starting at the bottom of the ladder in the Signs-4-Success merchandising department.

Barely.

With a sigh, she looked away. Turning thirty a little over a year ago hadn't bothered her. What bothered her was that over a year had passed, and she was still chasing her tail in this Big Eddie business.

Today had to change that. Whether the man was a ghost or simply a mascot for the underworld's nefarious dealings, the self-identified Big Eddie had gone too far in taking Bella's girl, and she would bring her back.

Her associate Drew would be listening in via an earpiece she would wear. He could feed her answers to questions she might not have anticipated, even with her immersive research. Although it might be too much to hope for a clear lead about Gianna, she would gain intel on every person in the suite, and, if she had to, flirt her way into any private conversations that looked promising. The black low-cut blouse and form-fitting dark-washed jeans she'd chosen to wear should help. The outfit teetered between business casual and *hello, hottie*.

Her flirting skills she attributed to her mom, who managed to attract men before and after her dad like sugar-water laced with poison attracted insects to their death. It was a skill she hated but served her well on the job. In real life, she didn't flirt and rarely wanted to. If a man didn't like who she was, he wouldn't be happy very long with who she might pretend to be.

Ethan didn't seem put off by her direct manners and sharp edges. Somehow, he even seemed to soften them.

She shook off the thought as she reached for her phone. There were no new texts. She hadn't heard from Ethan since his ER visit.

Not taking her up on her offer to drive him home had rubbed her harder than it should have. After all, if she were the reason for his wreck, she couldn't blame him for wanting to avoid her. Being driven off the road was some rotten *thanks* for getting back on her detail. Maybe he didn't have the heart to tell her to her face that he was done with her job for good.

He sure did have a heart, a big one. Her dad had a big heart too—until he couldn't take her mother's betrayal and abuse any longer. She never liked to think she was like her mother in any way, but it seemed as if she had done nothing but hurt Ethan since he started helping her.

Avery really was better off alone. That way, there was less collateral damage.

Her phone showed two missed texts from Bella. Avery's heart squeezed as she read them.

Text 1. *Any news?*

Text 2. *Hope your job tonight helps us find Gianna.*

She ground her teeth. No, there was still no news about Gianna. Whoever had texted her Gianna's picture had remained eerily silent concerning the exchange details. Maybe because they knew Avery and Sheriff Hannaford couldn't work on a court order concerning Russo until Monday. Maybe because they wanted her to squirm in sleepless nights and worry over the precious little girl. If so, they had succeeded.

No word yet, but it will come soon. And I will find her. Leaving for the job now. I'll call as soon as it's over. She shot off the text to Bella, then tucked her phone in her bag as well.

On her way out, she passed the Bible on the coffee table. She either needed to throw it away or read it. Having it lying around taunted her. She'd deal with it later. Right now, there was a job to do, and that little black book wouldn't have anything to say that could help her with it.

Chapter Thirty-Two

The private Buccaneers Suite at Raymond James was larger with a more sweeping view of the stadium than Avery had anticipated.

It was also a lot colder. As she followed Michael, the sales rep who was her ticket to this private business party, a chill raced down her spine. Although the room was inviting and luxurious, her investigator senses shivered from something sinister. It was a sensation she'd felt a few times, such as right before boarding the fishing vessel where Mario was killed.

There was no Bahamian drug smuggler waiting for her here, only businessmen dressed in expensive sports coats and sipping beers. A few chatted at the bar while others lounged in a circle of comfortable couches and chairs.

Who was this Weber? A rental that could accommodate twenty must have easily cost in the tens of thousands of dollars. Was there that much money to make in the signage industry?

Avery plastered on her best fake smile as Michael greeted the cluster of sales reps and introduced her as Amber Richards, his company's new merchandising specialist. Amber was her default alias and fake ID that she had used in the Bahamas. There was no fear reusing it here, since anyone who had known her under that alias was either dead or a tourist she would never see again.

To her relief, Michael explained she was here to listen and learn more about the industry and products she would represent in their annual catalog.

Most smiled patronizingly at her. These were "good old boys" several decades older than her. Some seemed annoyed. It didn't take a rocket scientist to recognize she was the only female present. She questioned to what extent Michael would risk his reputation with this group in honoring Hannaford's request to include her.

A tall, thin man with thick, gray hair and narrow eyes rose from a chair and extended a hand. She recognized him from his social media picture. "Bradley Weber. Glad to have you join us." The lightness in his tone did not match the coldness in his eyes.

"It's about time you included some young blood in this group." A thick man with a gray beard leaned forward in his chair. His frameless glasses magnified intelligent dark eyes that seemed to twinkle with—amusement? Something about him seemed oddly familiar.

Weber chuckled, but the sound caught in the back of his throat. "Our business is hardly something the more delicate sex find amusing."

Avery arched an eyebrow. Was there a double meaning in his words? Either way, sexism was clearly not dead in the signage industry.

"But the young must learn the ways of business," the gray-bearded man countered. "My dear, I will be happy to introduce you to our core products and our convenience ones—" His voice trailed off as his cell phone rang. "But ah, I must take this. Scusi." He pressed the device to his ear, retrieved the cane leaning against his chair, and walked toward the wall of glass windows that provided a wide view of the football field.

Scusi. The Italian expression for *excuse me* was one Bella used on occasion. Was that why this man felt familiar? What had he said his name was? Or perhaps he hadn't said.

"… Our new line of PPE apparel is taking off." One of the other reps had already engaged Michael in a new conversation, and she needed to focus.

Weber motioned toward a long table of appetizers. "Please, help yourself. I need to check with the caterer about something." With that, he strode toward the door right as it opened. A man dressed in black with a logoed shirt stood there, pushing a large beverage cart.

"We have plenty of ice," Weber said almost too loudly. "Bring more wings when you have a chance." With that, he shut the door in the man's face.

Avery added *rude* to her personality checklist for Weber.

Unfortunately, *rude* wasn't enough on its own to merit a search warrant. She helped herself to a soda from the cooler by the food table and placed a few hors d'oeuvres on a plate. If she needed to stall for a conversation, chewing on food would help.

Unfortunately, no conversation of interest happened before the kick-off, and at that time, the party moved to the theater seating by the glass. Avery strained to hear any private comments, but she was sandwiched between Michael and another rep who took great pleasure in shouting at the referees—as if they could hear him.

When the thick, gray-bearded man rose to get a fresh beer, Avery also excused herself. He had been the most welcoming of all, and perhaps she could learn something from him.

"Enjoying the game?" He peered at her with the same humorous glint in his eyes as before.

"From the nicest seat I've ever had." Avery reached for a water bottle. "I'm sorry, but I didn't catch your name earlier."

His lips parted to reveal polished white teeth. "Albert Costa, but you can call me Bert."

The name sounded like it should belong to a doting grandfather, not a dull sales rep. "Nice to meet you, Bert. How long have you been in this industry?"

"Probably longer than you've been alive."

Avery forced a chuckle, but it didn't match Bert's. The last thing she wanted was condescension about her presumed age, but she also wanted information. Her pride could handle the jibes about being young and inexperienced.

After all, she was. She'd studied merchandising and the signage industry for a few days.

"I'm sure there's a lot I could learn from you about the industry." Avery wasn't hungry, but she followed Bert along the food table. He piled chicken wings on his plate, while she opted for veggies and dip.

"There's a lot I could teach you." Bert glanced toward a high-top table where Weber and some colleagues seemed engrossed in a conversation. "The first lesson is: Watch your back."

Did he mean Weber? Avery blinked and faked a puzzled frown. "Come again?"

His eyes flashed a warning. "Not everyone is who they say they are. But surely you know that."

This time, a shiver raced down her spine. She wasn't who she was pretending to be, but Bert couldn't know her real identity. He must be referring to someone else in their party.

"I know sales is a dog-eat-dog world." She added some fruit to her plate. "That's why I like merchandising. It's more of a supporting behind-the-scenes role."

"As long as you stick to your place, you'll be fine." Bert paused at the end of the table and nodded toward the group at the high tables. "Weber's a mean one, but he's a puppy dog compared to others. They'd walk all over a little girl like you."

Avery's face warmed. "I am hardly little and not afraid of bullies."

"No, you're not so little." He scanned her from head to toe in a way that didn't fit the grandfatherly type she had pegged him as earlier. "But you should be afraid."

She flinched. Was he threatening her, or warning her?

The levity returned to his eyes, and he waved an arm toward the glass. "The second lesson: Business always takes a back seat to the game. Never interrupt a man and his sport." Bert balanced his brimming plate with one hand and pulled out a business card from his suit pocket with the other. "We should chat again later. I'd be delighted to spend more time with a lovely, rising star like yourself."

Wait, now he was flattering her?

Avery pinched the card between her fingers and offered him one of her own she had created for this event. "Thanks, enjoy the game."

He winked. "I always do."

Chapter Thirty-Three

At some point after midnight, Avery finally trudged through the door of her apartment and locked it behind her. *Weary* didn't begin to describe the ache in her bones and in her heart. Apart from Bert's warning about Weber and the invitation to meet again some other time, she left the game with zero leads.

She was no closer to finding Gianna, and Bella would be spending another sleepless night wondering about her missing daughter.

Avery had promised her a text as soon as the game ended, but she hated to let her down again. No news was not good news. No news was no progress.

Postponing the update made Bella's suspense worse, so Avery retrieved her phone from her bag and collapsed onto the couch.

As her fingers hovered over the keypad, a text came through.

A text with Gianna holding another cardboard sign.

Avery bolted upright in the seat and hungrily searched the photo for signs her goddaughter was unharmed.

The girl looked tired, but her face was clean and clear of bruises. The sign read, "Bucs game, next Sunday. Reynolds, bring Russo. Work alone."

Reynolds. That was her.

Working alone on the logistics with Russo was impossible, but she would have to give the impression of bringing Russo by herself. She immediately forwarded the text to Sheriff Hannaford and texted Bella the update.

At least she could give her a picture of her daughter, but what she wanted to give her was her actual daughter. Next Sunday seemed forever away, but so many logistics had to fall into place for the exchange to happen—

Her head started swimming. She needed sleep. Tomorrow's

hearing would start the process, and she would continue working from there with the sheriff's office and court system to provide the appearance of a release for Russo.

"We're coming, Gianna," she whispered. "Hang in there."

Monday dawned with a dull headache and a cell phone with blown-up text messages. Ethan silenced his snoozed alarm and squinted at his notifications. Twenty texts by six o'clock was never a good sign.

Half of them were from Jake, and the others were from Chloe. Dread tightened his chest, and he tapped hers first.

I'm okay, her messages began.

She knew her big brother so well, and how he worried about her, but he guessed there was more.

Someone slit my tires, and our security officers spooked whoever was tampering with our dorm's elevator. I gave our security team your message, and they're taking it seriously. Don't worry about me. I will be extra careful, but I wanted you to know these may not be idle threats you're getting. Love you.

Chloe had no idea that her tires and the elevator were merely a warning message—for him—that if he didn't back off Avery's case, things were going to get much worse for his sisters.

He shot off a reply text to Chloe and then dictated a message to Tori. He was partly relieved and partly worried she hadn't texted him too.

With a tightening sensation in his stomach, he moved on to Jake's texts. *A resident at Avery's complex found Luke unconscious this morning. Looks like someone clubbed him last night. He's at the hospital and stable. You still want back on Avery's detail? If so, call me when you get this. We need to meet with her and get her approval for additional funding for a two-man approach to her detail. I'm not sending my men in solo to her situation anymore.*

Ethan set down his phone and closed his eyes. Was he doing the right thing by helping Avery? His gut said yes, but what further pain was it going to cost him?

"God, I feel like I'm supposed to help her. You brought our paths together for a reason, and you know I'm starting to care for her. Help my reasons not to be selfish. Show me how to move forward."

His phone vibrated with another incoming text. He glanced at the screen.

Tori.

Hey big brother, Chloe told me what happened to her, and I've got a case of ditto. My tires are slit, and someone set off our dorm's fire alarms last night—for six hours on and off before security was able to chase away the culprit. I'm tired but angry. Whoever is trying to bully you, we can't let them win.

A smile tugged at his lips. Tori was so much like him, and her words gave him his answer.

He would do everything he could to make sure bullies like Big Eddie didn't win.

Ethan speed dialed Jake who answered right as Ethan thought he'd have to leave a voice mail.

"Hey, Ethan, I figured you'd call." Jake skipped the greeting. "I'm in another meeting right now, but Avery is coming by at ten. Can you be here?"

"Yes, sir," Ethan said.

"See you then." Jake's tone was clipped as he disconnected. Ethan didn't take it personally. His boss was a busy man. More than likely, he wasn't convinced Ethan should remain on Avery's detail.

But with Luke in the hospital and the plan to double up duty for Avery, Jake needed his help. After a jog and breakfast for him and Blackie, he took a quick shower and pulled his last clean security shirt from the closet. He threw in a load of laundry and was about to let Blackie outside for the day when he hesitated. If Big Eddie were already antagonizing his sisters, he wouldn't think twice before hurting his dog.

He grabbed Blackie's leash again instead. "C'mon, boy, you're going with me today." After loading his sixty-pound black lab into his rental SUV, he started the familiar trip. He had a good two hours before the meeting at work, and he needed to leave Blackie somewhere else. That should give him time to drive to the ranch. Plus, he needed to brief his parents and ranch hands about the recent security situation so they could also be on heightened alert.

"Call Dad," Ethan spoke into his phone as he started the familiar drive.

"Calling Dad," his phone replied with its artificial voice.

"Hey, son," his dad's deep voice rang with its usual warmth. "How are you?"

Ethan hadn't even had time to tell his parents about his accident. Had his sisters filled them in yet on what had happened? If not, he'd rather tell his parents in person that the danger he'd warned them about was proving to be very real. "It's been a bumpy few days, to tell the truth. Can I tell you about it in person? I can be there in less than an hour."

"Sure, your mom should be back from Bible study by then too."

His heart swelled. He hadn't told his parents his best news either, and his mom would want to hear it in person. How long had she been praying for him?

"Great, see you soon."

Even with all the problems in his world right now, joy surged through him. He had the best family. He had a great God, and he had hope like he hadn't felt in a long time.

What would it take for Avery to feel that hope? He didn't know. What he knew was that it mattered a great deal to him that she found it.

That *she* mattered a great deal.

As the traffic-laden roads gave way to less congestion and as the familiar streets led to his family's hundred-acre ranch, he wished that the next "girl" he brought home to his family might somehow be her.

Chapter Thirty-Four

Her car radio hummed a sleepy Nora Jones' song in the parking lot of Semper Security, and Avery rested her head on the steering wheel. She had tossed and turned last night until more sheets and pillows lay on the floor than on her bed.

The fact was that her brain had too many tabs open to let her rest, and no amount of coffee could fix this migraine-in-the-making. No amount of success could fix the widening hole in her bank account that security was costing her and her company. Against Jake Powell's advice, she had removed the security from her apartment but left the detail at her office. She couldn't afford both, and she couldn't afford more people she cared about getting hurt.

Unless a miracle happened, Reynolds Investigation would close before its two-year anniversary, like so many start-ups that couldn't keep their heads above water. But the only miracle she cared about right now was stopping Big Eddie and saving Gianna.

Her phone lit up in the cupholder where she had placed it in the center console. The call was from Sheriff Hannaford. Her heart hoped for news of a scheduled Russo hearing.

"Talk to me," she said.

A large sigh hinted of more problems she didn't need. "I'm afraid I have bad news," Sheriff Hannaford said. "The court denied the request for a hearing on Russo. The logistics of releasing Russo to us for the appearance of a prisoner swap are too problematic for them. We will have to find another way."

"There is no other way." Avery closed her eyes in frustration but kept her tone level. "You know the people we're dealing with. They've already set their ransom. They will kill Gianna if we don't appear to deliver Russo."

"We could find a stunt double," Hannaford suggested. "Make

it look like we have Russo."

Avery ground her nails into her steering wheel. "You know that won't work. Stunt doubles are effective because the camera cuts away or isn't focused on them. Big Eddie's team will be watching us from under a hundred microscopes. They'll recognize the fraud, and then it will be game over for Gianna."

"I'm sorry, Avery, but my hands are tied. You know I'm up for reelection next month. I can't fight the courts right now on this. We will find another way."

It was her turn to sigh. There was no other way, and Hannaford knew it. "Thanks for the update. I'll check in again later." After his goodbye, she disconnected.

Bella would go mad if she lost Gianna, but if the courts wouldn't budge, there would be no pretend swap.

Her phone screen lit up again, this time with a message. She accepted it, and Gianna's picture flashed on the screen.

No.

How could they already know?

Once again, Gianna held up a cardboard sign. *Too bad the courts said no. What are you going to do, Reynolds?*

She texted back. *Name your price, and I'll get it for you.*

Seconds later, another picture came through. This time, there was a gun to Gianna's head, and the girl was crying. Her sign read: *We already have. Will you get Russo, or are we done here?*

Terror like she'd never felt shot through Avery. She slammed her fist on the steering wheel and didn't care that the horn went off. Texting furiously, she replied. *No, don't hurt her. I'll get Russo.*

What was she saying? The courts had already made that impossible. But how could she say anything else? Gianna's life was hanging by a thread.

Another picture text came through. The gun was gone from Gianna's head, and though dark rims circled her eyes, she was no longer crying. The sign read. *Failure is unacceptable.*

Failure. Unacceptable. The word choices were eerily familiar.

All Avery knew was that she had made yet another impossible promise, and this time, she had to find a way to keep it.

Someone knocked on her window, and she turned to see

Ethan standing there.

"You okay?" His voice came muffled through the window. "I heard your horn go off as I was walking to my car."

She glared through her window. "No, I'm not okay."

Ethan tensed. "Want to talk? There's a coffee place down the street."

"The less I tell you, the better," she mumbled.

He tapped on the glass again. "What? Can you lower your window, please?"

She didn't want to talk. She didn't want to lower her window, but for some reason, she couldn't refuse this man. With a groan, she turned on the car and lowered her automatic windows. "I've got more problems than time, and you have problems of your own."

"None of them are as important as you at the moment," Ethan said.

"You might change your mind when you find out." What was she saying? She couldn't tell him the infantile, idiotic plan taking shape in her head.

Ethan leaned against her doorframe. "Find out what?"

What did she have to lose in telling him? He would think she was crazy, or maybe he would have some idea she hadn't considered yet.

"Find out that I'm going to break Russo out of prison."

The nutty aroma inside his favorite Buddy Brew coffee shop couldn't still his hands from shaking a little as Ethan returned to the bucket chair seating Avery had chosen in the far corner. The cozy shop was crowded as usual—several college students collaborated at a long wooden table, teens overcrowded a couch while playing on their phones, two men played chess at a table, and a woman talked noisily on a headset. The busyness served to provide static to drown out their conversation.

He handed Avery a large black coffee and cautiously sipped

his own before taking a seat. "Okay, try that. That tastes like America and freedom and possibilities. You won't taste that sitting in a jail cell the rest of your life."

Avery rolled her eyes and took a sip of hers. "Yes, it's good coffee, but that doesn't change the fact that if I don't deliver Russo, Gianna will die. Life in prison sounds much friendlier than trying to live with her death on my hands."

Ethan groaned. This woman was as stubborn as the day was long. "The police are looking for Gianna too. There has to be another way."

"Even Sherlock Holmes wouldn't be able to find her at this point." She winced as if the coffee was too hot. Maybe it was—but it wasn't as hot as this job was turning out to be. "Hannaford can't jeopardize his reelection by pressing the courts. He suggested a stunt double, but we both know that will never work. There is no other way."

"Did you tell him about this harebrained plan?"

"Of course not." Avery blew on her coffee. "He'd stop me, but maybe if I can get Gianna back, return Russo, and catch Big Eddie at his game, he will forgive me."

He choked on his coffee. "Forgive you? Avery, this is not *National Treasure*, and you are not Nicolas Cage."

"Yes, but I'm not stealing the Declaration of Independence. I'm stealing—borrowing—a felon for a short amount of time." Avery shrugged her shoulders as if she were merely suggesting an everyday occurrence.

"Last I checked, *borrowing* a felon, as you so delicately put what everyone else calls *prison breaking*, is still a felony."

Avery waived her hand in the air as if to clear the space. "Whatever. I already have another virtual call scheduled with Russo for Wednesday with an in-person meeting pending approval later in the week. If you can come up with a better game plan before then, I'm all ears."

Close your eyes. Count to ten. It was one of the cliché coping techniques one of his therapists had recommended, and though it didn't help his anxiety, experience had taught him it did help his temper.

When he opened his eyes, Avery was studying him with her intense blue eyes, a furrowed brow that seemed quirkily kissable, and lips tentatively posed to try another sip of coffee.

"I can't build a relationship with a woman who's spending life in prison," he blurted.

Avery's lips froze mid sip. "Wha-at?"

Ethan ground his teeth. Of all the stupid things he could have said, that one complicated the situation one hundred times over.

But it was the truth. "I know we're professionals, and I know I shouldn't have said that, but if you're planning to spend the rest of your life in prison, you might as well know that people—that I—care about you."

"You want to date me?" Coming from her, the direct question didn't surprise him, but the curious tilt to her lips did.

"When this is all over—and I'm not under contract to help man your detail—the thought has crossed my mind." He took a swig of coffee. "I guess it never crossed yours."

She took a cautious sip. "I don't date. Not anymore."

"Am I allowed to ask why?"

A shadow fell across her face. She set down her coffee and crossed her arms. "You don't look like a guy who takes no for an answer, so you might as well know. My verbally abusive and faithless mother chased my dad away. He walked out of my life when I was seven and never came back for me. She didn't want me either. I tried dating in my twenties and found I'm too cynical about relationships to even give them a chance. So there, I don't date."

She glanced out the window. Clouds were starting to crowd the otherwise sunny afternoon. "Thanks for the coffee. I appreciate what you've done to help me, and I was a fool to blurt out my thoughts to you. Forget we ever had this conversation."

Ethan gripped his coffee which wasn't cooling off nearly as fast as the air between them. "Which one?"

Avery arched an eyebrow.

He offered a subtle grin. "The Declaration of Independence one or the dating one?"

She stood and swung her bag over her shoulder. "Both. Bye, Ethan."

No, she couldn't walk out like that. She had friend-zoned him fair and square, but she needed a friend—and she still needed God, more than she knew. "I'm going to APC tomorrow morning at nine. You should join me."

Her shoulders seemed less erect than typical Avery-fashion dictated. She must be feeling the weight of her world crushing in from all sides.

"You should come for Miss Martha," he pushed. "She likes you."

There. Finally, the hint of a smile at the corners of her mouth. "We'll see." With a backhand wave, she strode out of the coffee shop.

Ethan closed his eyes and sank deeper into the already-too-low-for-his-legs bucket chair. He wasn't scheduled for Avery's detail until this evening, and Blackie was at his parents. Might as well enjoy the rest of his coffee.

"Well, God," he said under his breath. "That ball is in your court now. I know she's a stubborn one, but don't give up on her—like you didn't give up on me."

Chapter Thirty-Five

His coffee had cooled down too much to drink, and the silicone face mask disguising his identity was starting to itch, but the conversation he'd overheard more than made up for the inconvenience.

Edison. It was his middle name that had earned him the nickname Big Eddie. He wasn't overly big in size—about average height and girth for a man in his sixties. Rather, he was big in reputation.

Just the way he wanted it.

His smile twerked the silicone mask. "Check mate."

One of his amateur field men—the first available at short notice—nodded his head. "Good game."

"Always." Big Eddie cut down the man's king with a flourish. "Good day."

The man bobbed his head again as the amateurs always did out of fear or raw nerves at being in his presence.

"Can—can I get you something?" The amateur rose and wiped his brow. He needed more training.

"Good. Day." Big Eddie growled so low no one else could overhear.

The amateur's eyes widened, and he finally remembered the job ended with those words. He nearly tripped over his own feet out the door.

Big Eddie might have reported the incident to the man's superior, but he was too busy appearing uninterested in the security officer slouched in the bucket chair. The officer looked comfortable, at ease—a poor trait for someone in security.

Never let your guard down. The man was a *bambino* for thinking a spontaneous coffee date would go unnoticed.

He would be easy enough to knock off should the need arise.

Reynolds herself—she was proving a disappointment as well. The tracker on her vehicle went undetected. When it started moving this direction, he acted and arrived before she did. Of course, she had reacted badly to the news of the hearing being denied, so naturally, she went to meet someone for coffee.

Too predictable.

Break Russo out of prison? Now that move, he hadn't seen coming. Still, she would have to beat him to it. If she did, then she could enjoy the spoils of her felony—prison time—after she delivered Russo and failed to save the child. If she didn't, she could writhe in misery knowing the child's blood was on her hands for failing to deliver Russo. Either way, he would destroy her reputation as a private investigator and shred any self-respect she might have.

The bottom line—she was ruined. Ruined like everyone else who dared interfere with his *casa*, his hood.

"Check mate," he thought and rose from his seat. After retrieving the cane hooked onto the table's edge, he slipped into the street and disappeared into the busy Tampa scene the way he always did—undetected.

Chapter Thirty-Six

Avery flipped her laptop closed, banged her head against her bed's headboard, and pressed her weary eyes closed. Another workday had started at five in the morning, but three hours later, she had little to show for her research. If the FBI took one glance at her recent search history, she'd be in jail before she even set foot near Russo.

Every plan she had for getting custody of the woman was asinine. Her training had prepared her for keeping people safe, for putting felons like Russo where they belonged—not breaking them out.

Her contacts and her clearance could certainly gain her access to Russo, but escaping a secure facility with the woman in tow was another matter. So much depended on Russo herself. How fit was she? Could she scale a wall? Get to the roof? Getting above the security nets seemed to be the most commonplace method prisoners used to escape, but most of those breaks were also in less secure facilities than Russo's.

Would Russo even want help breaking out, and what would keep her from throwing Avery under the bus before they even escaped? The woman delighted in being difficult. She would probably think watching Avery get arrested was more fun than getting free herself.

Ethan had it backwards. What Nicolas Cage did was easy. The Declaration of Independence didn't talk back, try to trip him up, or dig in its heels.

Her one achievement of the morning was ordering custom silicone face masks from a Halloween shop. The expedited shipping was painful, but with the spooky holiday coming up this weekend, the order shouldn't raise any immediate eyebrows.

With an infantile plan formed, she had ordered two masks.

Whether she used one or both or none, they seemed her best bet for breaking out Russo—or providing the illusion that she had.

Ethan would much prefer the latter, and so would she. Destroying her reputation and living in a prison cell had never been her goals. Could a mask convince Big Eddie long enough for her to get Gianna though? She doubted it.

The thought of Ethan made Avery open her eyes and scan the sheets for her cell phone. He had said nine o'clock this morning for going to APC. She could stop by to help for an hour or so before heading into the office to work the rest of the day from there.

What was wrong with her? Spending time with him clearly spelled trouble, especially after his confession from yesterday. Dating him—or anyone—was impossible, but seeing the earnestness in his eyes almost made her wish it wasn't, almost made her think Ethan could be different from her dad who had quit on her.

She had confessed her harebrained plan, and he had still invited her. She needed to know why—why that didn't scare him off or make him report her. He was a security officer, after all. In a different capacity, he was also in the business of keeping people safe and dangerous people like Russo from changing that.

Is 9 still okay to meet you? She texted before she could talk herself out of sending it.

Her phone pinged almost immediately. *Yep. See you there.*

A slow smile tugged at her lips. He must really want to see her again. No wonder he was meeting with Kaley for professional counseling.

Avery slid off the bed and padded toward her bathroom. Then again, she was the one researching how to break out a felon and spending time with the security agent who had botched her sting earlier in the month.

Maybe she needed to start seeing Kaley for therapy herself.

As Avery pulled into the parking lot adjacent to the main

warehouse building for Ayuda Para Cuba, Ethan's truck was markedly absent.

Oh, right. She was responsible for that vehicle getting totaled.

Still, she doubted the white compact car or large minivan were his rentals.

The driver's side door of the white compact swung open, and out stepped a woman whose short stature and wiry curls could belong to one person. Miss Martha.

Avery shrank lower in her seat. If the woman spotted her, there was no chance she could ride out the time until Ethan arrived in silence inside her vehicle.

The spry woman waved a baseball cap her direction before donning it—and marching straight to her car with her purse dangling from one arm while balancing a drink carrier in the other.

Swallowing a groan, Avery straightened in her seat and lowered the window. "Good morning—"

"Every morning is a good morning," Miss Martha quipped. "I woke up again, my heart is still beating, there's work God has given me to do, and there's people He's sent my way to help me do it. I believed you'd come back, and I'm glad you did. Have coffee with me before we get started?" She pushed the drink carrier toward Avery. "Pick any one. They are all the same—my favorite. I always buy extras for my helpers."

Avery didn't know what flavor "favorite" was, but she selected a hot cup and placed it in her cupholder. "Thanks."

"Oh, bring that with you, dearie. Looks like you needed some caffeine in your system yesterday."

This woman was blunt, perhaps the one quality they had in common. It was refreshing. Avery retrieved the coffee, dumped her keys and phone in her bag, and then hurried to follow Miss Martha who was already on her way to the warehouse entrance.

Avery took a cautious sip of the coffee as Miss Martha unlocked the door. It was a bold and black, the second thing she and Miss Martha had in common. "What's on the agenda for today?"

"The truck last night brought in a bunch of first aid supplies as well as prescriptions to fill about fifty specific orders."

"Orders?" Avery repeated.

Miss Martha dropped her purse on a metal office desk and glanced at the phone which blinked red, probably indicating voice messages. "Yes, it's hard to get the care and medicine needed in Cuba, so we have an online system for communicating needs and fill them as we are able. Generic only, but something is better than nothing."

Avery drummed her fingers on the lid to her cup. "How do you find the individuals who need help?"

"They find us," Miss Martha said. "Word of mouth spreads fast, and my network inside Cuba is growing daily. I wish I could keep up with the demand, but my team does what it can. The generous Cuban immigrants inside the States and elsewhere are the backbone of APC. They remember what life in Cuba was like, and they want to help."

Ethan had also shared that Miss Martha's own pockets—and generosity—ran deep, but she admired the woman for not taking credit. "Do you think your network could find people someone was concerned about?"

Miss Martha's fingers paused on the desk phone handle. "Probably. Who do you know in Cuba to be concerned about? You don't look Hispanic at all."

Avery nodded. "Fair question. I'm not, but I know—or knew—someone from Cuba who was very concerned about his cousins living there."

The older lady sighed and took a seat in the swivel chair at the desk. "I hear that story every week. Applying for an immigrant visa is an involved process. To be successful, someone needs to be sponsoring the would-be immigrants. That could be either immediate relatives who are now legal U.S. citizens or a potential U.S. employer. But how do you get businesses, other than Cuban-owned businesses, to stick out their necks for people from another country who may not even speak English yet?" She sighed again.

"Sounds hard," Avery agreed.

Miss Martha straightened. "Fortunate for you, that's their cousin's problem, though it's nice of you to be concerned."

Avery picked at the cardboard sleeve on her cup. "Actually,

it is my problem now."

The woman's gray eyebrows shot up to her forehead. "Oh?"

A lump formed in Avery's throat. Could this woman help her with her promise? The odds seemed slim, but she had to ask. "Miss Martha, have you ever made a promise you couldn't keep?"

The woman studied her with keen, but sad black eyes that spoke of loss. "Yes. I have let people down, and others have let me down. I try not to dwell on it."

"Well, I can't stop thinking about it." Avery paced the small space in front of Miss Martha's desk. "I mean, I promised a dying man I'd help his cousins get their freedom. It was idiotic of me, but now my promise haunts me."

Miss Martha slid a notepad on the desk toward her. "What are their names? I can't promise help with their visa applications, but I can ask my network to see if they can find them, to see if—"

She didn't finish her sentence, and she didn't need to. If they weren't alive any longer, Avery couldn't begin to help them.

"Would you?" Avery reached for a pen from an old cup on the table and wrote the names Jayna had supplied after Mario Delgado had pleaded for his cousins with his dying breath. *Gabriel and Camilo Delgado.* She slid the notepad back toward Miss Martha.

Retrieving her phone from her purse, the woman snapped a picture of the names and then folded her hands to study Avery. "I'll see what I can do, but here's a piece of friendly advice, my dear. You and I—no one—can live up to all that we say or want to do. That truth can either haunt you, like your promise has, or it can lead you to the most important discovery of your life."

Avery reached for her coffee again with a growing sense that Miss Martha's so-called discovery might be even more uncomfortable than Avery's haunting promise. "What is that?"

"Only God never breaks His promises. If you want to stop being overwhelmed by your own failures, accept Him. His sacrifice for your sins covers you and gives you a fresh start. That is the most freeing truth you will ever discover."

To her relief, the phone rang. To her dismay, Miss Martha didn't answer it but kept staring at her, as if expecting an answer.

Avery thumbed toward the door. "I'll wait outside for Ethan. You can get that."

"I can call them back," but she reached for the phone handle anyway. "Just don't you get to the point in life where God has called you so often that you can no longer hear His invitation."

Out of respect, she nodded before stepping out through the door back into the morning sun. Despite its warmth, she shivered.

She hadn't heard from God since He answered her seven-year-old pleas with silence. Miss Martha had it all wrong. God didn't call people. He answered them on a selective basis.

He hadn't answered her. That was on God.

The thought satisfied her mind, but her heart remained uneasy. What if she was wrong, and Miss Martha was right? Where did that leave her?

Chapter Thirty-Seven

Ethan sped his rental SUV into the APC parking lot faster than he should have, but the time was later than he liked. Spotting Avery's silver Mercedes already in the parking lot didn't help the rush in his veins that told him he was late.

Would she think he was sloppy for inviting her and then not being there when she arrived? He slammed his door shut and strode toward the entrance. The familiar door chime greeted him, but the reception room that doubled as an office was empty. Everyone must already be in the warehouse working.

He paused in the doorway that opened to the warehouse work room. Several people packaged supplies at tables, but his gaze roamed the room until he spotted Avery's ponytail. She was at a smaller table, her focus jumping between some pages in one hand and a packing envelope in the other.

His chest swelled with admiration. Even with all the problems in her world, she was making the time to help others. The woman had a big heart, even if she didn't know it. He hoped she'd share that heart with Jesus—and maybe a piece of it with him, one day.

Striding thorough the door, he started toward her, but a hand on his arm made him pause.

"Hey, Ethan. I've seen that look before."

"Hey, Miss Martha." He gave her a side squeeze. "I don't know what you mean."

"Don't lie to an old woman." She shook a finger at him. "Avery is doing fine over there by herself. There's something I want to talk to you about."

As if hearing her name, Avery glanced their way. He waved, and she jerked her chin up to acknowledge him before going back to work. At least she knew he had showed up like he said, but what he really wanted was to talk to her, not Miss Martha.

The manners he'd learned from his mom kept him rooted to hear the lady out. "What's on your mind?"

"Have a seat." She motioned to two metal chairs around a fold-up table where packaged boxes waited for shipping.

His frustration rose. "I told Avery I'd meet her here. She's got a lot on her plate right now."

Miss Martha settled onto a chair and patted the one beside her. "This will just take a minute."

With a sigh, Ethan took the seat, and Miss Martha started right into her question. "How long have you worked for Semper Security?"

Ethan blinked. He had been twenty-eight when he was medically discharged from the Coast Guard, and he had been working for Jake ever since. "It's been about five years. Why?"

"Do you hire only veterans?" Miss Martha asked.

"Well, I don't hire anyone, but yes, my boss hires Coast Guard vets. Most of us have PTSD of some kind. It's his mission to help us find our footing again."

Miss Martha leaned forward. "Has your boss ever considered expanding his mission?"

What was she driving at? "Not that I know of."

"Would you say you have seniority?"

Ethan crossed his arms. "A few guys have been with him longer than I have, but I suppose you could say that. What are you driving at?"

"I'd like to meet him. Do you think he would talk with an old lady like me?" The sparkle in Miss Martha's eyes defied her reference to age.

"Miss Martha, you have to tell me what's cooking in that head of yours, because I'm not following you," Ethan said. "Why would you want to talk to Jake?"

"I have a proposition for him about potential job candidates." She pulled out her phone and scrolled. "You should already have my number since I have yours, but I'll text you anyway. All I'm asking is that you ask him. If he says no, that is fine."

Ethan shrugged. "Okay, I'll ask my boss, but I can't make any promises."

Miss Martha tucked her phone back in her pocket and nodded in Avery's direction. "I'm not asking you to. Now go talk to Avery about whatever it is that is eating you."

He rose and half-smiled. Miss Martha didn't need to know she had the situation backwards. He wasn't the one "eaten up" with worry and regret to the point of making bad decisions. Avery was.

However, he was the one God had put in her path to help her.

"Have a good chat with Miss Martha?" Avery asked without looking up from her work.

"She had something she wanted to talk about." Ethan leaned against the table and studied the woman who wormed herself deeper into his heart the more she pushed him away. Her tired eyes betrayed a sleepless night, and the lack of color in her cheeks concerned him. "Anything you want to talk about? A plan B to a future in prison perhaps?"

That comment cracked a small smile. "Maybe, but I'm not making any promises. I'll have a better idea after my video call with Russo."

"When's that?"

"Tomorrow. Not that you need to know." Avery slanted her gaze toward him. "Are you going to help me with these orders, or are you going to stare at me?"

He straightened. "Help—if you show me what you're doing—and let me buy you some lunch since I'm guessing you skipped breakfast."

Her cheeks colored. "You're not my nurse maid. I'm fine."

"No, you're not taking care of yourself, and your cylinders can't run on empty. You need fuel to be on your game."

Avery's lip quivered. "You're right. I just—" Her voice cracked. "Gianna." She gulped. "What if—"

She had never looked so vulnerable. He wanted to wrap her in his arms, but she would never allow that. He settled for a quick shoulder squeeze. "God's watching out for Gianna."

"Is He?" Her eyes flashed. "Or is that a nice platitude people say?"

Ethan picked up an envelope and a copy of the orders. "I believe He is. He knows exactly where she is right now."

"Then why doesn't He drop me a line?" Avery's words dripped with resentment. "Why doesn't He *do* something?"

His throat felt dry. How could he explain something He didn't fully understand? "Avery, I wish I had answers for you, but I'm new at this myself. All I know is that He is real. He loves us so much that He died for us. A Savior who would go to such lengths for a sinner like me is Someone who deserves my trust." *Your trust*, he wanted to say but didn't.

Avery shrugged and turned her focus back to her work. "I'm glad religion works for you, but it's never worked for me."

Frustration rose until his cheeks flushed. "It's not some crazy religion. God is real. I wish you could understand—"

She held up a hand. "I don't want to argue with you. I can only volunteer an hour, and then I need to get to the office. If you want to buy me lunch, I won't say no, but you should look in the mirror. When's the last time you slept?"

He swallowed down the rest of what he wanted to say. Nothing he said would prove to her God cared for her too. He was going to have to leave that job up to God Himself. "Fair enough. You eat. I'll get some sleep, but if something comes up, call me."

"As the security officer on my detail or as my friend?" For once, her tone was sincere, not sarcastic or defensive.

Friend. She was still offering him a connection, and he wanted it more than he could let on. Ethan whispered a prayer he would answer the right way.

"As whichever one you need."

The rest of Tuesday ran together like a blur, and Wednesday morning dawned with de-ja-vu. Sleeplessness left invisible toothpicks in Avery's eyes, which she failed to wash away with a cold shower. Maybe she should call Ethan for tips on surviving insomnia.

Scratch that. The last thing she should do was encourage more contact with the man who made her feel confused but also strangely comfortable at the same time. With her video call scheduled with Russo for mid-morning, she didn't need to invite any more thoughts that might fog up her tired mind.

After a quick shower and a smoothie she drank on the way to work, Avery unlocked her agency's door, only to find the lights already on.

Who was working earlier than she was? It was barely past six.

Fingers typing on a keyboard drew her past the conference room and her office to the cluster of cubicles where her employees and fellow investigators worked.

When she spotted a man's Irish red hair, she stopped mid-step. "Liam Bracken, what on earth—"

Liam whirled in his swivel chair and greeted her with a broad grin. "Hey, boss."

"—are you doing here?" Avery dropped her bag onto the table in the center of the cubicle cluster.

He arched an eyebrow. "It's been a week and a half, okay? It was one bullet. I even got a doctor's note, since I figured you'd want one. I'm healing nicely, just need to avoid heavy lifting for a little longer or any strenuous activity. I figured I could at least come into the office for a few hours to check on you."

"Check on me?" Avery crossed her arms. "I'm not the one who got shot."

"No, but you haven't been answering my messages or emails." Liam pointed a finger at her. "That means you're working too hard."

"You're not supposed to be working at all. You still have a target on your back."

"And you don't?" Liam stood. "Avery, I'm an investigator. It's my job, and it's yours. I'm here to help watch *your* back."

Avery retrieved her bag and nodded toward her office door. "Let me get through a few emails, and then stop by my office." She paused. "How is Jayna holding up?"

"She's doing better than most girlfriends would be." He chuckled and lowered himself back into his chair. "As you know, she's gone through her share of danger, and I'm making sure she's taking precautions herself."

Precautions seemed pointless with Big Eddie behind the wheel, but if they helped Liam sleep at night, she wouldn't nitpick his personal life. "See you in fifteen," she called over her shoulder as she started down the hallway.

After stowing her bag and powering up her laptop, Avery studied her calendar. Russo's call was four hours away. Did she dare tell Liam her plan?

No, she would stick with the facts. Maybe he would see another option or propose another idea. Liam was the best investigator she had worked with, but he was a man of honor. He would never agree to breaking out Russo.

Chapter Thirty-Eight

Liam had offered to monitor her call with Russo, but Avery had told him that wasn't necessary. Her colleague's skin remained a shade paler than his usual everyday Irish complexion, so thankfully, he hadn't argued and had gone home after a few hours.

Now, as she opened the video call, Avery steeled her expression, but her stomach felt queasy with uncertainty. Liam, Miss Martha, and Ethan would all tell her to pray if she was anxious. She must be getting desperate to even consider that idea. Pretty sure God, if there was one, wouldn't smile on an investigator entertaining the idea of a prison break.

"If you have another idea, I'd like to hear it," she mumbled as the video call connected.

The scowl on Russo's face was certainly not a promising sign. "What do you want now?" Valentina Russo's eyes looked red and the crow's feet around her eyes, more pronounced. Clearly, prison wasn't a party.

Avery folded her hands. "I want to see if you've developed a conscience."

"Sorry, wrong number." Russo mimicked hanging up a phone.

"So you don't have a problem with child abduction and the prospective murder of an innocent girl."

For a moment, Russo hesitated. "I never hurt a child."

"In a sense, you have. Big Eddie kidnapped her on your behalf."

Russo snorted. "Big Eddie lives by his own rules. You're wasting your breath if you think I have any influence over him. I could tell him to let her go, that I'd rather rot here for the rest of my life—which I don't—but it wouldn't make a difference to him. What it sounds like to me is that you need to up your game and rescue her yourself."

"I don't know where to find her."

"Can't help you there."

Avery glared. "Can't help or won't? You could start by telling me how to find Big Eddie."

Russo exaggerated a yawn. "We've already had this chat, and you already know I can't do that."

"Right, or Big Eddie will somehow reach behind bars and kill you."

"Yep."

"So you'd rather he kill a child." Surely this woman had a small heart that could be reasoned with.

With a sigh, Russo propped her chin in her hands. "Listen, honey, I feel bad for the kid, but it sounds like you're lazy and can't keep up with Big Eddie. Maybe try harder and you'll find her before Sunday."

Interesting. Russo knew about both Gianna and the deadline. She'd love to know how, but that didn't matter right now.

"If it will help you sleep at night, you can rest in the assurance that I actually have a heart for kids." Russo batted her long lashes.

"Really."

"Yeah, really." Russo straightened and stretched. "This Friday, I'm parading my prison-uniform-clad self to the local high school for the prison preventers program. I'm putting myself on Exhibit A for the unglamorous nature of prison life."

Avery's pulse quickened. Russo had mentioned that program during their last chat, but she had forgotten about it. If the celebrity-felon were out from behind bars at a local school event, gaining access to her would be much easier.

"… think I deserve some credit for how humiliating that will be."

"So humiliating." But Avery's mind was racing. Could she get permission to attend the event? Maybe as a last-ditch effort to appeal to Russo's conscience on Gianna's behalf in a setting where young adults are everywhere? Or maybe on a professional level, as the detective who put her behind bars?

"Well, cupcake, you've got three minutes left to this delightful conversation." Russo's sarcasm pulled her focus back to the screen.

"That's three more minutes for you to reconsider your life choices." Avery mimicked her syrupy tone. As if Russo cared at this point in her prison career what Avery thought of her, let alone what anyone thought of her.

"I'm not the one about to be responsible for failing to save a child," Russo shot back.

Avery ground her teeth behind a stern scowl. "I'm not the one responsible for jeopardizing a child in the first place. You know who is, and yet you fail to provide the clues to help me find her. Guess you feel pretty cozy with your life sentence."

A devilish smile snaked up Russo's lips. "Oh, I'm not cozy with it at all, and we've already discussed why."

Yes, Avery knew why, and she hated the check-mate Big Eddie had cornered her into.

The ex-Hollywood producer picked at a nail and then tapped her wrist as if saying *time is up*. "As you've already made clear, Big Eddie wants me for the kid. It's rather ironic, isn't it? Unless you figure out how to get me out of here, you will fail again."

Fail. At this rate, it would be the epitaph on her grave.

Russo exaggerated blowing a kiss. "Thanks in advance for getting me out of here. See you soon."

Avery closed the video call in disgust and slapped her laptop shut. She would like nothing better than to kick-box a punching bag with Russo's face on it.

Instead, she had to plot how to break-out the former icon during her stint at the prison preventers program.

"Maybe I'll give you your taste of freedom, but don't get too excited," Avery mumbled. "You're going right back into the slammer—even if I have to join you."

Ethan pulled into the parking lot of the hole-in-the-wall Cuban diner and shook his head. No doubt he was about to have the best Cuban cuisine of his life, but exactly how Miss Martha had convinced Jake to meet them both for dinner a day after Ethan had shared her phone number with his boss was a mystery.

Miss Martha should run for president. She'd probably win.

Bongo music pulsated from speakers no one had tried to disguise as Ethan followed a walkway to the hostess stand. Families and couples crowded onto some benches, and he waited his turn to check with the hostess. If Miss Martha didn't have a reservation, they'd be here a while.

His phone pinged. It was Miss Martha herself. "Come around back when you get here. Our table is on the patio."

He gave the text a thumb's up and grinned to himself as he retraced his steps to find the side entrance. Of course, Miss Martha already had a table.

A flash of red in the parking lot signaled Jake had arrived in his oversized SUV. Ethan waved and waited at the edge of the pavement. No surprise, Jake had one of his dogs with him. The Siberian Husky everyone at Semper Security knew as Titus jumped out the back door.

So that's why Miss Martha had a patio seat. She was accommodating Jake's dog, which was a check in favor of whatever proposition she wanted to discuss.

"Hey, Jake." Ethan greeted his boss and then offered a hand to Titus to smell. The dog's piercing blue eyes relaxed as he recognized Ethan's scent, and the beautiful animal greeted him with a slobbery kiss.

"Smells like a great little place." Jake shortened Titus's leash and led the way to the backyard seating. "I'm curious to hear what your Miss Martha has in mind."

"What did she tell you?" Ethan pushed past a palm frond to reach the surprisingly large patio. At least a dozen tables fit in the space, and all were taken. From the far corner, Miss Martha waved them over.

Jake chuckled. "She started by sharing her faith with me and that she is the founder of the non-profit called Ayuda Para Cuba where you volunteer. She asked point blank if I am a man of faith—I told her yes—and said she wanted to know my vision for Semper Security and if I was open to a proposition that might expand my business and benefit the Cuban community. She invited me to dinner at this place and said you'd be here too. Frankly, I have no idea what she has in mind, but I'm intrigued."

None of that surprised Ethan. Miss Martha was persuasive and persistent with a charisma about her that drew people to her. He greeted her with a hug and introduced Jake.

Miss Martha shook Jake's extended hand and motioned for them to sit down. "Thank you both for coming. I've already ordered half a dozen items on the menu, so there will be plenty of food."

Ethan hid a smile behind a glass of water. Miss Martha was wasting no time with whatever she had in mind.

Jake secured Titus' leash to his chair and poured half of his water glass into a collapsible dog bowl he'd brought with him. "I'm sure it will all be delicious. Now, tell me your idea."

Miss Martha leaned forward in her chair. "First, I want to understand if your vision for Semper Security is strictly for Coast Guard veterans. I respect your answer either way."

"Thank you for that," Jake said. "I'm sure Ethan has told you part of his story. My reason for starting my security agency, outside the obvious business element, was to provide new purpose and community for vets like myself who were medically discharged. Most have some form of PTSD. Coming back to "normal" life feels anything but normal to those of us used to always being "on" during active duty. We're a band of brothers who have each other's back— and the backs of our clients."

A waitress arrived with more food than they could possibly eat: Cuban sandwiches, pulled pork on rice and beans, something Miss Martha called tostones or fried plantains, a large salad, and Cuban bread coated in butter. He didn't follow some of the other menu item names, but he gladly tried anything Miss Martha piled on his plate.

After Miss Martha prayed for the meal, she turned back to Jake. "I admire your vision," Miss Martha said, "but I am hoping you are willing to expand it."

Jake swallowed a bite of his Cuban sandwich. "I'm listening."

"Right now, it is difficult for my people to obtain immigrant visas without sponsors. Usually, that sponsor is a relative who is a U.S. citizen, but many do not have relatives here yet. In that case, a prospective U.S. employer can fill out the petition on their behalf and act as their sponsor."

Miss Martha paused, and for the first time, doubt flickered across her features. "I hope I am not too forward to ask if you would consider being a sponsor. You could start with one or two under the umbrella of your employment, see how things go, but my people are hard workers, and so many want a second chance at life, at freedom."

Ethan glanced from her to Jake. His boss didn't seem phased at all but nodded his head as if interested. "I have been asking God this year what plans He has for me, for my security agency, and perhaps this is His answer. But I will be honest. I wouldn't know where to start with becoming a sponsor or filling out a petition."

A smile lit up Miss Martha's face. "I can help you with all the paperwork. Would you pray about it and let me know if you'd like to start?"

Pray about it. Praying before acting was new to Ethan, but he liked the idea of trusting God for direction. Maybe he should start doing that with Avery instead of trying to solve her problems the best way he could figure.

"I will." Jake sipped his water. "Thank you for asking me—and for this amazing dinner. Don't know that I can eat much more though."

Miss Martha laughed. "That's okay. Cuban food is good leftover too—especially when you're single and don't want to cook." She glanced down at Jake's hands. "No ring that I can see. I'll get some to-go boxes."

Jake chuckled as she darted away. "Nothing gets past her. No need to explain that men in our line of work don't wear rings for several reasons."

"The primary one being that we're single." Ethan's tone came off more sarcastic than he intended.

"Might not always be that way," Jake said. "I didn't think anyone could handle my baggage until I met Laura. God can work in two hearts to make them right for each other."

"Yeah," was all Ethan said. What would it take for God to get a hold of Avery's heart? He feared the answer.

Chapter Thirty-Nine

Friday morning couldn't dawn soon enough. Like every day since Gianna was taken, Avery woke before her five o'clock alarm after a nightmarish sleep.

At least today she would be doing something and hopefully not getting arrested.

Sheriff Hannaford hadn't questioned her motives when she asked him to introduce her to the authorities in charge of the prisoner prevention program Russo would be participating in. The coordinators were delighted at the prospect of pairing a detective with the felon she'd placed behind bars for the high school demonstration and even asked Avery to give a presentation. She'd thrown together some slides she could share from her laptop of careers in law enforcement.

It was ironic, considering the forecast of her own career after today.

She paused for only a second as she passed the Bible collecting dust on her end table. Did it have anything to say to someone about to do something wrong for a right reason? Avery shook her head, grabbed her bag, and headed out the door. She had a drive ahead of her, and she couldn't waste time thumbing through some thousand-page religious guidebook hoping for help.

Two hours later, she pulled into a parking spot at Creekside High School and shot off a quick text to Ethan. She'd been ignoring his texts the last two days, and she at least owed him a thank-you for all the trouble she'd put him through.

Hey, I want to say thanks for your help the last few weeks and want to wish you all the best. Ugg, it wasn't great, but she owed him something.

Almost immediately, she received a response. *That sounds*

like a last will and testament text. What's going on? Where are you?

Was Ethan a mind-reader? With a grunt, she shot back. *Just working but had a sec to spare. I'm sure you're busy too, so I'll let you get back to it.*

She unbuckled her seatbelt as her phone pinged again. *Never too busy for a friend.*

Her chest tightened. Why were there some people that no matter how hard she tried to push them away, they kept coming back like a boomerang? Liam and Ethan were both like that. She couldn't let them get too close, or they'd try to stop her from ruining herself. That's who they were.

But someone had to get Gianna back for Bella, and that someone had to be her.

She casually tapped a thumbs-up emoticon and then repocketed her phone in her bag. Enough procrastinating. It was showtime.

How little sleep could he function on? Ethan ran a hand over his face, readjusted his pillow, and stared at his cell phone. It remained quiet. Avery was clearly not going to respond to his last text.

His shift had ended three hours ago, and he had been in the middle of sleep when his buzzing phone jolted him awake. Being a light sleeper had serious disadvantages. The time now was a little after nine o'clock. What had prompted Avery's text that sounded like a goodbye?

He should close his eyes and go back to sleep. Avery wasn't his problem right now. Still, her unsettling confession that she might break Russo out herself had been haunting him the last few days.

The least he could do was check in with Liam, make sure she was okay. Liam had touched base when he returned to Tampa, and odds were, the man was as much of a workaholic as Avery.

Hey, man, do you have sec? Avery sent an odd text, and I'm curious if she's in the office today. I want to check if she needs any extra security. There. If Liam didn't respond, Ethan could rest knowing he had tried.

Moments later, his phone pinged. *No, she's in the field, doing a presentation at a prison prevention program. What did she say?*

Warning sirens went off in his brain. Why would Avery volunteer for some program when her deadline for Gianna's ransom was two days away? Something didn't fit.

Nothing much, but it didn't sound like her. Where's this program? Maybe I should check it out, from a security standpoint. It would be like Avery not to tell us where she might need her detail to focus today.

After he hit send, Ethan chewed his cheek. A few days ago, he wouldn't have thought twice about that message, but now, it seemed like a half-truth. He wasn't scheduled to be on Avery's detail again until late tonight. Right now, it was none of his business where she was or what she did.

That was his problem. He wanted Avery to be his concern, whether he was on the clock or not.

"God, what am I supposed to do?" he groaned. "I care about her, and I don't want to see her get hurt—or make a rash decision that will ruin her life."

Maybe Liam wouldn't respond or tell him where she was. That would end his dilemma, and he would have no choice but to go back to bed.

No such luck. His phone pinged moments later with the address of the school where Avery was volunteering with the program. The location was two hours north.

"Service above self." Ethan quoted the old Coast Guard slogan and tossed his covers off. He had made his choice. The nagging question was if he could reach her before something went south.

Chapter Forty

"Reason one hundred and one you should not be like me is that these jumpers come in only bright orange for felons." The ever-indomitable Russo strutted back and forth in front of the classroom of high schoolers. "There is no pink or chic black option. Your sense of fashion will fall by the wayside." She held out her cuffed wrists. "And these are the best you get for bracelets."

Avery rolled her eyes and raised an eyebrow in the direction of the supervising prison officer who stood with her arms crossed a few feet away. The woman matched her eye roll and stepped closer to Avery. "This diatribe was nowhere in the speech Russo promised she would give."

As if Russo would ever stick to a script. "Want me to interrupt her?"

"Please."

Avery strode forward to the podium where she had already set up her laptop with the projection system. "Thank you, Ms. Russo, for your enlightening demonstration, but these students already have a strong fashion sense. Let me share the daily reality of your choices with them."

Valentina eyed her with a secretive grin, the way she had been ever since Avery showed up in the classroom. It was as if the woman knew Avery was here to get her out, and she was going to milk the upside-down situation for everything it was worth.

"Let me fill you in on what Ms. Russo failed to tell you." Avery rubbed her finger over the mousepad to wake up her screen. "She had everything—in fact, a life many can only dream about. She was a respected Hollywood producer who had just won her first Oscar. You would think that would be enough.

"But it wasn't, not for a woman entrenched in crime. She became privy to murder, kidnapped a woman to help cover her part in a fraud scheme, and then threatened murder to keep her silent. She threw away her star-studded career for a life sentence in a prison cell where going to visit a class of highschoolers is the most exciting outing of her entire year."

Avery paused to study the rows of high schoolers in front of her. She had gotten their attention. Many sat up straighter, and no one smiled.

"I don't want to bore you with the details and consequences of becoming a felon, because you've probably seen enough true crime shows to know crime doesn't pay. Instead, I want to share about career options that each of you young people can pursue in either public or private law enforcement that perhaps you've never considered—and how the choices you make today can prepare you for a bright future."

Snickering came from the corner where the prison officer had latched Russo's handcuffs to a desk. Avery ignored her and began her multimedia presentation. As she touted the profession of law enforcement, her gut twisted. Could she go against everything she believed in and commit a crime herself? What would happen to Gianna if she didn't? Would Bella ever forgive her if she failed to save her daughter? What family would she have then?

What about the students in front of her? What example would she be setting for them? Would she be prisoner exhibit A at next year's prevention program?

"Any questions?" She finished and let out a breath.

No one spoke. Either the students didn't have any questions, or they had been pretending to be interested in what she had to say.

"I can't raise my hand, but I have a question," Russo drawled from her corner.

"Does anyone *else* have a question?" Avery ignored Russo and scanned the students. Many looked at Russo, and one girl raised her hand. "I'd like to know what her question is."

Giving Russo the figurative microphone back spelled trouble. "She needs permission from her officer to speak," Avery explained. "You see, you lose basic rights when you become a felon."

The same girl craned her neck to locate the prison officer. "Can she ask her question?"

Why was this girl so gung-ho for Russo? Did these prison prevention programs accomplish nothing but to make students more curious about crime?

With a sigh, the officer nodded. "Permission granted."

"Thank you." Russo squinted at her officer and cleared her throat. "I have a scenario question. What if there's a little girl, and a cop knows the only way she can save her is by committing a crime? Should the cop commit the crime to save the girl and become a criminal herself, or follow the law and let the girl die?"

Avery's smile froze on her face. How dare Russo—

"I'm sorry, but I'm taking actual questions, not hypothetical scenarios," Avery said sharply.

"It's not so hypothetical," Russo purred. "Just answer the question."

Avery swallowed. She had to speak the truth, even if she were about to act against it. "It is never right to do wrong."

Valentina arched an eyebrow. "So, the cop should let the girl die?"

"Absolutely not," Avery shot back. "The cop should find another way to save the girl."

"What if there is no other way?" Russo insisted.

Avery shook her head and turned her back on Russo. "If there are no other questions, that concludes my presentation. Thank you for your time."

The teacher made her way to the front of the class and thanked Avery for her time and the information, but Russo's question seemed to hover over the room and taunt Avery's mind.

What if there is no other way?

If he had wasted two hours of gas, at least he had a caffeine rush to commemorate it. Ethan snagged the last parallel parking spot across from Creekside High School, turned off his car, and banged his head against his headrest. The throbbing behind his eyes was no doubt due to the double espresso shot he had consumed to stay alert.

If there were laws against driving over-caffeinated, he would have lost his license by now.

Also, too much caffeine messed with his critical thinking skills. What was his plan now? He couldn't go on a school campus without obtaining a visitor pass, and he had no reason to request one. His clients at Semper Security had never involved school security, so this was out of his element. Besides, the campus was large. Aside from the main two-story building, several portable classrooms jutted out on both sides, connected to the main building by covered walkways. There was no telling where Avery was.

Wait.

The thought came out of nowhere, and his over-stimulated brain slowed. Wait for what? Liam said Avery's program ended at noon, and if nothing happened by then, he might as well find a decent lunch spot around here to help balance all that caffeine with some healthy calories.

Pulling up a map, he noted a large park past the school in one direction, and in the other, a shopping strip, home to a Mom and Pop's Bar-b-que and a Mediterranean Buddha bowl place. Bar-b-que it was.

Ethan was scanning the menu when a car backfired, and he jolted to attention. A revving engine warned him someone was speeding his way.

Flattening himself against his seat, his gaze darted between his side and rear-view mirrors. A black SUV with tinted windows zoomed in and around other cars toward the school entrance. Without braking, it jerked into the empty car line and came to a screeching stop.

How stupid could this person be? A security guard would chew him out for sure, but no such guard was in sight.

The time was two minutes to noon, so Avery's class and probably many others, were about to end. Still, it wasn't the end of the school day, so why was this car waiting with all engines ready? Maybe a student had a doctor's appointment? That idea didn't fit this bill, and he knew it.

Seconds later, the side door burst open, and two large men wearing sports coats and face masks darted toward one of the portable classrooms.

Not. Good.

Ethan snatched his cell phone and dialed 9-1-1.

An operator answered, "What's your emergency?"

"I saw two men wearing face masks charge onto school grounds at Creekside High School."

"Officers are on their way."

"I'm a licensed security officer." Ethan slid his concealed carry into his belt holster. "I can help."

"Stand by. There's security on the campus."

"The men targeted an outdoor modular classroom."

The operator hesitated. "Did you see any weapons?"

"No, but they were wearing face masks." Ethan kept the sarcasm from his voice. It wouldn't sound professional on a 9-1-1 recording.

"Whatever you do, stay on the line."

It was the closest thing to permission he was going to get. "I'm transferring the call to my watch so you can listen in." With that, Ethan pushed open his door and jogged down the sidewalk, looking for a clearing in traffic to cross the street. A police car with sirens blaring sped past him to the school's entrance.

Gunshots made Ethan hit the pavement. The police car swerved, then slid to a stop, though its sirens continued to blare. Ethan's held his watch close to his lips. "Black SUV in the car line fired shots on the police. The patrol car stopped moving, and there's no response from inside. Send EMS."

"10-4." The operator's voice was stony but calm. "Where are you?"

"I'm on the sidewalk across the street." Ethan scanned the open ground between himself and the school. If he went any direction other than the one he'd come from, he'd be an easier target than the patrol car.

"Any sign of the masked intruders?"

"No—wait, there's a small group of people running back toward the SUV." Ethan strained his neck behind another parked vehicle for a clearer look. "The masked men are holding handguns with extended magazines. There are two women—" His throat went dry.

The first was Valentina Russo, and the second was Avery.

Chapter Forty-One

Ethan didn't have time to gawk and couldn't afford to expose himself if he didn't want to get shot. Staying flat against the pavement, he shielded himself from view as the SUV in the car line shifted from idling to race mode the moment the doors closed behind the two masked men and two abducted women.

Was *abducted* the right word? Russo was probably thrilled someone had broken her free, and Avery—was she a hostage or the mastermind?

Ethan felt sick at the idea Avery might be behind the escape, but he couldn't forget her words to him from a few days ago. It sounded like she would go to any length to save Gianna, but breaking the law and consorting with people who shot at police was inexcusable.

"God, let her be innocent and let her be okay." The alternative of her as a hostage didn't sit well with him either.

As the SUV shot down the road, Ethan jumped to his feet and raced to his rental. The dispatcher kept talking in his ear, but he heard only a fraction of what she said. Frankly, he needed space to process what he had witnessed, and he didn't want to confess that he was about to pursue. "Suspect SUV is heading west. I've lost visual and need to disconnect the call."

With a breath of relief, he ended the call and welcomed the silence as he completed the fastest three-point-turn of his life and accelerated westward, past the bar-b-que place he had planned for lunch, and toward the large park he'd seen on the map.

The SUV could have taken a turn anywhere, and he had no way to trace Avery, but maybe Liam did. Pulling into the park's entrance, he dialed Liam.

"Hey, Ethan, what's up?" Liam's voice rasped, as if maybe

he should be taking pain medication for his healing gunshot wound but wasn't.

"I drove to that school to check on Avery—and got here in time to witness two masked men haul her and Valentine Russo from a modular classroom. By the time I got back in my car, the black SUV was gone. Do you have a way to trace her—a shared app or something?"

Liam would have a hundred questions after that explanation, but true to his training, the man focused on the immediate problem. "Yes, hold on."

The line was silent as Ethan chose a shaded parking spot overlooking a large baseball field with adjacent bathrooms, vending building, and playground. A few moms watched their kids on the playground, but otherwise, the park wasn't busy.

"She must have turned off her tracking," Liam muttered. "I'm not seeing her."

That news made his heart sink and suggested something premeditated. *Oh, Avery, what have you done?*

"Did you call the police?"

"Yeah, I was on the phone with a dispatcher the whole time until I got back in my car and tried to follow, but I was too late."

"I'll call my contacts at the sheriff's department to find out what happened in that classroom and let them know you were the caller who reported it. They might have more questions for you."

He had more questions of his own. "Sure, you can give them my number," he said instead. "Keep me posted."

The call ended, and Ethan banged his head on the steering wheel. He should have stayed in bed. This day had gone from bad to worse. What he had hoped would be a pointless drive had confirmed his fears about Avery.

"God, what am I supposed to do now?" He couldn't protect a woman who was bent on her own undoing, and he couldn't defend a woman who stooped to work with criminals.

There was nothing he could do now except leave Avery to the professionals, and he had a two-hour drive back home. Might as well use the bathroom before going through a drive-through for lunch.

He had just rounded the building in search of the men's entrance when he froze.

There, in the parking lot on the other side of the restrooms was the black SUV with its tinted windows.

And there, standing with the hatch open while barking orders to someone inside and cuffing two unconscious men sprawled on the pavement was Avery.

With a huff, Avery slammed the hatch shut and glanced at the thugs. Good thing for her, those two were all muscle and no brains.

Leaving them here would cause plenty of questions for whomever found them, but she couldn't afford to have them waking up and causing more problems for her than the woman she'd tied up in the back seat already had.

On the bright side, she hadn't had to break out Russo. Big Eddie had sent his own thugs to do that job.

On the downside, she was still technically committing a crime by not turning in Russo to the police right away. "Borrowing" a criminal sounded civilized, but the law wouldn't see it that way.

She spun toward the driver's door but came to a screeching halt. A man stared at her from the edge of the bathrooms, and not any man, but Ethan Bridger himself.

No. Way. This was a horrible case of déjà vu. He could not ruin her plans again.

"What are you doing here?" They both asked the question at the same time.

His mouth gaped. It wasn't a good look, but the concern etched in his eyes was endearing. "You—I—drove up here to check on you, but you—" Ethan didn't seem to know how to finish his sentence. His jaw tightened, and he stepped forward. "Tell me one thing—did they take you, or did you plan this?"

Avery glanced in the back seat. Russo was squirming on the floor. "I did not plan this, but I'm taking advantage of it. The less you know, the better."

"Is Russo in there?"

She glared at him. "The less you know—"

"Avery, these men took you and Russo at gunpoint from a school campus."

"You saw that?"

"Yes." He waved his arm as if the whole world had seen it. "Police are everywhere looking for them and for you. You've got to get back there and tell them what happened."

Avery shook her head. "The teacher can tell them what happened. I must save Gianna. You can be the hero and take those two back to the police, but I have to go."

He stepped even closer, and she backed against the SUV. "Avery, listen to yourself. This is crazy. You're going to destroy yourself and your reputation."

She blinked back angry tears. Did he think she hadn't considered those angles already? "I have to save—"

"The only one doing any saving is God," Ethan cut her off. "He's ultimately in control of what happens to Gianna. You aren't her savior. And even if you go through with this crazy plan of yours, she might still die."

Her fingers froze on the door handle. She hated him right now for being right. She could fail and lose everything. "What am I supposed to do?"

"Do the right thing, and trust God," Ethan said. "I'll help you get these three to the police and we can explain your situation. Maybe they'll reconsider and let you use Russo since you've been helpful."

She snorted and gripped the door handle tighter. "You are a dreamer. That's never going to happen."

"Or maybe they'll agree to put her in solitary confinement somewhere so at least Big Eddie won't know that you don't have her. Either way, don't destroy your reputation because your emotions are running high. That's what Big Eddie wants."

Avery wanted to jump in the car and forget Ethan, but deep down, she knew he was telling the truth. She would be driving the getaway vehicle. She might not even get down the street before getting pulled over. And maybe, the prison authorities would agree to one of those ideas. If not, she would at least be a free woman with her career who could keep fighting for Gianna a little longer.

With a tense nod, she pulled her phone from her pocket. "Put those two in the back? But check on Russo first. That woman is a cat, and she might have clawed her way out of the bungee cord I used to tie her up."

"How did you even take on these three?" A smile cracked the corner of Ethan's mouth for the first time in their conversation.

"I'm not as fragile as I look." She dialed the local sheriff's department to make her report and call for back-up. Giving up Russo felt like giving up the one playing card the day had given her, but Ethan's words echoed in her mind. Perhaps she had been about to walk into Big Eddie's trap by getting caught with Russo and getting taken out of the game.

An operator put her on a brief hold to transfer her to the sheriff's direct line. She glanced at Ethan as he checked on the two men and tightened the bungee cords she had used to bind their legs. This was the second time Ethan had ruined her plans, but maybe there was a reason.

"Yes, sheriff? This is private investigator Avery Reynolds. Yes, the same one taken from the school today—I'm okay. I was able to overpower my abductors and Russo—with the help of a security officer. Can you send back-up? We're at the park west of the school." After thanking him and assuring him the only ones who might need an ambulance were her abductors, she hung up with a sigh. "They're on their way."

"Good." Ethan wiped his hands on his pants and slammed the SUV's hatchback door closed. "Think I'm going to leave them on the pavement. The cat inside is hurling expletives, and there's no point putting them back inside when the police are going to take them away in different vehicles."

"True."

Sirens sounded nearby, and Avery leaned against driver's door. "I suppose I owe you a thank-you—"

A gunshot exploded through the side of the vehicle beside her, and something sharp punctured her leg. Avery swore at the pain and staggered. How had Russo gotten free and gotten a gun? There must have been one hidden in the SUV.

In her peripheral, she saw Ethan crouch against the pavement, then glance her way as the ground beneath her began to swim.

"Avery!" was the last thing she heard.

Chapter Forty-Two

Her head hurt more than the scratch that had caused so much drama a few minutes ago. "You are one lucky woman." The paramedic checked the tourniquet that had all but stopped her bleeding. "If that cut had been any deeper, it would have hit your femoral artery, and the bleeding wouldn't have slowed so fast."

Avery looked away and out the window from inside the ambulance someone had put her in without her consent. She was fine. The actual bullet had missed her, but shrapnel from the door had cut her thigh. Her ruined jeans lay at her feet. Someone must have cut them off her but at least had the decency to cover her with a hospital gown.

"I have to get back there," Avery told the man.

"You need stitches and rest. Leave the mess back there to the professionals."

Avery ground her teeth. She was the professional. She was the one who had caught the bad guys single-handed. Now what was going to happen? Would Ethan advocate on her behalf about Russo, or was everything she had hoped for slipping out of her grasp?

"Where's my phone?"

The paramedic eyed her. "Might be in your pants—no wait, I think I saw it on the ground. Not sure what happened to it."

"Can you check my pockets?" She couldn't attempt to reach it, thanks to being strapped down with an IV in each arm. Total overkill.

"Nope, pockets are empty. Now try to rest. We'll be at the hospital soon."

Avery closed her eyes out of misery. Losing her phone meant losing any chance of controlling the situation. She would borrow a phone when she got to the hospital and dial the office. Someone there could get a pulse on the situation and what had gone down after she blacked out from blood loss.

She should've eaten more for breakfast. This was a scratch and minor setback. She had to have plans A, B, and C ready to get Gianna back in two days' time.

Ethan might have his faith, but Gianna needed a savior with hands and feet, not invisible angel wings.

Ethan paused a moment outside Avery's room at the ER. The strong antiseptic odor brought back memories that were still too fresh of his own ER visit a few days ago.

There was no wall to knock on, so he slowly pulled back the curtain and called, "Knock, knock."

Avery bolted upright in her bed and blinked rapidly. "Please tell me you have my phone."

"Good to see you, too." He handed her the overpriced flowers he had purchased in the lobby. This woman needed to slow down.

"I'm sorry—these are nice, thanks—it's just that no one here will give me a phone, and I have to call the office." She set the flowers on a tray and held out her hand in expectation. "I think the nurse is taking forever with my discharge paperwork out of pure spite."

A smile tugged at his lips. "Why would she do that? I'm sure you've been the perfect patient."

Avery continued to hold out her hand. "Don't make me snarl at you too. Phone, please."

He sighed and retrieved her phone from his pocket. "Here's your precious phone, but it needs a new cover. It must have cracked when you hit the pavement."

"Whatever, I can work with this for now." Avery scrolled furiously.

"I have your sidearm too. It's in my trunk. You're welcome."

Avery sighed. "Okay, thank you. Now tell me what happened after I left. Where do we stand with Russo?"

Ethan pulled up a hard chair, straddled it, and propped his elbows on the back. "Can you tell me how you're doing first? We can talk shop in a minute. You look pale."

"I'm. Fine." Avery grunted. "The stupid scratch is more painful than it should be, but it's not going to slow me down. You'd better have good news about Russo, because you're the one who talked me out of my initial plan."

"Which would have gotten you killed," Ethan pointed out. "Russo would have found that gun in the getaway SUV sooner or later, and if you were driving down the road, she would have blasted it into the back of your skull."

Avery stilled. At least he had gotten her attention. "If you're waiting for a thank-you, then thank-you," she said. "But I've got a little girl who needs to be home with her mom and dad, not in the clutches of Big Eddie's kind. And I need my bargaining chip, Russo."

Ethan rubbed his chin. Sharing this piece of news was something he had been dreading the whole drive over. "There was a small gunfight after you conked out. Russo refused to exit the vehicle and shot at the police. They returned fire, and—"

He stopped as what little color remained in Avery's cheeks vanished. "Russo was hit. I don't know how badly, but paramedics were working on her when I left."

"No." Avery croaked. "Big Eddie will kill Gianna the moment he finds out."

Ethan lowered his voice to above a whisper. "I explained that to the detective on the scene, and he ordered the paramedics not to reveal her condition to anyone. They said they would treat her and take her to an unnamed, secure confinement facility. No one will know her condition until after Sunday."

"But we need to know her condition." Avery jabbed a finger toward him. "If she's breathing, I want permission to use her."

"Avery—"

"Don't *Avery* me. I want the lead detective's number, and I want to talk to him."

Ethan had expected no less. "I have his card for you, but you're not getting it until you've been discharged. The signal is horrible here anyway."

Avery opened her mouth as if to argue, but the nurse returned with a sour expression and a clipboard. "I need your signature on these, and then you can go."

"Finally," Avery muttered. It was all Ethan could do not to laugh at how charged the air felt between those two. He must have missed a show before he arrived.

"Where are the rest of my clothes?" Avery asked.

"The EMTs had to cut off your pants, ma'am. Didn't your boyfriend bring you something else to wear?"

Ethan coughed and cut his gaze toward Avery whose mouth gaped. She glanced at him and looked perhaps the most helpless he had ever seen her.

"Sorry, I didn't think to get any," he answered for Avery. "Do you have anything here she can use?"

The nurse tossed another hospital gown onto the edge of the bed. "You can wrap that around your back and tie it to the front one to stay decent. Check out with the nurse at the end of the hall when you're ready." With that, she slipped out of the small room and yanked the curtain back in place.

Avery glared after her. "Of all the—"

Ethan hopped to his feet. "I'll wait outside until you're ready."

He gulped down the chuckle rising in his throat. Avery's expression was complete mortification at wearing hospital gowns out of the emergency room, but from his perspective, it was a much better alternative than an orange jumpsuit or a body bag.

"Thank you, Jesus, for putting me in the right place at the right time, and thank you that Avery's isn't badly hurt," he whispered. "Help me know what to do next—and keep that little girl safe."

God did answer prayers, but there were still a lot of messy unknowns Ethan would have to trust Him for—including the fiery investigator whose choices kept bringing her closer and closer to disaster.

Chapter Forty-Three

It had to be a windy day. Avery gritted her teeth and forced her chin high as the automatic doors of the emergency room exit closed behind her and a breeze tried to flip up the hem of her hospital gowns.

Ethan strode by her side as if to shield her from unwelcome stares, and thanks to his size, he didn't make a bad wind shield.

How was this man always turning up at the worst times?

He pressed the key fob for his rental car. "Let me get your door."

Normally, she would refuse, but she didn't dare let go of the gowns which she and a puny string tie held together.

With a grunt, she eased into the passenger seat and tried to ignore the pain in her leg. "Thanks."

"You're welcome."

Could he stop smiling for a minute? There was nothing good or funny about how this day had turned out.

At least she had her phone back, and a delivery notification in her email told her the packages she ordered had arrived at the office. Once she got a change of clothes at her apartment, she could head there, make a lot of phone calls, piece together a plan for Sunday, and fill the pain prescription she'd gotten in the ER. Normally, she wouldn't take medicine that strong, but she needed to feel invincible for Sunday.

"You okay?" Ethan asked as he pulled out of the parking lot.

If only they didn't have a two-hour drive. She would give anything to have real clothes on right now. Sitting next to Ethan in a flimsy hospital gown was worse than him rescuing her wearing her hooker costume. Maybe because she now cared what he thought of her.

When had that happened? She shoved the thought aside. Now

was not the time to think about her personal life.

"Been better," she mumbled, "but thank you for taking me home."

"You're welcome." His phone buzzed, and he stuffed an earpiece in his ear to answer. Whoever it was, he didn't want to feed the caller through the speaker for her to hear.

Fine by her. She had her own work to do. Avery shot her office manager a text to retrieve the packages as soon as possible and started a second message for Liam when a groan from Ethan made her glance his way.

"Wow, I'm glad you called and told me. Is the fire contained?" Ethan asked.

Fire. The word triggered images from Gianna's dance recital. Bella's frantic eyes. The message *failure* burning into the fence.

Avery closed her eyes. She wouldn't fail Bella. She couldn't. Yet today felt like a failure. The one thing she had succeeded at was keeping Big Eddie from getting Russo. That was something. If he had reclaimed Russo himself, he would have no reason to make a trade for Gianna.

A shudder coursed down her spine. Maybe she hadn't failed yet anyway. As long as Russo was alive, she could hope for a trade—or at least the illusion of a trade.

"Thanks, I'll see that she has a safe place to go. I'll let you know once I've talked with her." Ethan cut his eyes her direction, and her heart sank.

No. No, no, no. Was he talking about her?

Ethan ended the call and swerved off the road into the drive-through of a restaurant that boasted about its burgers and shakes.

She gripped the hems of her mock dress even tighter. "What's going on?"

"We're getting lunch." Ethan studied the menu.

"Was that call about me?"

"I'll tell you after we eat. Do you like burgers? What kind of shake?"

Her stomach growled the way she wanted to at this impossible man. "Yes, but stop avoiding my question. Tell me what's going on."

"After you get food in your belly. It's well after two o'clock, and neither of us had lunch. I'm about to pass out."

"That's comforting. Maybe I should drive."

He cracked a grin. "You don't have three hands, and I can't imagine you're going to stop clutching the edges of your gowns."

Heat rushed to her cheeks, but she kept her chin high. "I don't care if you make fun of me."

Ethan's smile faded to sympathy which was so much worse. "I wasn't making fun of you. C'mon, you can relax around me. I'm on your team."

"Maybe, but that doesn't change the fact I'm not—wearing real clothes." She bit her lip. Right now, she wanted to be anywhere other than in a car with Ethan.

"I think you wear that sack as well as anyone could, but if you're self-conscious about it, you can use my jacket." Ethan reached around her seat and brushed her shoulder as he retrieved a dark hoodie.

Goosebumps radiated from the contact. Well, it was a cool day after all.

"Thanks." Avery wrapped her fingers around the thick fabric and spread it out over her legs. "Now about that phone call—"

"Order when you're ready," an employee called over the intercom.

"Two burgers, fully involved, a large fry, a strawberry shake, and a chocolate shake. That's it."

Ethan pulled forward before she could even comment on the order. "Aren't you making some assumptions? How do you know I like my burger all the way?"

Ethan passed the worker a credit card and turned to face her. "Because you don't do anything half-hearted."

"And the shake?"

His eyes twinkled for a moment. "You strike me as the kind of girl who only lets her hair down at home when she eats chocolate ice cream straight out of the tub, but if I'm wrong and you prefer strawberry, that's fine too. I like them both."

He was either a psychic or had a pin on her freezer's contents. "Well, you still could have asked," she huffed.

"I did, and you didn't answer. Normally I would have given you more time, but one, I'm starving, and two, we need to move fast to get somewhere we can regroup and you can rest."

His tone held a weak attempt at humor, but the firm lines around his jaw told her trouble was brewing, and she was about to find out what it was.

"Thanks," Ethan told the worker while passing her the bag of food and seating two of the biggest shakes she'd ever seen in his cupholders.

He drove the car to the stop sign as a stream of traffic headed their way.

"So?" She prompted, eyeing the chocolate shake.

Without warning, he reached for her hand while keeping his left hand on the wheel. "Dear Lord, thank you for this food and for keeping Avery safe. Guide us through what's ahead. Amen."

His grip was gentle and firm, polite but intentional. She slid out of it. What had just happened? Had he prayed for her or for the food or both?

She took a sip of the chocolate shake. It was pure bliss. "You're pretty serious about that religion stuff."

"Yeah, I am." Ethan eyed the bag on her lap. "I'd like to talk to you more about it soon, but would you pass me a burger please? Then I need to tell you about Jake's phone call."

"The one involving fire." If only the velvety ice cream could cool the dread that had been growing in her stomach.

"Yes." He peeled back the wrapper on the burger the second she passed it to him. "I'm sorry, but I've got to eat something. I haven't slept in over twenty hours, and I need calories to keep going."

"You really should let me drive."

"You don't know where we're going."

She paused mid-sip of her shake. "Excuse me? You're taking me home."

Ethan took another bite of his burger and swallowed. "There's no sugar coating this news. Jake just heard that your apartment complex is on fire. Firefighters think they have it contained, but they aren't letting anyone inside until they've assessed the structural integrity."

The chocolate ice cream threatened to come back up. "Then we need to go to the office. I keep a change of clothes there."

"Nope, that's exactly what Big Eddie expects you to do," Ethan talked between bites. "He's playing you like a pawn on a chess board. You've got to get off the board until Sunday, and I know the perfect place."

Avery choked and set down the shake. "Not *your* place."

"Of course not." Ethan fished his straw through the strawberry shake's lid and grinned at her. That trademark grin made her toes tingle and sent sirens off in her head at the same time. "I'm taking you to meet my parents."

Chapter Forty-Four

The last time he had brought a girl home to his parents was before he lost Troy. But then again, his girlfriend at the time had wanted to meet them.

Those were just two ways Avery differed from Lindsey. Avery wasn't his girlfriend, and the look in her eye told him she wasn't at all excited about meeting his parents.

Wearing two hospital gowns roped together.

Ethan hugged the edge of the narrow road leading to his parents' ranch and repeated the line he hoped would help calm her agitated state of mind. "It's for one night, assuming your apartment complex gets cleared by sometime tomorrow."

"You've already told me that twice." Avery picked at the sleeve of his jacket on her lap. "I suppose I should be thanking you, but I'd rather take my chances and go straight to my apartment."

He bit his lip. Telling her no one would take a woman wearing a hospital gown seriously was something she didn't need to hear.

"You'll have plenty of privacy and can use either of my sisters' old rooms. Pretty sure they both left clothes in the closet for when they visit during the holidays, and I think Chloe is about your size, maybe shorter."

"And you cleared this with your parents?" Doubt flickered across her features. This self-assured woman was having one rough day.

"Not really," he said. "I sent Dad a text to let him know I'm bringing company."

"What?" Her eyes widened. "Isn't that rude?"

"That's family," he said. "My parents have an open-door policy with us kids, as they call us. Come home often and make yourself at home. It usually involves significant others, not private investigators, but it won't make a difference in their book."

Avery's fingers stilled on his jacket. "Must be nice—to have family and significant others." Her voice was above a whisper, as if she were talking to herself.

"Family, yes. Significant others—that's more my sisters' department right now." Ethan turned his full attention to the road. Now wasn't the time to talk about his own hopes and dreams when Avery's career and a little girl's life were hanging by a thread.

He nearly ran over a squirrel when he parked behind his dad's pickup in the circular driveway. His mom's birdfeeders attracted the rodents like bees to honey and were a source of frustration to her. She'd be disappointed he had missed.

Ethan hopped out and circled around the car, but Avery wasn't letting him get her door twice in one day. She was on her feet and tying his jacket around her waist. Her cheeks lacked their usual color. The pain meds from the hospital must be wearing off.

Circling to the back of his rental, he popped the trunk. After seating his own concealed-carry in his inside-the-belt holster, he offered Avery hers. "Let's get you inside, and then I'll pick up your prescription."

She nodded and tucked her handgun underneath his jacket. "After you. Any chance I won't have to meet your parents looking like this?"

Ethan's pulse quickened. Why should she care what his parents thought about her? Unless—

The door swung open, and his mom filled the entrance. Her brown hair tinged with gray bounced in curls to her shoulders, and a flour-dusted apron made him anticipate whatever baked goods were on the menu for dinner.

"Mom!" He strode forward to wrap her in a hug.

She suddenly pulled back and frowned. "What is that on your forehead?"

He ran a finger over the fresh scar forming there and waved her off. "Just a scratch. Nothing to worry about."

"Uh-hmm."

Nothing got past his mom. He needed to change the subject. "But how did you know we were here so fast?"

She beamed up at him. "Dad finally installed that alarm on

the gate like you asked so we know whenever someone is coming or going on the property. I didn't recognize the car, but our family app told me it was you."

Avery flashed an unspoken question his way.

"It's an app on our phones that lets us keep track of each other, another of my security ideas," Ethan said. "But I'm being rude. Avery, this is my mom, Nancy Bridger. Mom, this is Avery. She's a—"

"Fashion designer," Avery cut in. "Hospital gowns are all the rage now."

Ethan choked on a laugh as his mom's eyes twinkled with humor. "I'm sure there's a story behind the fashion statement, but you don't have to tell me, dear. Any friend of Ethan's is welcome. Come on in."

Avery's tight facial features softened. "Thank you, ma'am."

Ethan closed the door behind them. "Mom, I told Avery she could borrow some of Chloe's clothes."

"Of course, Chloe won't mind." His mom motioned toward the stairs. "You know the way. Come meet me in the kitchen when you're ready, because my banana bread just finished baking."

He kissed her cheek. "Thanks, Mom. We'll be down soon."

"Take your time—but not too much time." She winked at Avery and retreated to the kitchen.

Avery's mouth hung open. "She doesn't mean—"

"C'mon, Miss Fashion Designer." Ethan placed a hand on the small of her back and led her to the stairs. "My mom raised me right, but she probably thinks we're dating since you didn't let me introduce you. Now I don't mind if we let her think that way, but something tells me you do."

Avery actually grinned. "I suppose *girlfriend* is a lot less complicated than *private investigator*. But your mom seems too nice to lie to, and I don't want to disappoint her when she learns the truth."

"Then maybe we make it the truth when Sunday is over." The words rushed out before Ethan could stop them.

He meant every one of them, but he'd told himself now wasn't the time.

A sad smile replaced Avery's grin as she took a cautious first step up the staircase. "You don't want to date a mess like me."

"You're no more of a mess than I am." Ethan kept his hand on her back as she inched up each step to avoid irritating her stitches. To his relief, she didn't pull away from him.

Her blue eyes clouded. "After today, I think I may have you beat."

How he wished he could give them a reason to sparkle again. "Who's keeping score?" He asked gently.

"Big Eddie."

The mention of his name broke the magic of the moment. Avery hadn't said *no*, and he would hold onto that.

For now, he had to help her stay focused on —taking down the elusive mob boss and saving Gianna.

He nodded toward a door at the top of the hallway. "Chloe's is the one on the right. Help yourself to whatever you need in the dresser and closet. Text me your prescription information when you have a chance, and then come downstairs whenever you're ready."

Avery paused at Chloe's door and turned to face him. His hoodie still wrapped around her narrow waist, accenting the hospital gown which made her suddenly look vulnerable. It took all the restraint in him not to wrap her in his arms. "Thank you, Ethan. I know I'm a miserable patient and difficult client. Thank you for being on my team."

He swallowed and gripped the staircase railing. "It's my pleasure. Now, take your time."

She shook her head. "Time is exactly what we don't have."

"We have till Sunday, Avery," Ethan said. "First, we take care of you, okay? Then, we make Big Eddie wish he never messed with you."

That made her smile. "Deal."

Chapter Forty-Five

A timid rap sounded at the door to his executive office at Epic Enterprises. Albert Costa knew the sound of failure before he even glimpsed his secretary's face.

"Come in."

Ambrose shuffled inside with a fresh mug of coffee, probably his attempt at an apology. His coffee was as offensive as his lack of confidence.

"Weber is on line two."

"I don't want to talk to Weber. I want to know the job is done."

His secretary's hands shook as he placed the mug on the edge of his mahogany desk, bumping his nameplate. Ambrose caught it before the plaque crashed to the floor. "Yes, sir. Sorry, sir."

"You know I hate apologies. Get out."

Ambrose retreated like a three-legged dog as Albert took the waiting call. "Why are you calling me at the office?" He growled into the phone.

"This is a secure line?" Weber asked.

He hated when his associates answered a question with a question. "Yes." His ensuing silence would do the threatening for him.

On the other end of the call, Weber cleared his throat. "Everything was going according to plan with a cherry on top. We had Russo and the investigator."

The *but* was coming. Albert closed his eyes and wondered what it would take to find one good man he could always rely on.

"I don't know what happened, but my sources say Arlos and Evans are in custody, Reynolds checked out of a nearby hospital an hour ago, and Russo is missing."

"Missing?" He hissed. "People don't just go missing. I want

to know where she is and what happened. Have you gotten Reynolds back?"

"She hasn't showed at her apartment, which is still roped off from the fire. We expected that would bring her running."

"Someone with a brain better than yours is helping her." He swore into the mouthpiece. "I want video footage of her leaving the hospital. Now."

"My guy is hacking into the ER security cameras as we speak." Weber paused. "Wait, he's got it. I'm pulling it up and sending it to your inbox."

Albert swatted his mouse to wake up his computer screen. "Who's with her?"

"Don't recognize him from this angle," Weber said. "He's the size of a linebacker. I'll run a scan on his face, but this footage is fuzzy."

His download was in progress, and Albert squinted once the clip loaded. How did Weber not recognize the security officer Albert had paid him to get off Reynold's case? Ethan Bridger was a fool not to take his hints and leave Reynolds alone. It was time to wreck him.

"It's Bridger," Albert said. "Check his place. No, he wouldn't have taken her there either, but in a pinch, he might have run to a family or friend's place."

Furious tapping made Albert smile. Maybe Weber wasn't totally useless.

"Bridger graduated from a local high school. Odds are his parents still live here."

"Then why are you talking to me? Make Bridger pay and find out what happened to Russo." Albert slammed down the receiver and then adjusted the plaque on his desk his incompetent secretary had bumped. The early afternoon sun beaming through his office windows made his engraved name glint.

Albert E. Costa.

Few knew what the E stood for, and those who did would not recognize the rest of his name. His middle name was a tribute to his grandfather who had paved his family's path into the Tampa underground. It was also a nod to the genius Edison, though some people suggested Edison stole Tesla's ideas to benefit himself.

Who knew if that were true, and the truth didn't matter to him.

What mattered was that he shared a name with a lineage of big men, and he aimed to be the biggest of them all.

Big Eddie.

Avery twisted to check her reflection in the floor length mirror of Chloe's bedroom. The dress was a little shorter than she'd like, but the gash in her leg ruled out any chance she'd be pulling on skinny jeans.

The problem now was how to conceal her gun. Avery checked the bottom dresser drawer and found a pair of shorts. She carefully slid them over her bandage. Wearing shorts under the skirt made her look hippy, but she wasn't here to impress anyone.

Why, then, did she feel self-conscious with the shorts?

"Get over it," Avery told herself and seated her handgun inside the waistline of the shorts under the dress. Why Ethan should want to date someone like her meant he must not be in his right mind, and she certainly wasn't if she entertained the idea, under the current conditions.

She checked the mirror once more. Her Glock bulged under the dress.

Nothing a sweater couldn't fix. She shrugged on a dark blue one. Paired with the yellow sundress, she must look like a happy summer day. She felt anything but.

The numbness around her stitches was wearing off, but nothing was worse than her fear that her one bargaining chip was on her way to the morgue. She needed to call the detective on the case to find out Russo's status, but first, she had to be polite to her host.

Taking the stairs slower than usual, Avery met silence in the entryway. Maybe Ethan was in the kitchen with his mom, and his deep voice wasn't echoing in the hallway. She followed the scent of banana bread to the kitchen where Nancy was cutting generous slices of bread onto two plates.

"No offense, but that dress looks like a million dollars on you compared to your fashion statement." She winked and passed her a plate. "I hope there was no serious reason you were wearing a hospital gown?"

"Thanks, it's only a scratch," Avery said.

To her credit, Nancy didn't press for details about her real occupation.

The warm bread smothered in butter made her somehow feel at home. "This is delicious."

"Thank you, it's one of Ethan's favorites." Nancy motioned to a bar stool. "Please, make yourself at home."

Avery slid onto the low stool which didn't put pressure on her stitches. "Speaking of Ethan, where is he?"

"He left for your prescription." Nancy poured her a glass of water. "You don't have to tell me what happened, but a mother knows what understatement looks like. You're welcome to rest back in Chloe's room or the living room. Your face tells me you could use it."

Avery chuckled. "Is that mother's intuition speaking?"

"Yes, it's a mothering instinct. Wait for your turn. You'll see."

Avery sipped her water to avoid saying something she'd regret. Her mother never exercised *motherly* anything, and Avery had long since let go of the idea of being a mother. The risk of being as rotten at parenting as her mother was not worth taking, though she hoped that somehow, she'd be different.

A chime sounded from somewhere nearby, and Nancy moved toward a monitor on the counter. "That was fast. Ethan must have—" But a frown creased her brow, and she didn't finish.

Avery set down her glass and slid to her feet. "What is it?"

"Ethan's rental car is silver, right?"

The hesitation in Nancy's tone formed a pit in Avery's stomach. "Yes, why?"

"The security monitor we set up showed a black car entered our driveway. Frank—my husband—is at a ranching show, and I don't recognize that vehicle."

Avery strode to the monitor. "Can you see the car now?"

Nancy shook her head. "No, this is more of a head's up for when our guests and kids come to visit. It's not a security system or anything."

"Do you have a safe room?" Avery asked.

"You mean like a kitchen pantry? Why? What's going on?" Nancy's eyes grew wide.

"I don't know, but I'm beginning to think coming here was a mistake. Wait in the pantry until I come get you—and call Ethan to let him know we have a visitor."

"But maybe it's a neighbor or someone needing directions."

The sinking feeling in her gut told Avery otherwise. "Maybe, but nothing is happening to you on my watch."

Nancy's mouth fell open. "Your watch?"

"I'm not your typical fashionista." Avery pulled up her skirt to draw her gun and held it at low ready. "Wait in the pantry, please?"

"When will Ethan ever bring home a nice girl and not a coworker?" Nancy mumbled as she retreated behind a door in the kitchen.

Avery couldn't help but smile. A simple, nice girl was what Ethan needed. She'd be sure to tell him so when he got back.

But first, she had to take care of whatever problems had found her at his family's home.

Chapter Forty-Six

Avery hugged the edges of the hallway and paused at the wall before the entryway. Ahead of her was the front entrance and double doors. A frosted glass panel on one side gave her a glimpse of a person poised by the door.

The bell rang. The shadow disappeared.

Avery waited. The person was probably hiding out of sight, waiting for someone to answer.

Any other day, she might take the offensive and try to get around him by exiting the house from a different entrance, but she didn't know the house or the grounds, and Ethan's mother didn't seem like the type to stay in a pantry for long.

Plus, her leg felt like someone was pricking her with half a dozen needles, and until she had more pain meds in her system, it would slow her down.

So, she waited some more. She patted the dress for her phone but came up empty. Must have left it in Ethan's hoodie in Chloe's room.

"Well, are you going to answer the door or not?" Nancy's whisper behind her sent her heart to her throat.

Avery waved her away. "Get back in the pantry."

Nancy crossed her arms. "It's been fifteen minutes, and I'd like to know what's going on."

A shadow reappeared in the glass beside the door, and Avery pushed Nancy behind her and held a finger to her lips.

There was a scratching sound, and the knob turned. Nancy shrieked and retreated, while Avery raised her handgun and aimed with her finger hovering above the trigger.

"Don't shoot. It's Ethan."

She sighed in relief and lowered her weapon. "Is it clear out there?"

"Yeah, all except for a large bouquet of flowers and a box of chocolates that the squirrels already got into." He poked his head around the corner. "Where's mom? I tried to call, but she didn't answer."

Avery tried to seat her handgun in her holster out of habit, but it met the silky fabric of her dress. "She was too busy ignoring my orders to stay in the pantry until I gave her the all clear."

"Ethan!" Nancy came running around the corner. "What a relief you're here! Did I hear you brought flowers?"

Ethan caught her in a hug while Avery stepped toward the doorway to inspect the delivery. Something still felt wrong. She surveyed the porch, and her gaze froze on what she saw past the bouquet of daisies.

"No, Mom, but someone did I think all the hype was a floral delivery."

"Oh, I love flowers! Let me see—"

But Avery whirled and blocked her path. "Ethan, please take your mom to the kitchen, and call poison control."

Nancy's face flushed, and she turned to Ethan. "Now, really, what is this about?"

But Ethan's focus shifted to Avery, and his eyes searched her face. "What is it?"

"You can thank whoever delivered those chocolates and flowers for serving as pest control." Avery swept her arm toward the porch.

There, two squirrels lay dead, with empty chocolate wrappings within reach of their rigid paws.

Blackie pushed a wet nose into Ethan's open palm, waking him with a start. Ethan ran a hand over his face and glanced at his phone on the bedstand. The time read a few minutes after six in the morning.

Even at his parents' house, he couldn't catch up on sleep, thanks to his dog who needed to go outside. Stiff from Audrey's too-firm mattress, Ethan tried to stretch. His muscles ached, probably still recovering from his crash. What he needed was a vacation.

"Let's go, girl." Ethan retrieved his gun and followed Blackie down the stairs. No son should have to carry on his home turf, but Big Eddie had brought the fight to his doorstep.

The thought of that delivery addressed to his mother made his blood boil. It was one thing to threaten a professional like him or Avery. Only a coward targeted innocent people like his mother.

Sure enough, the chocolates were laced with cyanide powder, which also coated several of the daisies. The white-colored powder could easily have been mistaken for pollen, but inhaling it—or ingesting it—could have sent his mom into a coma, seizures, unconsciousness, or worse. Avery had later shared with him that the analysis on Reef and Kaley's wedding cake sample showed it had also been tinged with cyanide. Coincidence? He doubted it.

Ethan scanned the fenced back yard for any litter, debris, or other packages before opening the screen door to let out Blackie. If Big Eddie was out to hurt his family, the man certainly wouldn't discount throwing something in the yard that would kill his dog too. "Make it quick, girl. Then I'll get your breakfast."

Blackie darted onto the lawn, and true to her training, came right back. With a sigh of relief, he closed and locked the door once she was back inside. While Blackie downed her dog food, Ethan started a pot of coffee. Liam promised to bring by Avery's packages this morning, and knowing Avery, she was already up and working on her phone.

She had certainly impressed the detective assigned to the school incident by apprehending Big Eddie's two thugs and putting Russo back in custody. The last report was that Russo hadn't been badly injured, which made Avery seem optimistic she would get permission to use her for Sunday.

Ethan pulled the largest mug he could find from a cabinet. Too bad he didn't share Avery's optimism. The odds of getting hold of Russo for tomorrow seemed slim to none, and since Russo was responsible for Avery's hospital visit, he didn't exactly want to see her anyway.

There had to be another alternative. Maybe when Liam arrived, the two of them could help Avery find a better plan B.

The hardwood floor in the hallway creaked behind him, and Ethan spun to find Avery there, wearing another of his sister's sundresses. This one was green, his favorite color on Avery, though he couldn't tell her that.

It fell above her knees and gave her the appearance of a much-younger woman. She had also left her hair down, and it was still damp and wavy from a shower. His chest tightened. He wanted to tell her how pretty she was, but she would never accept that compliment.

"You look rested," he said instead.

"I don't feel it." She beelined for the coffee. "Who knew a scratch could make it so hard to get comfortable and sleep."

Ethan pulled a second mug from the kitchen cabinet and slid it toward her. "Did you take the meds I picked up?"

"I forgot before bedtime, but I took some a few hours ago and now I feel like superwoman. Sometimes, I think my best work happens at five in the morning."

He knew better than to offer her cream. "When this is all over, you need an intervention—someone to take away all your electronic devices and put you on a cruise for a week."

She wrinkled her nose. "You make me sound like a teen who needs rehab."

Ethan sipped his coffee instead of responding. Was there such a thing as rehab for workaholics? He'd have to look into it.

"Anyway, I caught up on my texts and emails." Avery filled her mug to the brim. "There was an interesting text from Bert Costa. Did I tell you about him?"

"Nope, but I have a feeling you're going to," he said with a smile.

"He was one of the good-old boys in the signage industry I met at last weekend's football game and the only one who deigned to have a conversation with me. Anyway, he texted me late yesterday, inviting me to lunch with him today about a new product he thinks would be a good fit for the catalog I'm working on." Avery paused to gulp her coffee. "This is good."

Ethan needed more sleep or more coffee, because he had no idea what she meant. "Wait, what catalog do you mean?"

"It's a catalog for a sign company," Avery said. "Of course, it's kind of a problem since I don't actually work for the company. I told him I had an accident but could reach out next week. If all goes well Sunday, I won't need to."

Ethan topped off his mug. "I don't see how he could help either way."

"He knows Weber, who we suspect is somehow working for Big Eddie." Avery leaned against the counter. "Anyway, the odd part to me is that he invited me to lunch on a Saturday, which isn't a business day."

"Maybe he lost track or is simply a workaholic and assumes everyone else is too." Ethan topped off his mug. "Anyway, I have some news too. Jake checked into the situation with your apartment complex. He said they're letting people back in to get personal items today. I'd rather you not show yourself at the apartment, but he offered to get anything you need if you happen to have a hide-a-key somewhere."

Avery wrinkled her nose. "Yeah, I can't exactly wear a sundress to the stadium tomorrow. Doesn't your sister wear anything but shorts and dresses?"

He held up a hand. "Sorry, Chloe is a girly girl. Tori is more of the tomboy, but she's built differently than you." Ethan hoped that didn't sound offensive to either woman. They were both beautiful, just different.

"No problem, I appreciate these for today, but yes, I'll text you what I need and where he can find my spare key. I'd rather get the items myself, but I get what you and the detective are trying to do with both Russo and me, and I appreciate it." Avery pulled her phone from a pocket in the dress. "Thank goodness this one has pockets at least," she mumbled. "I've got a conference call with the case detective and Sheriff Hannaford at nine, so fingers crossed—"

"You two can talk shop on the porch." His mom appeared and grabbed her apron off a peg on the wall. She pecked his cheek like a mother-hen. "Now shoo, so I can make breakfast and not have to dance around you."

He laughed and kissed her cheek. "Yes, mother. We'll take our coffee and leave you alone."

Ethan held the porch door for Avery, and she settled onto a rocking chair. "More coffee?"

She held up a hand. "No, if I drink much more, I'm going to start shaking. I need my head on straight for the call."

Ethan claimed the rocker next to her. It sure felt good to be starting the day on the porch overlooking his childhood backyard. How nice it would be to have a home of his own like this one day, but he needed to focus on the present. "You think they're considering your idea about Russo?"

"They'd better be." Avery's bare feet tapped on the wooden floor as she pushed back and forth. Paired with the sundress, she looked like such a different woman than the no-nonsense investigator front she wore most of the time. He liked this laid-back version better.

"And if they don't?"

She turned to meet his gaze. "That's why Liam is delivering my package later today."

Ethan gave her space to explain, but she didn't, and he didn't press her. He'd see soon enough what plan B this woman had designed.

He prayed that whatever plan they orchestrated tomorrow, it would be the one that worked.

Chapter Forty-Seven

Good news was better than any pain killer. After that conference call, her natural adrenaline made Avery feel like Wonder Woman.

A car door slammed outside. She pulled back Chloe's curtains but couldn't see the driveway. It was probably Liam. She shot off a quick text to Bella, promising to call later and assuring her everything was falling into place for the exchange tomorrow.

She hesitated at the door and glanced down to her feet. She missed shoes, and she wasn't about to wear the disposable ones the hospital had sent her home in. Chloe's feet were smaller, so even her flipflops were uncomfortable. If Ethan's colleague couldn't get her clothes and shoes today, she would have to go shopping.

For now, she would plan tomorrow's operation barefoot.

A woman's voice coming from the entryway made her pause halfway down the stairs. The hallway echo muffled it a bit, but she knew that voice. "Jayna?"

Jayna spun toward the sound of her voice, causing her light gray dress to swish as if she were back on a modeling runway. "Avery!"

Avoiding her hug was about as impossible as preventing Bella's, so Avery didn't try. "What are you doing here?"

"I came with Liam to deliver your package, though I have a confession." Her olive complexion flushed.

"Where is Liam?" Avery used the question as an excuse to pull away from Jayna's hug.

"Oh, he's in the kitchen with Ethan. I was coming to find you and make sure you weren't working too hard." She smiled. "But about my confession. You see, Liam was on a call when he handed me the package, so I assumed it was for me. He's a terrible gift wrapper, but he knows gifts are my love language, and I was so excited he'd gotten me something that I tore into it before he realized what I was doing."

Love language? Avery's mind was spinning just trying to decode Jayna's sentences. What did that phrase even mean?

"So anyway, I'm so sorry, but nothing is damaged. I don't understand—"

"It's fine," Avery cut her off. "The good news is I won't be needing them now."

Jayna's face puckered in a question. "I don't understand why you would need them in the first place."

Avery winked. "And that, my dear, is why you should stick to baking and leave the investigating business to me."

Jayna rolled her eyes. "Remember that you once told me I'd make a good detective."

Their close call in the Bahamas had revealed a bravery she'd never expected from the ex-model and travel blogger, but the last thing she wanted was to see Jayna mixed up in any more dangerous situations. "Stick with your baking business. It's much more tasty and far less messy."

Liam stepped into the kitchen doorway at the end of the hall. "Thought I heard voices. How are you, Avery?"

"Better now." Avery hadn't felt this hopeful in weeks. "The lead detective is beyond grateful for what I did at the school and apprehending the two men and Russo. He personally knows the officials in charge of Russo's prison, explained the situation with Gianna, and convinced them that if I could handle all three by myself, I could babysit Russo for a mock exchange and see that she's returned. I'm coordinating all the details with the prison so that Russo and I arrive at the stadium together. They are going to work with Sheriff Hannaford's undercover team to monitor us and provide security."

Avery paused for breath. She'd been talking too fast and mostly to Ethan, who understood better than Liam how high the stakes were to rescue Gianna.

"That's great." Ethan was mid-bite into a leftover biscuit from his mom's Southern breakfast. "I'm kind of shocked they agreed to let you have Russo. Wasn't she shot trying to escape yesterday?"

If she believed in fate, Russo's gunshot wound location was her saving grace. "It was a shoulder injury, and it probably hurts like crazy, but her two feet still work. With some pain killers and careful bandaging, she'll be fine."

Jayna circled past her to Liam's side. He picked up an opened packing envelope on the counter. "So, I'm guessing you won't be needing these?"

The custom silicone masks Avery had ordered were the reason for Liam's trip today. "Thankfully not. Those were a backup plan in case—" She paused and glanced at Ethan. As far as she knew, he hadn't told anyone her other crazy plan to get custody of Russo.

"That's Russo's face?" Jayna wrinkled her nose as she glanced at a slip of paper poking out the envelope. It was the proof copy Avery had approved. Jayna then pulled her phone from her back pocket and started typing something into it.

"That's her." Avery stepped around her to reach into the package and select one of the two masks she had purchased. She held it up for the group to see. "The resemblance is decently accurate, but the quality isn't the best. From a distance, it could work, but close-up, we wouldn't fool anyone."

"I found a picture of her online." Jayna flashed the image on her phone. "The mask isn't bad, and if someone like me wore it, I could be fairly convincing since my skin tone is similar and I'm—" She blushed and didn't finish.

"You're a curvy model who could more than match Russo's Hollywood glamour," Avery finished for her. It was true, after all. "But I would never let you go undercover, let alone around the same group that got your ex-fiancé killed." Maybe she was too blunt, but the look in Jayna's eye made her worry what ideas her friend might be having.

"How exactly were you going to pose as yourself and as Russo?" Liam crossed his arms.

"Don't worry about it." Avery inserted the mask back into the envelope. "You should be focusing on your own rest and recovery, but I appreciate you driving out here to deliver my package."

Liam arched an eyebrow and exchanged a look with Ethan.

"Rest and recovery? I've done plenty of that. The woman who was in the ER yesterday needs to do more of that herself."

Avery shrugged off the comment. "I'll take a break after that sweet girl is back in her mama's arms. Until then, I have work to do."

Ethan stepped to the sink and turned on the water, probably to wash the remnants of biscuit off his fingers. "*We* have work to do." He caught her gaze, and the look in his eyes made her chest swell with something that felt like hope.

Avery nodded. "Let's bring Gianna home—and take Big Eddie down."

Chapter Forty-Eight

It was game day. It was go-time.

Avery flexed her toes inside her black suede boots, the only piece of her outfit that seemed fitting for the black SUV limousine. She had traded her usual dark-wash jeans for stretchy black cotton pants that would rub less against her stitches. As for her charcoal blazer—well, its job was to conceal her Glock 19.

Across from her, Russo sat handcuffed, and the ex-Hollywood producer seemed unusually tight-lipped. Maybe her gunshot wound was smarting, or maybe she was inventing a hundred possible ways to escape the minute her handcuffs were off.

Let her try.

The adrenaline pumping through Avery could take down a dozen Russos.

Avery's one doubt was that today's plan seemed too perfect. The stretch limo had been Sheriff Hannaford's idea, and it was brilliant. It was the flashiest way to attract attention—and let Big Eddie know she was here, she had Russo, and she meant business.

His last cell phone communication had been vague on details but showed a timestamped picture of Gianna holding up a cardboard sign that read, "Ready?"

She had immediately texted back, "Ready with Russo," and the response she'd received was, "Pick up your tickets at Will Call. See you at the game."

So Big Eddie was buying Russo's and her tickets. How generous of him. Her one concern with that plan was he was calling the shots. A sniper could take her out once he confirmed Russo was seated beside her.

Ethan had wanted her to tell Big Eddie no, she had bought her own tickets, but Avery refused to do anything that might jeopardize Gianna. If she took a bullet to the head, she took a bullet to the head. Besides, even if she didn't sit in the seats Big Eddie had handpicked, the man had more eyes than a sea scallop.

But she had her own contingencies—Ethan and some of his partners from Semper Security, Sheriff Hannaford's undercover team, and security from Russo's prison who were monitoring her movements using the GPS tracker bracelet on her ankle. If Avery took a hit, they'd handle Russo and hopefully recover Gianna without her.

"You have to know you're going to lose." Russo arched a manicured eyebrow.

"Says the woman wearing handcuffs and a tracker." Avery yawned into her palm. "Hope you enjoy your taste of freedom today, because your field-trip privileges have been permanently suspended after your stint at the school."

Russo shrugged. "School programs aren't really my thing. Football games and high stakes prisoner exchanges are more my style."

This woman needed a reality check. "You don't have style anymore, Russo. You have a life sentence. Don't forget the reason you're here is to save a child's life. Today is not about you."

With a bored chuckle, Valentina nodded. "Oh, I'm sorry. You're right. Today is not about me. Today is about you—the end of you."

Avery ignored Russo and checked her phone. The woman was trying to crawl under her skin, and Avery wasn't giving her that satisfaction. She shot off a message to Ethan. "When you're bored one day, listen to the recording of this car ride. It will make you spit out your coffee."

On second thought, she shouldn't be texting her driver.

A glance out the tinted windows showed the stadium looming ahead. The October afternoon sky shone a cloudless blue as the Buccaneer flag greeted stadium goers, who seemed decked out in costume more than ever because the game fell on Halloween.

"What a party this is going to be," Russo purred as Ethan slowed to a stop at the drop-off area near Gate D.

"Isn't this spot for people with disabilities?" Russo laughed.

"You don't need to know the plan, Russo." Avery unlocked her cuffs and snapped on a wrist leash that connected Russo to herself. "You do exactly as I say, understand?"

"Oooh, so I get to act like a disabled person, is that it?" Russo inspected her new locking wrist cuff and the bright yellow coil that connected her to the matching cuff on Avery's wrist.

Avery hoped her glare would shut her up. "You don't need to act anything. People with disabilities are much nicer and deserve far more respect than you do. Now, let's go."

Whatever Russo mumbled was lost in the buzz coming from fans entering the stadium. After a stop at will-call to get their tickets, Avery kept a firm hand on Russo's back as she led them to the specified entrance for security personnel.

While another security agent scanned Russo, Avery completed her own screening and then slid her hair over her ear to help conceal her tactical earpiece with mic. "We're in. Over."

"Roger," Liam replied almost instantly. He hadn't been happy about being left out of the action, but managing the comm seemed to console him.

As they exited security and rejoined the crowds headed to find their seats, Russo flipped her wrist so the bungee cord between their wrist cuffs moved like a jump rope. "Watching you fail is going to be so fun today."

Avery reeled in the bungee cord and squeezed Russo's arm. "Watching you fall on your face because you're not paying attention will also be fun. Now be quiet and follow my lead."

Russo exaggerated an eye roll but complied. Finding their seats took less time than Avery expected, and soon, they were climbing over other fans eating hot dogs and drinking large sodas to get to their seats. It would have been more convenient if Big Eddie had purchased aisle seats.

"I'd like a soda." Russo sank into her seat and pouted. "You could at least keep me hydrated."

Avery ignored her complaints to examine their seats. A visual inspection didn't show any type of tampering. She looked under her seat before folding it down. All clear.

"Check under your seat," Avery told Russo.

"What?" Russo leaned back. "I just sat down."

"Use your hands. Or get up and look."

"Eww, no." Russo wrinkled her nose. "I'm not slapping someone's old gum."

Avery tugged at the bungee cord to jerk Russo's arm into action. "It wasn't a request. Do it."

"Oww! That's my hurt shoulder," Russo whined. "You owe me a soda for that."

"I owe you nothing, but I might get you a soda if you behave."

Russo leaned forward and reached under her seat. "Hang on. There's something taped here."

"Get up and let me look."

For once, Russo didn't argue but traded seats with her. She probably expected a bomb and didn't want to be the one blown up by it.

But the taped device wasn't a bomb. It was a walkie talkie.

A smirk snaked across Russo's lips as Avery pulled off the last of the tape. "Let the game begin."

She wasn't referring to football. "Liam, we found a walkie talkie under my seat. I'm expecting contact soon. Over."

"You can expect more than contact." Russo waggled her eyebrows. "I can almost taste my freedom—and that soda you still owe me."

The words had no sooner left Russo's lips than the walkie talkie crackled, and a man's deep voice spoke. "Make your way to the nearest concession stand."

Avery frowned. She hadn't been expecting a warm hello, but the simple command rubbed her the wrong way—as if she were a programmed robot following commands.

Her feelings didn't matter. What mattered was following the instructions and getting Gianna back.

Ignoring another comment from Russo about wanting a soda, Avery led them back up the stairs toward concessions. "Following instructions to go to concessions," she spoke into her discreet mouthpiece.

"We're tracking you," Liam said, "and I'm monitoring you on the surveillance cameras too. Don't be a hero if something isn't right. Backup isn't far away."

"Roger that."

The line for soda, hotdogs, and popcorn wound like a rope that needed straightening.

Russo tipped up her sunglasses to study the menu. "I'd like some popcorn too. You've got to have popcorn to watch a show. It adds to the entertainment value."

"There's not going to be a show, Russo."

"Oh, I think there is. You've got this cut and dry plan in your head, but you should know by now that nothing goes as planned when Big Eddie is involved." She shook out her long, wavy hair. "In fact—"

Avery stopped listening. A guerilla of a man strode toward them, like a missile on a target. Something told her popcorn wasn't on his mind. Oddly, he seemed familiar.

Tugging Russo closer, Avery spoke into her mouthpiece. "Suspect wearing a Bucs jersey and wide brim pirate hat—"

The man grabbed her by the elbow before she could finish. "Don't say another word and come with me." He hooked his arm around hers as if they were best friends and pulled her from the line.

Avery tensed but followed his lead with Russo skipping like a schoolgirl a few feet behind them.

You're fine. This is what you want. He's taking you to Big Eddie. You're going to have Gianna back.

Her self-talk did little to quell the alarm bells sounding in her head. The man's hat would obscure his face from security cameras. Liam's voice in her ear requested an update, and she didn't dare give him one.

He could track them, using Russo's ankle bracelet. Even if they couldn't see this man's face, they would recognize her and Russo in the surveillance cameras.

As if reading her thoughts, Liam spoke again in her earpiece. "Cameras have gone on the fritz, freaking out. I need you to talk to me."

Seconds later, Ethan's voice broke into the one-way conversation. "Avery, do you copy?" The tenseness to his tone made her breath hitch. He was worried.

Avery gritted her teeth and focused on their trajectory. Her memory of the stadium layout from last week's job suggested they were heading toward the lower-level suites. Big Eddie would be sinking at least ten thousand to rent one of those during the game.

Her guerrilla gatekeeper paused in front of a family restroom. "Get in."

Avery dug her heels into the pavement. She wasn't going down until she had Gianna. "Not with you."

With a grunt, the man tapped his ear and said, "Put her on." Then, pulling out his earpiece, he handed it to her. She swallowed and held it close to her free ear.

Someone sniffled. "A-Avery?"

Avery's heart squeezed. "Gianna? Is that you?"

"Avery! Please, please come get me. Take me home—" But there was a cry, and Gianna's voice disappeared.

Avery thrust the earpiece back at the man. "Take me to her. Now."

"Not until you follow orders." Her nodded toward the family restroom again. "Get. In."

"Fine." She yanked open the door and stepped inside. She had taken down two thugs at once. She could handle him.

"Ooh, wait for me." Russo hurried in behind the man. "Don't want to miss this party."

The door thudded closed, and Avery braced herself. The man held out his hand. "Earpiece."

Avery had guessed as much. She pulled back her hair and removed the discreet ear and mouthpiece combination. The man tossed it in the trash.

Russo stood by the door as if to block her exit and crossed her arms. "She's got a gun."

The man's gaze swept over her. "Hand it over, or I take it."

Avery's hand went to her hip. "This is a prisoner exchange, not a disarmament."

The man's face remained like stone. "You want the girl to die? Give me the gun."

Exhaling her frustration, Avery retrieved her Glock and

handed it to him. As before, he tossed it in the trash can.

"Anything else, Val?"

His familiarity with Val set off more warning bells and triggered her memory. "Wait, are you—"

"Yes, he's my darling Louis Caputo's cousin," Val purred. "Isn't that delicious? Big Eddie doesn't miss a beat when it comes to details."

Louis Caputo. Val's henchman Avery put behind bars the same time as Val.

"I'm first in line to snap your neck." His words were a low growl.

"Now, now, Cappy, that's no way to talk just yet." Russo petted his arm the way someone might pet a Doberman. "The fun is only getting started, but I need this ankle bracelet gone first."

Still leveling her with his eyes, "Cappy" pulled a pair of cutting pliers from under his jersey. "Watch her."

"Oh, she'll behave." Russo pulled up the bottom of her jeans to expose the ankle bracelet. "She doesn't have a choice, do you, sweetheart?"

"You can save your sappy sarcasm, Russo." Avery tried to ignore the hollow space in her holster. "You're going right back in the slammer after today."

"Oh, princess, you've got such spirit." With a sharp clip, Russo's tracker fell to the floor, and "Cappy" tossed it in the trash with the rest of Avery's contingency plans. "I wish I could stick around long enough to watch Big Eddie crush it."

"Yada yada yada." Avery twirled her finger in a *let's wrap this up* motion. "I've heard all this before. Can we move on?"

Russo snapped open the door. "With pleasure."

"Cappy" once more claimed her arm, pinching it even more tightly in his, as they navigated through crowds and continued their descent to the lower-level suites.

Finally, they stopped in front of a suite door, and Caputo's cousin released her arm while mumbling into his own mouthpiece. Russo smirked beside her like a snitch with a secret she couldn't wait to sink her teeth into. That woman would be the death of her nerves.

Or the death of her. Period.

The door to the private luxury suite cracked open enough for "Cappy" to shove Avery through.

She whirled in time to watch Russo blow her a mock kiss. "Au revoir, darling. Thanks for my ticket to freedom. I've got a ship to catch."

Heat flamed Avery's cheeks. She wasn't Russo's ticket. Russo was hers. Without Russo, where did that leave her?

"Avery!" Gianna cried, and Avery turned in time to catch the little girl as she jumped into her arms.

Avery fell to her knees, cradling the child. "Oh, Gianna, you're all right? I'm so sorry for all this. I'm taking you home."

"Ciao, bella. You're not going anywhere."

That voice. It couldn't be. Avery wrapped Gianna more tightly in her arms. Dread chilling her core, Avery's gaze swept past Gianna to a man with a cane.

Chapter Forty-Nine

"She's gone dark. I repeat. Avery has gone dark." Liam's words drove a knife into Ethan's gut. The scenario he had dreaded was happening.

Phone in hand, Ethan jogged toward the nearest stairway. He had been waiting on the level above Avery's location, following her orders not to shadow too closely. "Russo's tracker has stopped moving, but you probably see that too," he spoke into his mouthpiece.

"Yes." Liam's grim tone expressed exactly how he felt.

"I'm almost to the tracker's location." He took the stairs by two. With the game having started, the walkways were less crowded. He paused in front of a family restroom and tried the handle. "It's a restroom. Unoccupied."

He breathed a prayer Avery wasn't here. If she was, she would probably be dead. "I'm going in."

Using his foot, he tapped the door open and used the wall as a shield in case someone was waiting inside.

But the bathroom was empty. Slipping inside, he locked the door behind him to inspect further and immediately checked around the trash. Nothing.

The bag was nearly full with used paper towels. He shook it, and something thudded. There was something heavy inside. If only he had gloves, but now wasn't the time to be squirmy about germs. He wrapped clean paper towels around his hands for some protection and reached into the trash.

Halfway down, his makeshift glove caught something.

Russo's ankle bracelet. That wasn't good.

Avery's earpiece wasn't far beneath it. His heart sank as he caught sight of a gun at the bottom of the bin. No doubt it was also Avery's.

Gagging at a smell he'd rather not identify, he retrieved the Glock, the same model she carried.

As he scrubbed his hands and arms with soap and water, he made his report. "She's unarmed and muted. I found her gun and earpiece, along with Russo's bracelet. Any luck getting the surveillance cameras to work again?"

"Yeah, they acting fine now." Liam snorted. "Security said it must have been a glitch."

A very convenient glitch.

"I have Russo's bracelet now, so you can track me that way." He dried his hands with a paper towel.

"She could be anywhere," Liam said. "And if Russo escaped Avery's custody, Big Eddie will have no reason to return Gianna."

Or keep Avery alive. His throat went dry at the thought.

"Hold on!" Liam's voice rose an octave. "We've got something."

"You found Avery?" Ethan tossed the paper towel into the bin. He never wanted to dig around in one of those again if he could help it.

"No, but Hannaford's team monitoring the surveillance cameras spotted Russo heading toward an exit, accompanied by a man. No sign of Avery."

"Tell them to catch her and find out what happened."

"They've got two teams converging on her now, but knowing Russo, she won't talk. She never has cooperated with us."

Ethan grunted. He'd make her talk. That wasn't a Christian thought, was it? "I've got to find the route they took after leaving this bathroom." Ethan exited the restroom and scanned the hallway. A caterer pushed a large cart down the walkway. He would start with him. "We'll find them. The last report Avery made was about someone wearing a Bucs jersey and pirate hat."

"That describes the man with Russo now—and pretty much half the fans in this stadium." The exasperation in Liam's voice wasn't lost on him. "Maybe we need to play Big Eddie's game."

"Buy a Buc's jersey?" Ethan asked.

"No, hold a few surprises in our hand."

"Are we talking about Big Eddie or about a card game? I'm

not following." Ethan had almost caught up with the caterer. "Listen, I need to go."

"Go do your search. Hopefully Hannaford's team will catch Russo. If not, I'll work on plan B. Over."

Whatever plan B Liam had in mind, Ethan hoped they wouldn't need it.

Avery jumped to her feet and tucked Gianna into her side as Albert Costa tapped the floor in front of her with his cane. "You. It was you all along?"

Gone was the grandfatherly façade. The intelligent eyes no longer twinkled. They smoldered and gloated.

"I thought I might have found a worthy nemesis in you, Avery Reynolds, but you can't see the nose on your face. You are both a fool and a failure and frankly not worth my time."

"Then I won't take any more of it." Avery backed toward the door. "You have Russo, and now I have Gianna."

"You have nothing." Costa flicked his wrist, and two men snapped into place in front of the door, blocking her exit, while two other men waited behind Costa.

Avery's pulse pounded in her ears. She was unarmed. She couldn't protect Gianna or fight her way out of this one.

"I thought the mafia had morals." She spat and gripped Gianna's shoulders more tightly. "You called this deal, and now you back out of it? I know Big Eddie to be a lot of things, but I never guessed *coward* was one of them."

"I am *not* a coward." He smacked his cane so hard against the floor that even the walls must have winced. "You simply have nothing to barter in your possession. I had Russo before you even arrived."

Avery glared back at him. "Because I followed your instructions."

"Your mistake." Costa whispered something to the man at his right, and he strode toward the bar, returning moments later with a large, enclosed beverage service cart.

"Don't let them take me again," Gianna whimpered and buried her face in Avery's side.

Avery hugged her even tighter. "Let her go, Costa. You can keep me if you want, but she's a child."

Costa inspected his nails. "Can't. I've already got a buyer—and a high ticket one at that. Some men prefer children, you know."

Bile rose in her throat. She had to get Gianna out of here. "You're despicable. Let her go."

In a flash, Costa swung his cane at her face. Avery jerked back, and it missed by mere inches. "No one tells Big Eddie what to do." His words were a growl.

The men by the door were too close, and Avery couldn't fight them with Gianna clinging to her. "Trust me," she whispered in the girl's ear. Louder, she said, "At least tell me this–where do you get *Eddie* from Albert Costa?"

A crooked grin traced across his dull lips. "It's from Edison, my middle name. From one genius to another, you could say."

"A genius doesn't trample on others to make himself great."

"Oh, I don't trample people." Big Eddie edged closer. "They bow."

Her time was out. In one smooth movement, Avery pushed Gianna under the adjacent bar and temporarily out of anyone's reach. She ducked to avoid the men grabbing at her from behind and rolled toward Big Eddie, sweeping one leg ahead of her to knock the cane from his hand and his feet from underneath him.

Pain shot through her leg. She'd ripped her stitches. Didn't matter. She had to get that cane.

His thick hand landed on top of hers and squeezed like a meat cleaver, but she refused to let go of her grip on the cane. She elbowed his rib cage, which elicited a string of profanity and a brief release of his hand.

But she couldn't move the cane fast enough. Three boulders of men tackled her. One jerked the cane from her grip, while the others pinned her to the ground.

A fourth man extended a hand to Big Eddie, who kneeled next to her, but he waved him off. "Syringe. Now."

It couldn't end this way. Their oppressive strength and fear of her own ability to move were suffocating. She screamed in rage and tried one last thrust to extricate herself, but their grips tightened. Gianna's sobs nearby made her skin crawl. She had to save her. She had to—

A needle stabbed her neck, and she groaned in pain. The room began to fade quickly. "Failure. You are a failure," Big Eddie hissed in her ear.

Yes, she had failed. Failed Bella. Failed Gianna. Failed them all.

Chapter Fifty

Ethan jogged toward the beverage cart attendant and tried to mentally phrase his question.

Have you seen a kidnapped woman? Have you seen the woman I'm falling in love with? Have you seen a beautiful woman who is also fiercely brave, stubborn, and intelligent?

None of those would do.

"Excuse me! Have you seen a woman with blondish-brown, kind of red hair—maybe in an argument with someone?" He blurted instead.

The man jumped as if lightning had struck him. "Uh no, I can't help you." He picked up his pace as if Ethan had a disease.

Odd.

Ethan strode after him. "You mean you haven't seen anyone come this way?"

"No." The man muttered.

But the stadium was buzzing with fans, and this hallway, though fairly quiet, was far from empty.

"Can I at least buy a beverage then?" Ethan asked.

"All out."

A beverage cart worker without a beverage to sell? Something wasn't adding up. What also wasn't adding up was how hard the man was pushing the cart. Soda cans couldn't weight that much. Also odd was that the cart had one large door on the side, not a series of smaller drawers like other carts he'd seen.

Ethan wasn't here to make friends. With a running start, he slid into the cart and pulled at the door handle. The man swore as it swung open—

And a woman tumbled out.

Her hands and feet tied, she struck the floor with her head.

The attendant sprinted for the nearest exit.

Ethan wanted to chase him, but the woman was sobbing—and other people were gawking at them, or more specifically, the woman who was wearing a mini skirt and tight sports top. The makeup on her face couldn't hide bruises.

There was no point asking the woman if she was all right. She clearly wasn't. Ethan stooped beside her. "Who did this to you? Where are they?"

"Th—thank you for finding me." She continued to sob while hugging her knees to her chest. "G—get me out of here. D-on't give me back to the man with the cane."

Maybe she would share more once she felt safe. "I need backup now near the lower-level suites," he said, more loudly than he probably needed to for his earpiece to pick up. "I've found a possible trafficking victim. Her handler fled. Avery must be close, but I can't pursue until this woman is safe in our custody."

Liam's response came quickly. "Hannaford's team is on their way."

"Tell anyone watching surveillance to look for large beverage carts. The woman was inside one."

Liam whistled in his ear. "You're kidding me. In a beverage cart?"

"Yeah, a modified one with two large panels."

The small crowd gathering was the last thing Ethan wanted. "Give us some space. Police are on their way." The poor woman on the floor buried her head in her arms.

What felt like an eternity later, two members from Hannaford's team arrived. Ethan briefed them and then took off running toward the door the man had exited. Propping it open revealed a service door, but pursuing might take him out of the stadium and farther away from Avery.

"Where are you, Avery?" he whispered.

"Hey, Ethan? You there?" Liam's voice cut through his thoughts.

"Yeah, talk to me." Ethan stepped back into the hallway.

"You're not going to believe this, but we've spotted five suspicious service carts. Two aren't far from you. Keep going down the hall you're on to find the first one."

Liam didn't have to tell him twice. Ethan took off sprinting.

"Slow down, you're close—"

But with the cart in view, Ethan sped up. The fans in the hallway—and this group's fear of exposure—were his best weapons.

This attendant was twice the size of the last one, but the eyes on his beard-crusted face widened in surprise when Ethan rammed into the cart and jerked the door open.

A small form crumpled out, and Ethan's heart twisted in his chest. *Gianna.*

The man lunged for her, but Ethan jumped on top of him. "Liam, I need backup!" He grunted as the man's elbow connected with his stomach. Ethan kneed him in the groin and hopped off to avoid an elbow to the face.

As the man tried to limp to his feet, Ethan pulled his gun and ignored a woman who screamed a few feet away. "Freeze. Put your hands in the air where I can see them."

Slowly, the man complied. Ethan glanced at Gianna, who hadn't moved. "What's wrong with her?"

"Drugged," he snorted.

"Where is he?" Ethan demanded.

"Who?"

"You know who."

The man shrugged. "I'll never tell."

"Ethan, we've got Russo in custody, but there's a problem," Liam's voice broke into his thoughts. "Also, the other carts are about to exit the stadium. I've got agents tracking two of them, but the others we can't get to fast enough."

Avery. Was she in one of them? But he had Gianna, and he had to make sure she was safe. That was what Avery wanted the most.

Ethan's gaze darted to the man's posterior and a cell-phone

bulge in his back pocket. In one swift motion, he snatched the phone from his pocket.

"Hey!" the man growled and turned.

"Hands on the wall!" Ethan barked as footsteps pounded the walkway behind him.

"Team 2 should be there," Liam said.

Sweet relief. He nodded his welcome to the police officers, who made quick time of cuffing the man. Ethan bent down and checked Gianna's pulse. It was sluggish but steady. "She's breathing, thank God."

"What's wrong with her?" a female officer asked.

"Drugged, apparently. We need a medical team." The words no sooner left his mouth than the woman called in an order on her phone.

Ethan's focus shifted to the phone he had snatched from the man's pocket. It showed a message to unlock using a fingerprint ID. The second officer had the suspect's hands cuffed behind his back. Perfect.

"I need his print." He flashed the phone at the officer, who nodded. The suspect grunted in protest when Ethan snatched his wrist and pressed his index finger onto the scanner.

Bingo. Ethan quickly navigated to settings and disabled the security feature so the phone wouldn't lock on him. A glance through his email revealed the man's username as Burt Not Reynolds. At least the guy had a sense of humor.

Scrolling through his text messages revealed one number called The Job. That had to be the one he needed. He started typing a new message.

Burt Not Reynolds is in custody, and we have Russo. If you want to see Russo again, meet me with Avery in one hour at—

"Liam, can you suggest a nearby meetup location?" Ethan's fingers hovered over his new message to The Job. "I'm going to use this thug's phone to send a message—swap Russo for Avery."

"Yes and no," Liam said. "Busch Gardens and Lowry Park Zoo are nearby, but both require passes. Rowlett Park is close, and there probably isn't a fee to enter."

Ethan imagined not. The park wasn't in the greatest section of town, but that would be right up Big Eddie's ally. Plus, if he told him to meet near the dam adjacent to the park, Ethan would have an open view of when they arrived. "Great, I'll suggest the park."

"There's a problem, but I'm handling it," Liam added.

"What?" Ethan's fingers hesitated over the phone's touch screen.

"Russo is on her way back to maximum security. No way will they agree to let us use her again when she almost escaped."

"But without Russo, we've got nothing." Ethan's gaze swept over to the suspect in custody. "Big Eddie could care less about one underling."

"We've got Avery's masks. I've already got Jayna enroute with them."

"Wait, what?" Ethan jerked the phone to make sure he had heard right. "You're bringing Jayna into this?"

"She wanted to help, and we don't have much time to get Avery back. When people disappear into Big Eddie's underworld, they don't return."

Never seeing Avery again was not an option. "Okay, I'll text and demand an exchange at Rowlett Park in one hour. Does that give us enough time to get ready?"

"We can't afford to give Big Eddie more time than that. We don't even know if he'll take the bait," Liam said.

"Can you get me a screen shot of Russo getting taken into custody from the surveillance cameras? That will be our bait."

"Give me two minutes."

While waiting, Ethan finished typing his message and prayed their plan would work. If it didn't—no, he wouldn't think that way.

His phone pinged, confirming Liam had sent the image. Ethan snapped a picture of it using Burt Not Reynold's phone and added it to his message.

He pressed send and then glanced up as paramedics rolled onto the scene with a stretcher for Gianna. The female officer hovered as the EMTs lifted Gianna into it.

Ethan hurried over to her. "Could you stay with her? She's been kidnapped for a week, and we can't let her fall into the wrong hands again."

The officer nodded. "Sheriff Hannaford briefed me, and I can stay with her until her parents meet us at the hospital. Hannaford contacted them, and they're on their way."

"Thank you." Relief seeped through him. Avery would want to know Gianna was cared for. "Here's my number. Call me if you need anything."

"Will do."

Burt Not Reynold's phone vibrated, and Ethan held his breath as he opened the message that contained a simple thumb's up.

Ethan gritted his teeth and jogged toward the closest exit. "I'm coming, Avery."

Chapter Fifty-One

Golden hour lacked its usual warmth. Ethan attached a cargo ramp to the back of Liam's borrowed truck he had staged in an empty parking lot at Rowlett Park. Using Burt Not Reynold's phone, he texted the pin of his exact location to The Job so Big Eddie and his men would know where to find him.

Then, Ethan navigated a first utility cart, then a second, down the ramp. He had weighed both down with an even number of bricks so they dragged as if a person were inside. The carts weren't identical to the beverage ones in the stadium, but Big Eddie would get the idea.

Jayna, disguised as Russo, was not actually inside either one. Instead, she and Liam waited at the park near the dam, posing as photographers. Jayna was dressed with a face scarf so no one could see her mask.

Two of Liam's colleagues were also stationed nearby where they could jump into action or call the sheriff's office if their plans went south. Ethan's own boss Jake had volunteered to launch his kayak into the waterway for an extra pair of eyes.

Hannaford and his crew were still sorting through the mess at Raymond James where a second woman had been recovered in another beverage cart. They were also searching for evidence in the suite she was able to direct them to. Of course, Big Eddie was long gone by then.

Ethan could only hope he was on his way here with Avery, but he was no fool to think he would come alone. Ethan certainly hadn't.

The phone vibrated with another thumbs-up and the words, ETA 1 minute.

"Be with me, Lord," Ethan breathed and stationed himself between the two carts. He focused on the road to the parking lot.

Any minute, Avery could be here.

One minute ticked away, then two, then five. The phone remained silent.

Ethan retrieved his personal cell and texted Liam. *They said they'd be here five minutes ago. No show.*

Liam texted back almost instantly. *A boat entered the waterway a few minutes ago. Someone yanked off a tarp ...*

His phone rang. It was Liam. He wasn't supposed to call. "Get over here, man. The tarp was covering a beverage cart. They're shoving it toward the edge of the boat. They're close to the dam."

Ethan bolted into the truck's driver's seat, leaving his utility carts behind. If Avery were in that cart, every second counted. He sped past a dog park to where the grass ended and the river began.

He speed-dialed his boss. "Jake, can you get to the dam? Liam's spotted a boat there, and it looks like they're about to dump a beverage cart."

"I see them. I can get there in less than five minutes." Jake disconnected.

Jumping out of the parked truck, Ethan spotted Jake's kayak and the boat as two men shoved the utility cart overboard right next to the water pounding the base of the dam.

No! His heart lunged into his throat. Swimming would never get him there in time. Jake was his only hope.

Dear God, help Avery.

The hair on his neck prickled, and he spun, expecting to see someone there.

But there was no one. Ethan searched the vicinity. He knew that feeling, the feeling of being watched.

There. In the distance, where the earth met the dam, was a lone man with a cane.

Big Eddie smiled as he watched his men haul the beverage cart over the side of the boat into the water near the dam falls. He could have gotten a pretty price for Avery, but this end to her story was much more satisfying—especially because of Ethan Bridger's reaction.

The man had thought himself so clever to arrange a swap for Russo by staging his own carts. But those had proven empty like Bridger's poorly executed plans.

Whether Bridger even had Russo in his custody was debatable. Even if he did, Big Eddie could care less. Russo had served her purpose. He didn't need her.

There were plenty of other pliable women he could leverage for his purposes. With Avery out of the way, no one was even attempting to dog his path. There would no doubt be more run-ins with the sheriff's office, but Hannaford didn't have the manpower to dedicate to chasing a ghost.

Yes, Big Eddie was a ghost. Uncatchable. Unstoppable.

And Avery? She was many things, but she wasn't a fish.

He blew a mock kiss toward the dam's falls. "Caio, Bella."

Slam! Her head collided with metal, and water sprayed onto her face. Where was she? Why was breathing so hard?

The rolling motion gave her no time to think. Her prison rammed into something else, and a door burst open. Water gushed inside.

She had to move. Kicking through the opening revealed a new problem.

Her hands were bound, but her eyes could now focus. She was underwater, in fresh water, since her eyes didn't sting. The cart she'd left crashed into a rock just ahead, and she thrust upward to miss hitting it.

So close to the surface.

But her legs couldn't kick hard enough to make up for her bound wrists. She sunk back down and tried to ignore her screaming lungs. The water wasn't that deep, but if she couldn't get air—

God, help.

She couldn't die this way. She had so much left unfinished. She had no faith there was an afterlife, and if there was, she wasn't ready.

With her last ounce of strength, she kicked off the rocky floor one more time.

Almost there, almost—

Something darkened the water overhead. She stretched out her cuffed hands, hoping to touch the surface.

But she was sinking again. Sinking. She cried out, but water filled her lungs, choking her.

You can't save yourself, but I already died to save you.

She must be hallucinating. She forced herself to look up.

A hand plunged toward her, grasping the cuffs binding her wrists and jerking her upward.

Chapter Fifty-Two

The cool evening air slapped Avery's face. All she could do was sputter and gasp for breath. Whoever had reached under the water was holding onto her shirt and pulling her onto the side of his kayak, which wobbled hard with her extra weight.

"Hang on!" The man's voice seemed familiar, but she couldn't place it. With one hand, he gripped her shirt, and with the other, he tried to navigate the river with his paddle.

Hang on? The guy had a twisted sense of humor. She could only do so much with her wrists in cuffs, but her hand found an indent in the kayak, and she dug in her fingers.

This must be the Hillsborough River. The gator-infested Hillsborough. But gators were the least of her concerns.

Something splashed behind her. "I'm coming, Jake!"

Ethan! A thrill of hope coursed through her.

"Shove her onto my kayak," Jake said. "Then I can paddle us to shore."

Ethan's strong hands grabbed her waist. "It's going to be okay."

She wanted to believe him.

Even though the water must be over his head too, Ethan hoisted her onto the kayak, and Jake pulled her the rest of the way.

"You good?" Jake asked, now able to grab the paddle with both hands.

She sucked another fresh breath of air. What a gift it was. "I am now."

"You holding on back there?" Jake called over his shoulder.

"Yep." Ethan said. "I'll swim with the kayak if you steer."

They soon reached the shoreline, and Ethan sloshed around the kayak toward her. Though dripping wet, he had never looked better. His eyes shone as he reached for her.

"Whoa—" She started to topple on the shoreline, but Ethan caught her, wrapped strong arms around her, and breathed into her hair. "I love you, Avery."

Jake tossed his paddle onto the shore and snorted. "Knew it." He didn't sound angry though.

"I—" Avery gulped. What was she supposed to say to that?

As if reading her thoughts, Ethan put a finger to her lips. "Don't say anything. I had to get that off my chest. I would never have forgiven myself if you'd died without knowing."

"I knew." She was thankful for the water dripping onto her face so maybe he couldn't make out the tears. Why he felt that way about her made no sense. She had done nothing but rebuff him.

She could sort through those feelings later. "Thank you—both, for saving me, but we must find Gianna. Big Eddie still has her."

"No, he doesn't." Ethan wrung out his shirt, but it still hugged his chest in a way she shouldn't appreciate so much. "She's at the hospital for observation, and her parents are with her."

Avery collapsed onto the shore, relief seeping into her chilled skin. Gianna was safe. That was what mattered most, though once more, she had failed to catch the mastermind behind so much mayhem. "What about Big Eddie? Do we have any leads?"

Gunfire answered her question, and Ethan dove on top of her. She choked under his weight. "What is going on?" she whispered. "And can you please get these cuffs off?"

Jake hit the ground beside them. "Call 9-1-1," he spoke into his phone.

While he made the report, Ethan inspected her wrist. "I need cutters, but about the gunfire, my guess is Liam and Jayna found Big Eddie."

"What?" she hissed. "You sent them after him?"

"He was watching you drown from his perch near the dam." Ethan nodded in the dam's direction. "I couldn't let him walk away, but when I saw those men throw the cart in the river—"

Avery let the reality of his words sink in. He'd chosen rescuing her over capturing Tampa's most notorious under lord.

Ethan cleared his throat. "Anyway, I called Liam and reported

Big Eddie's location. Jayna was already in her Russo mask, so I figured they would come up with a plan."

Trying to process everything that had happened while she was imprisoned in a beverage cart was giving her a headache. "Wait, Jayna was wearing the silicone mask I ordered? Whose crazy idea was that?"

"Liam's." More gunfire sounded from the park beyond them as sirens wailed in the distance. Help was coming, but would it be soon enough for Liam and Jayna?

Once more, Avery felt helpless.

"God, please protect Liam, Jayna, and our men and women in blue," Ethan whispered beside her.

Her heart pounded. Pray. Should she pray? She and God needed a long heart-to-heart, but her team might have mere seconds before a bullet caught them in the crossfire.

She closed her eyes, her face toward the ground and her head nestled into the crook of Ethan's arm. *God, I'm here. I'm lousy at this. You don't have any reason to listen to my prayer, but I believe You're real and can save me—and You're bigger than Big Eddie and his web. Bring him down. I can't.*

Jake crawled farther up the riverbank. "Back up is here. You two hang tight, and I'll scope out the situation."

For once, Avery didn't mind waiting. Her whole body ached, and were it not for Ethan's warm body hugging her side, she would be freezing cold. Even if her hands weren't cuffed, she couldn't hold a gun steady enough to shoot it.

"We're going to get through this." Ethan's hot breath on her hair gave her even more goosebumps. "God's got us."

For the first time, she believed him.

Her bath towel still smelled mildly like smoke, but it felt so good to be home. Ethan had wanted her to spend the night with his family again, but she insisted on going back to her apartment since her complex had been cleared and declared safe.

Avery collapsed onto her couch. What. A. Day. All had ended well, but she couldn't take credit for any of it.

The craziest part was Big Eddie's fate. Disguised as Russo, Jayna had exaggerated spotting Big Eddie as he approached his parked car and then started a pretend fight with Liam. Shoving Liam to the ground, she then ran as fast as she could toward Big Eddie who waited for her—his mistake. She didn't stop running but barreled into him, hoping to give Liam time to reach her moments later and arrest him.

But there had been no need. Big Eddie had hit the pavement with such force that he cracked the base of his skull and died minutes later.

The under lord who had evaded justice for so long met it unsuspectingly when an untrained woman tackled him. Liam had called her a regular Jael, a name he had to explain to Ethan and her. Liam told them the Bible story about a mighty warrior named Barak who went out to fight against Sisera, the infamous commander of an oppressing king. A prophetess named Deborah told Barak he would be successful but would not be able to take any glory, because Sisera would fall by the hands of an ordinary woman.

That woman was Jael, who invited the fleeing Sisera into her tent under the pretense of "hiding" him—but instead drove a tent peg through his skull while he slept.

Big Eddie's death wasn't that gruesome, but he had indeed fallen by the hand of an ordinary woman.

Not by the driven private investigator who had sworn to avenge her foster brother. Not by her.

Avery didn't mind. She was too sobered by the fact that she had almost met her own end today. She would have drowned if Jake hadn't been there. She couldn't shake the feeling that his hand reaching down to her was God's way of reaching down to her too. She'd even told Ethan as much, and he hadn't made fun of her.

Ethan. He was the real hero. Bella had called Avery sobbing for joy, praising her for saving Gianna, but Ethan was the one who had ultimately rescued her goddaughter. She owed that man so much.

Her phone pinged, and his familiar name on the screen made her smile. As she swiped to open his message, her breath hitched.

It was an artist's rendition of Jesus. He was blurred and out of focus above the water, but He plunged His hand below the surface and held it outstretched, as if to pull someone who was sinking. Ethan had typed below it: *You should read Matthew 14, starting in verse 22, for this picture's inspiration.*

She would, but not now. Her heart swelled as tears pricked her eyes. Jesus had reached down to save her today, even though she had rebuffed Him more times than she could imagine. He hadn't given up on her. He had never walked out on her. He was the loving Father she had desperately wanted. He had been waiting all this time for her to let Him into her life.

And she had. She finally had.

Chapter Fifty-Three

Ethan leaned forward on the bench outside the Italian restaurant and glanced at his phone to check if his table was ready. Maybe he should have made a reservation. He had assumed that six o'clock on a Tuesday night wouldn't be busy.

Everyone must be craving some good Italian tonight, but most probably weren't celebrating for the reasons he was.

He exhaled and looked up at the sky where the lowering sun cast an array of colors onto a backdrop of clouds. "Thank you, God," he murmured for the hundredth time.

Thank you that Avery finally believed in Him.

Thank you that Avery, Gianna, and their team were safe after Sunday's events.

Thank you that Big Eddie wouldn't be darkening Tampa with his deeds any longer, though the good guys still had their work cut out.

Thank you that even though insomnia plagued him and the cold sweats still woke him, the nightmares didn't haunt him.

Thank you that Avery had said *yes* to dinner with him.

They barely had time in the last twenty-four hours to exchange more than a text message. Reports, testimonies, and evidence had to be filed, and Avery had spent her spare time yesterday with Bella, her husband, and Gianna. The little girl had been released Monday morning with hardly a scratch on her, though her emotional scars from the experience would take time to heal. Avery had already recommended Kaley for counseling, and Bella planned to book sessions for Gianna as soon as Kaley was back in the office after her honeymoon.

He had so much he wanted to ask Avery—and tell her—but that surprise would wait until later this evening.

Avery's familiar silver Mercedes pulled into the parking lot as his phone buzzed with the notification his table was ready. Perfect timing.

His mouth went dry when he saw her. Avery, the non-nonsense private investigator who usually slayed in her jeans and blouses, was wearing a dress.

Not just any dress, but the same emerald, green number he had admired her in at Reef and Kaley's wedding in Beech Mountain. With her heels, she stood as tall as he did.

Ethan dared to greet her with a kiss on her cheek, and to his delight, she didn't scold him.

A blush crept up her neck. "You're staring. It's awkward."

"Sorry but not sorry." He opened the door for her. "I thought that dress was reserved for weddings and funerals?"

"And special occasions."

"Oh? What's the special occasion?"

She cut her gaze toward him as she walked thought the door. "You are."

If the smile on his face grew any wider, Avery would smack him. "I'm honored."

"You should be." Her laughter was light, lighter than he had ever heard. She was the same intelligent, brave, and stubborn Avery, but there was a new sweetness to her that nothing other than God's love could produce.

The hostess seated them at the long table he had reserved and left them to study the menu. Avery set hers down on the table and folded her hands. "I have to tell you, Ethan, that picture you sent me—I ordered one for my apartment. It captures so well what God did for me last weekend. He saved me from not only physical drowning, but also spiritual drowning. I was so close to gone—to closing off my heart to Him forever. It took breaking me down, letting me fail time and time again, to finally see how much I need Him. I can't do this life on my own."

Ethan reached across the table to squeeze her hand. "I have prayed so hard to hear you say those words, Avery. I am so happy for you."

Avery's eyes filled with tears, which she blinked away to keep from falling. "Thank you. I'm happy too, though I'm sorry for all the time I've wasted. I'm also sorry for how I treated you. You've been nothing but kind to me, and I've been rude and unfeeling. I can't believe you stuck around for as long as you did."

"I don't plan on going away either, unless you tell me to get lost." There was a chance that after all the dust settled, Avery would disappear into her work again and forget him.

Avery picked at the menu. "I've been thinking about what you said, about—about us. Maybe we could start going to church together? I've got a lot to learn, and I know you're new to this God stuff too. Maybe we could learn together and get to know each other at the same time. I don't know what a relationship with God at the middle should look like, but I want to learn."

"I do too, as long as you let me take you out. I know you don't date, but trust me, dating is fun. I've already got a list of things I want to do with you." He paused. Maybe he was going too fast.

Avery laughed. "Okay. Also, what is a love language? Jayna used that term, and I have no idea what she meant by it."

"Same, but like you said, we can figure it out together." He put on his best serious face. "I do have a big ask."

Her laughter caught in her throat. "Yes?"

Ethan took a deep breath. "Join my family for Thanksgiving? My mom already likes you, and my sisters will lose their minds if I bring you home."

Avery's hand shook as she reached for her water glass. It spilled all over the table. "I—I'm sorry."

"You don't need to apologize." Ethan swallowed the lump forming in his throat and braced himself for the hard *no* that was about to come from her lips. He shouldn't have pushed her.

She grabbed a napkin but didn't mop up the water. She mopped the tears streaming down her face.

Chapter Fifty-Four

Avery blew her nose louder than any lady wearing heels probably should, but she couldn't help herself. How many years had she dreamed of what Thanksgiving would be like with a family? On a rare occasion, she'd spent Thanksgiving with Bella and hers, but most years, she made an excuse to spend the day working.

Now here was Ethan, inviting her to spend Thanksgiving at his parents' beautiful home with his sisters and him. It would be like the Thanksgiving she'd never had.

A lie whispered in her ears that she didn't deserve this joy, that she should say no, but she shoved that thought aside. She was part of God's family now. Why couldn't she share in Ethan's family's celebration?

She sipped what was left of her water and took a steadying breath. "I would love to join you."

Ethan's face lit up. "You would? That's awesome! My sisters are going to love you."

Other than her spilling water all over the place, the evening could not have been more perfect. The food was great. Ethan was even better.

The waitress returned to check if they wanted dessert, and Avery started to waive her off, but Ethan nodded. "The hostess put something in the back for me. Could you bring it out in five minutes?"

"Oh, that's yours," the woman said. "Sure, I'll be back soon."

What was Ethan up to? "I really can't eat a bit more." Avery stared at the remnants of her fettuccine weesie and second-guessed her choice to eat most of it.

Ethan smiled smugly. "Excuse me. I'll be right back."

She caught him pull out his phone as he strode away and took the opportunity to check her messages as well. There was one from Bella. It was a picture of Gianna at dance practice with the caption,

"Can you believe the studio reopened today? That was a fast recovery from the fire! Gianna begged to go, so I took her. She's going to be okay. I just know it. Let's get together again soon."

Avery hearted the picture. *So glad. We'll talk again soon.*

As she slipped the phone back into her bag, movement in her peripheral made her turn.

A lady wearing heels probably shouldn't gape either, but she couldn't help it. There, heading her way, were Ethan, Liam, Jayna, Reef, Kaley, Miss Martha, and Jake. Now the long table made sense.

Avery jumped to her feet. "What are you all doing here?"

"To celebrate!" Jayna greeted her with a hug, and Avery allowed it.

"You are quite the hero." Avery pulled away. She still had her limits on hugs.

Jayna's olive complexion paled. "The accidental one, truly. What happened to Big Eddie was in God's hands. Let's talk about something else, though." She hooked her hand through Liam's arm, and he patted it as though to reassure her.

Reef pulled up a few extra chairs. "Yes, like all the good news."

Avery squeezed Kaley's shoulder, hoping to avoid another bear hug. "Congratulations to the newlyweds! But I thought you guys were on your honeymoon?"

Kaley smiled and mercifully didn't hug her. The new bride seemed to glow—and it wasn't because of the tan she'd acquired on her honeymoon. "We came back yesterday, and when Ethan invited us to join you tonight for dessert, we couldn't wait. He told us what went down on Sunday, but that's not why we're here to celebrate."

"It's not?" Avery scooted back onto the bench and made room for Miss Martha beside her.

"We're here to celebrate you and Ethan becoming part of God's family." There was no avoiding Miss Martha's hug, but somehow, Avery didn't mind one from her. "We're also here to celebrate one other piece of news."

"You want to tell her, Jake?" Ethan made room for his boss next to him while Jayna and Liam pulled up two more chairs on the other end of the table.

"I think Miss Martha should," Jake said. "It was her idea, after all."

Miss Martha's curls seemed extra mischievous, as did the shimmer in her eyes.

"What are they talking about, Miss Martha?" Avery asked.

"Well, dear, the long and the short is that my Cuban contacts found Gabriel and Camillo like you asked, and that Jake is a generous man. He's offered to front them jobs at his security business to help expedite their immigration process to the U.S."

Avery's eyes smarted with tears for the second time tonight. She had promised Mario to help his cousins but hadn't been able to do anything in her own power. Once again, God was making a way where she could not.

Avery leaned forward to look at Jake. "I can't thank you enough."

"I'm glad to help. Everyone needs a second chance, don't you think?" The light in Jake's eyes matched the hope filling her chest.

Jake turned to Ethan. "Now that Semper Security is expanding, I realize I need to delegate more, and I'd like my first move to be making you my security supervisor. You'd still have field jobs, but you'd also help train, integrate, and oversee new hires." He paused. "I think God might want to use your story to give hope to men in the thick of navigating their pasts or PTSD."

Her heart squeezed at the opportunity this would be for him—both personally and professionally. She held her breath as his eyes widened in surprise, then squinted as a smile spread across his face. "I'd be honored."

"I was hoping you'd say that," Jake said. "We'll talk more on Monday."

Just then, the waitress returned, carrying a large sheet cake. Someone had decorated it with the words, "Welcome to the family."

Her gaze met Ethan's, and he seemed relieved for a reason to get the attention off himself. "Think you can find room for a small piece?"

"Absolutely." She had found her family—God's family. For the first time she could remember, she finally felt home.

Author's Note

There were times I didn't think I could finish this book. My young son was sick at least four times in four months and went through the brutal eighteen-month-old sleep regression while I was trying to finish. The weekend I anticipated writing the climax during his two-hour nap, he skipped his nap due to a fever, and I wanted to cry.

Reviews seemed to suddenly freeze on books one and two in the series. Self-doubts about my writing soared.

Then I started praying. This much resistance to a book meant Satan didn't want me to finish, that someone needed to read Avery and Ethan's redemption story.

I could never have finished without God answering my prayer for inspiration and for my husband's help with our son and his encouragement not to quit.

When will I write my next book? Is writing more stories the right goal for me in this wonderful but messy season of raising a toddler? I don't know. But I know the One who holds tomorrow, and I trust that if it is His will, I will write again, and He will open the doors.

For now, I am thankful for the privilege of sharing this story with you. I pray it blesses you and that you draw something from it that stays with you long after the last page.

In His Grip,
Kristen

Sign up for Kristen's monthly newsletter at:
KristenHogrefeParnell.com and receive a free story.

Romantic Suspense by Kristen:

Crossroads Suspense
Take My Hand
Hold Your Breath
Watch Your Back

Young Adult Fiction by Kristen, published under her maiden name
Kristen Hogrefe, includes:

The Rogues Trilogy
The Revisionary
The Revolutionary
The Reactionary

Discussion Questions

1. Have you ever tried to rationalize a wrong to make a right? What was the outcome? At one point, Avery considers committing a crime for the "good reason" of rescuing Gianna. Thankfully, Ethan crosses her path in time to keep her from making a choice she'll regret. In the Bible, a couple named Abram and Sarai rationalized a wrong choice for a right reason. God had promised them that they would have a son, but they remained childless—and Sarai's biological clock was ticking. Read their story starting in Genesis 16. What was the outcome of their choice, and do you think they regretted it?

2. Are you familiar with the term "love language" or know what your primary "love language" is? Avery doesn't have a clue what Jayna means when she uses the term, which was coined by Gary Chapman in his best-selling book, *The 5 Love Languages*. Whether you're married or single, this insightful book will teach you much about yourself and about others.

3. Is there some personal loss or tragedy in your past that makes you question God? If so, you're not alone—in fiction or in real life. For Avery, she struggles to view God as a loving Father since her own father walked out of her life when she was a child. Take the time to read Hebrews 13:5. What does it say God will never do?

4. Ethan struggles with feelings of guilt since he couldn't prevent the attack on his friend. Ultimately, he realizes that God wants him to come to Him just as he is—and let God work in his life. Has guilt over a past situation paralyzed your faith or ability to move forward with life? Read Hebrews 4:16 and I John 1:9. Does either verse help you see how to begin again after your own situation?

5. What do you fear you might "fail" at in life? Avery worries she might never bring her foster brother to justice, and Big Eddie capitalizes on her fear of failure to taunt her again and again. In real life, Satan also preys upon our fear of failure to distract us from the fact that our God is greater than any of our fears or failures. 2 Timothy 1:7 says, "For God has not given us a spirit of fear, but of power and of love and of a sound mind." Fighting our fears with truth and with the confidence that God is more powerful than any "failure" can help us regain our footing.